The Redemption Road

The Redemption Road

The Redemption Road

Sweet River Redemption Series
Book Three

By

Christa MacDonald

The Redemption Road
Published by Mountain Brook Ink
White Salmon, WA U.S.A.

The website addresses shown in this book are not intended in any way to be or imply an endorsement on the part of Mountain Brook Ink, nor do we vouch for their content.

This story is a work of fiction. All characters and events are the product of the author's imagination. Any resemblance to any person, living or dead, is coincidental.

Scripture quotations are taken from the King James Version of the Bible. Public domain.
ISBN 978-1-943959-60-0

The Team: Miralee Ferrell, Rachel Lulich, Nikki Wright, Cindy Jackson

Cover Design: Indie Cover Design, Lynnette Bonner Designer

Mountain Brook Ink is an inspirational publisher offering fiction you can believe in.
Printed in the United States of America

DEDICATION

To every woman who has ever doubted that they
were the sort of person who deserves love, this is for you.

ACKNOWLEDGMENTS

As this series comes to a close I want to thank every person who has ever beta read, critique-partnered, submitted a review, bought a book, signed up for my newsletter, joined my Facebook group, tweeted me, or stopped me on the street to say you read one of my books.
Your encouragement means the world to me.

As always, thanks to my mom, my first reader.

Thanks to my brilliant content editor, Rachel Lulich, who manages to point out the exact bits that need help.

Thanks to my family and friends who put up with me when I'm suffering from book angst.

To my husband Steve, my first editor and greatest support, thank you for loving me even when I'm a mess.

For giving me the words and the opportunity to share them, my thanks to God, the author of the universe, who loved me before I drew my first breath.

CHAPTER ONE

THE JINGLE OF SLEIGH BELLS RANG out as the door to the shop swung open. A blast of cold air swept inside along with a swirl of snow which twinkled like fairy-dust in the overhead lights. A man in an olive-green parka shut the door and stood on the welcome mat, stomping his boots and shaking off the new-fallen snow.

Annie watched him push back his hood and unwind a long scarf from around his face. Even with the wintry camouflage, she knew who it was. There was only one person who ever arrived almost every morning, rain, shine, or snow, right after she opened. She started up the espresso machine and took out the coffee beans, knowing his order by heart. A minute later, she looked up to see him standing at the counter in front of her, and she felt her lips form the smile that his presence always conjured. "Good morning, Alex."

He closed his eyes and sniffed the air. "What is that baking?"

"Gingerbread men. But you can't have any yet." Her smile broadened at his perplexed look. "They'll need time to cool so I can decorate them."

"I'll have to stop in later." His eyes fell on the glass case under the counter where sheets of scones, muffins, donuts, and other treats sat ready to tempt her customers. "What's the special today?"

"You'll love it." She walked into the back room for the tray of goodies. His face lit up as she returned.

"Cinnamon rolls? I thought you said you hated those."

"I hate making them. They're a pain, but I love eating them, and it's the Christmas season, so I'm feeling generous." She took a sheet of bakery paper, pulled a roll off the tray, and placed it on a plate. "Here you go." She slid the plate across the counter to him and scooted over to the espresso machine to finish his double macchiato.

"Speaking of Christmas, are you going to stay open over the holidays?"

She shrugged. "I'm not going anywhere. Business should be good with all the shops staying open. I'll have regular hours on Christmas Eve, but I'll close on Christmas. No one is likely to be out."

"You're not going home to your family?"

Annie managed not to wince. She'd had to answer that question a few times already. The simple answer was no, but few people let her leave it there. The real answer wasn't something she wanted to share. It made her feel broken–in a way, lesser-than. How was she supposed to tell people she still didn't know very well that she never spent holidays with her family? Talk about awkward. "My parents are traveling, so I'll be here. How about you? Are you headed home for Christmas?" She finished off his drink and slid it across the counter for him to take.

"No." He gave a brief shake of his head, his short-cropped hair unmoved by the gesture. His tone didn't invite a follow-up question, so she gladly changed the subject. Maybe Alex's long answer was as complicated as hers. In the many months he'd been coming to her shop he'd never arrived with anyone other than the warden who was training him to take over for him, Pete Coleman. She'd seen him and Pete together a lot—they were almost like father and son, but she'd never seen him with anyone else. She'd never seen him talking to anyone but her, either.

It made her heart ache to think of him alone. "If you're going to be in town, you might want to check out the candlelight service at the Calvary Church. The music will all be carols from medieval times through the twentieth century. It's supposed to be beautiful."

"I'll think about it."

Annie kept her expression neutral as a wave of disappointment rushed through her. It was followed quickly by embarrassment. This wasn't the first time she'd invited him somewhere and got the brush off. Annie found herself rushing to fill the space between them with words. "I'm planning to go. I love Christmas music, even the hokey stuff. My Aunt and I used to sit in her lounge and listen to the old records she had on this big, wood thing." She held out her arms to show its size. "The center had a lid you'd lift to put the records on, and it had cloth speakers built in. I loved it. Coming from my parent's place in New York where everything had a remote and was either steel, black plastic, or glass, it was quite a difference. I used to sit on this large poof she had in front of her chair and..." She stopped when she saw a smirk on his lips and realized she was rambling again. She could feel the blush creep across her cheeks. "Why do you let me run on and on like that?"

"You're fine." He waved it away.

Annie decided it was a good sign that he hadn't already run for the hills, or his usual corner table. She prized any time he chose to spend with her. It wasn't like she had handsome men tripping over themselves to listen to her prattle. Alex was patient and unfailingly kind. If a part of her worried he was only humoring her, that was her cross to bear. "Do you have any plans for Christmas?"

"Pete and his wife Lauren invited me over for dinner. If nothing comes up, I'll probably go." Strangely, Alex's expression clouded over. She wasn't sure what was in that look, maybe regret?

"You should go." She urged. "Lauren's a great cook. What I wouldn't give for her talent."

Alex lifted an eyebrow and pointed down at his cinnamon

roll.

"That's baking, it's totally different. Baking is science. I follow the recipe, and it comes out every time. Cooking is an art. It takes a certain degree of creativity to be any good at it, not to mention a level of courage I apparently lack."

He shook his head. "I don't believe it."

"No, really, I can do eggs and a decent stir-fry, but sauces or the fancy stuff? No way. I can't even make chili. It always comes out lackluster, watery, or off somehow."

"Bland chili is the worst. I use my mom's recipe, but I add a few things."

"See?" She held up her hand. "That's the creativity and courage part. I wouldn't know what to add."

"You need somebody to teach you the basics."

Annie huffed out a laugh and lifted a shoulder in a half-hearted shrug while her mind spun through all the possible responses. This was the moment where she could turn that opening into a witty reply about how if he was offering, she'd be happy to let him teach her. In her imagination, it wouldn't be a weird self-invite at all. He'd get it, and he'd give her one of his rare, real smiles, and they'd set up a time. Maybe it would even lead to another date, but instead of any of that she stalled, and the moment had all the time it needed to become awkward. Alex scooped up his coffee and cinnamon roll, giving her a little salute with it before heading to the corner table where, if it were like every other day, he'd sit and read while he ate. Annie tried to bury the disappointment like she had a dozen times before.

The door to the shop swung open again as Claire Murphy, her only full-time employee, swept in with another flurry of snow. "It is so pretty!" She pulled off her coat and hung it up. "The world is frosted over, not a scraggly brown bush or blade of grass to be seen." Claire took off her knitted hat and fluffed her long, brown hair. Annie thought Claire's hair had to be secretly magic. One fluff and no static, no hat head, only gorgeous waves of shiny brown. Magic.

"You're early."

"Hockey practice. Normally I drop the boys off and then go back to bed, but it took so long to dig the car out of the snow I didn't feel like doing it twice in one morning, since I heard we've got another four inches yet to fall. I figure I can help you with prep or whatever."

"There's always something." Annie quickly reviewed all she had planned for the week and knew there were probably a half-dozen tasks she could hand off to Claire. "Do you want to work on the menu?" She pointed to the blackboard where Coffee by the Book, the name of her shop, was written in block letters. The rest of the board was blank, waiting for the daily menu.

"Sure." Claire inspected the bakery case. "I see we got the delivery of the usual suspects. I can price those up, easy-peasy. By the way, one of the moms on the PTO asked me if you were going to do the peppermint latte through the season, or if she had to come get her fix before they were gone."

"That one has been super popular, which is a surprise. Coffee and mint together are gross. To be honest, I do not get the draw."

Claire's jaw dropped open.

"You're going to say that's sacrilege, I suppose?"

"No, the real sacrilege is that you own a coffee shop that also sells books, but that you prefer tea." Claire took a sheet of paper out of the drawer under the register and started marking down items and prices. "That's what you get for spending half your life in England. Tea is fine, but it's not coffee. Americans love their coffee."

"Good thing, since it's our main business."

"The books sell, sometimes." Claire squinted at the long wall of the shop that was filled, floor to ceiling, with the books

Annie had chosen. "And they're great ambiance."

"That they are." Annie's attention drifted from the shelves of books to Alex who sat in the corner, hand wrapped around his coffee, reading a book.

"I see 'tall, dark, and broody' has arrived." Claire jerked her head in Alex's direction.

Annie rolled her eyes and made sure to keep her voice low when she answered. "He's not broody, he's reserved. There's a difference."

"Whatever he is, he's in need of a reason to smile." Claire gave her a long look then fluttered the fingers of one hand at Annie, as if telling her to 'shoo.' "Maybe you could go discuss books or something. Don't you both read mysteries?"

"No. He likes suspense, I read mystery. It's two different things."

"If you say so." Claire went back to the list she was working on. "But he really is a bit too serious. It's probably why he's had trouble getting the locals to like him."

"What game warden is popular with the hunters?"

"Pete Coleman was before he retired."

"Pete's one of the nicest people on the planet. He practically adopted me when I first moved here. Of course he was popular. Alex has to enforce the law, so it's only natural he'll get attitude." Annie frowned, thinking Alex really did need to take her up on the town events she invited him too, not for herself, but to get to know the locals. "If people would give him a chance, they'd find out he has a good heart." Annie turned to see Claire staring at her with narrowed eyes, speculation all over her face. Annie could tell she was about a half-minute from asking some very personal questions about Annie's feelings for Alex, and that would not be good.

"Hey, can you mix up a bowl of royal icing?" Annie pointed over her shoulder at the back room with her thumb. "I've got gingerbread men on the menu today, and they'll be cool enough to decorate soon. I need to be at the school in a few hours, so if you can give me a head start that would be great."

"Sure," Claire answered brightly before heading to the back. "I love decorating."

"I know." Annie chuckled. With disaster averted and Claire distracted, she made a plan to buzz by Alex's table. He might need a refill, or she could ask how he liked the book she'd recommended yesterday. She couldn't help but notice he was reading it today, and it looked like he was more than a few chapters in. She wondered what he did in his off time since she never saw him around town if he wasn't either on shift or about to be.

As she got ready to leave the counter and walk to his table, she saw he was in motion already. He had his phone to his ear and was heading for the door. This was a familiar sight. He often had to rush out on a call. His coat was on before he whirled to face her, still holding his phone, one hand fishing through his pocket.

"You can pay me tomorrow." She waved him off. "Go. It's fine."

"Got it." He pulled the phone away from his head. "Thanks." He waved to her as he ran out the door and into the swirling snow. She looked at the coat rack and realized he'd forgotten his scarf. She left the counter and grabbed it, but when she peered out the glass door, she could see him pulling away in his truck. It was no matter. He'd be back tomorrow. As she rehung it on the pegboard, she could smell pine needles, wool, and bergamot. She wondered if he drank Earl Grey tea like her Aunt Delia or if the bergamot was his aftershave; another puzzling detail to Warden Moretti. Despite his daily trips to her store, she felt like he was still a mystery.

Roger Cook stood about a foot too close while he stuck his index finger an inch from Alex's face and continued to shout. His face was a spectacular shade of red, beyond florid and headed for heart-attack scarlet. Alex waited for the man to either run out of steam or throw a punch. It could go either way. The facts of the situation were undeniable. His snowmobile wasn't registered, and he'd been operating it on private land. Alex had gotten the call from the landowner during the hour he usually reserved for hanging out at Annie's, and he wasn't happy about it. All that was saving Roger from being slapped into cuffs and sitting in the back of his truck was the fact that Alex knew Roger wasn't really angry at him. From the scattering of previous years' registration stickers on the sled, Roger had probably realized that he could have avoided this drama by registering it as usual.

Alex had stopped Roger at the mouth of the trail and let him know the landowner had closed this path and it was posted. He had planned to let the guy off with a warning, but the unregistered snow machine turned this into a situation. He knew Roger was angry at himself and taking it out on Alex because nobody likes to be stupid. Knowing this made Alex calm. He could let the guy scream himself hoarse if that made him feel better about the ticket.

Roger spluttered to a stop as a car pulled up. A disheveled woman got out from the driver's side. It looked to Alex like she'd thrown a parka over her pajamas. As she stomped closer, he saw the pajama bottoms had little bunnies on them. Her feet were stuffed into a pair of unlaced boots, and a knit hat was shoved down over her long, brown hair. She rolled right up to Alex and got in his face despite being about a foot shorter. The pom-pom on the top of her hat bobbled as she yelled at him.

"What's going on? Roger called me saying you're towing

him?"

Between her getup and the way she was defending what he assumed was her husband, it was hard not to smile.

Roger stepped in between them. "Lucy, chill." Roger seemed to have found his calm. "I thought the snowmobile was registered this year, but I guess I forgot. No big deal." He shrugged. "My fault, babe." Roger's tone was placating.

"I told you to get that thing registered." Lucy wasn't chill. She didn't seem interested in being calm either. She had her arms crossed over her chest, her anger directed at Roger now.

"I know, I know. I said I forgot."

Instead of telling him off, Lucy seemed to deflate slightly. Her shoulders slumped a little, and her tone changed. "Like you forgot to order oil yesterday?" Her head tilted to the side, and her face softened. "I told you to let me take care of this stuff for you. You're working killer hours, Roger. You can't do it all."

Roger glanced over at Alex and drew his wife away a few feet. Alex pulled out his notebook and mindlessly scribbled trying to make it clear he wasn't going to listen. He watched though, and after only a minute or two he saw Roger nod. Lucy reached up to him and placed her hand against his cheek, her thumb stroking his whiskered cheek. It was a small gesture, but Alex was moved by it all the same.

"Hey," Alex called over to them. "Do you live close by?"

Roger looked up and nodded. "Number seven Oak. Two streets over."

"Okay." Alex radioed in and canceled the tow. "Here's what we'll do. You're going home and getting online. Go to this web address." He wrote it out. "And get this machine registered. Then you'll email me a screenshot of it." He added his email address to the paper before tearing it from his notebook and handing it to Roger.

"Seriously? Thank you." Roger seemed both shocked and

pleased.

"You get that done, and we're good. You don't, and I'll be at your door before the end of my shift with your summons." Alex raised the citation he'd been about to write so Roger could see it. "Have a good day, folks." He nodded first to Lucy and then to Roger and strode to his truck. He followed them for a bit to be sure they made it home. Once they arrived, he drove around the corner and up the long driveway to the house of the landowner who had called about Roger zooming over his fields. Once out of his truck, he waded through the snow that had yet to be cleared from the walk and up to the front door. He didn't need to knock since the homeowner was right there, waiting for him.

"I assume the situation is resolved?" The man was older, probably in his sixties, dressed in a cardigan sweater and wearing LL Bean slippers. His accent hinted that he wasn't a local product. He sounded like a transplant from Massachusetts.

"I know you said that the land is posted, but there's no sign at the head of the trail or at the exit at the road. I can help you with that if you'd like. I've got a few signs in my truck and can hang them for you. That would go a long way to keeping the ATVs and snowmobiles out."

The man shook his head. "No. Thank you. I wanted Cook to know he has to stay off my land. I can deal with the occasional trail rider."

"Uh, okay." That was odd, but Roger was this guy's neighbor, and if there was one thing Alex had learned in his six months on the job, it was that neighbors made the best enemies. "Give us a call if you need us again." Alex backed away, and the man shut the door in his face. He brushed off the insult since it was a rare one. Most of the time landowners were glad to have help. As Alex got into his truck and drove away, he thought over the call. He rarely gave anyone the kind of pass he had given Roger. For some reason, seeing his wife pull up and defend her husband had stirred something inside. He wondered what it would be like to have someone on his side like that. A 'ride or die' partner for life.

Annie would be that kind of partner. He thought about the first time he'd met her. He'd walked into the shop to order a coffee and had been rendered speechless when she'd looked up at him with those lavender eyes. She was short but built like a perfect hourglass. Annie had projected a kind of strength and kindness combined. He was left staring at her, taking in her heart-shaped face surrounded by black curls. He often wondered if it was natural or if she walked around her apartment in curlers. He smiled at the thought. Not that he was likely to ever be close enough to her to know. A stab of regret hit his gut. Annie needed, no she deserved, a good guy, a man who had a life he could be proud of. Alex was not that man.

"Shake it off." He'd told himself a hundred times that it was probably stupid to keep showing up every morning, ordering coffee, and eating whatever she'd made, pretending she'd made it with him in mind, but he couldn't stop. It was the one comfort he allowed himself. Every day he'd wait at the table until she came by with a refill or with a book recommendation. She'd sit across from him, and he'd pretend that they were indeed friends, or something more, something infinitely better. It never lasted, but if life had taught one lesson, it had taught him that nothing good ever did.

CHAPTER TWO

ANNIE SAID A PRAYER OF THANKS to the Sweet River DPW on her way to open up the library at the school. They had cleared the sidewalks with some kind of Elven magic, since it hadn't stopped snowing until dawn. Being a private school with more boarding than day students, Sweet River Christian Academy had more flexibility when it came to snow days. Most public schools were closed today to deal with the snow removal. SRCA had only a two-hour delay.

Annie was grateful for the late start since she walked to school. She managed to only slip twice on the way which prompted a 'note to self' that pretty and warm did not top traction in boot choices. Once inside, she slipped her boots off by the radiator outside the library and put on the flats she had added to her bag that morning. It reminded her of New York and how all the assistants at her father's company kept gym shoes in their purses to swap out their heels, so they could run or walk to the train at the end of the day.

Unlocking the doors, she pushed them open and took a deep breath of the library's distinctive air. She closed her eyes and inhaled the scent of old paper and wood. The library was a square, two-story addition built off the original school building. A large, center staircase connected the floors. Tall, nineteenth-century industrial windows lined two walls which flooded the space with light but made it downright cold three seasons of the year. Annie checked the radiators to be sure they were pumping out heat. She held her hands over their warmth for a moment and then switched the overheads on, illuminating the shelves of books.

She set her bag down on the oak desk by the windows, the

only space she claimed in the building. As a part-timer, the desk wasn't really hers, so there wasn't much of anything on it other than a small vase with a few candy-canes in it, and a picture frame with a photo of her and Auntie Delia outside the Queen's Theatre. They'd just seen Les Mis, Delia's gift for her sixteenth birthday. Looking at herself from a decade ago, she didn't feel the years. In so many ways, she was still that cautiously optimistic teenager hoping for the best but braced for the worst. Seeing Aunt Delia's smiling face set off a pang of grief, but it was a soft and familiar one. She did the math and realized it had been almost three years. If this upcoming anniversary was anything like the last one, her father would call, which would be nice.

He'd also find time during that call to nag her about following Delia's advice for her life instead of his. 'Why work so much when the reward is so small?' Her father did not understand that being a librarian, for her, was a reward in itself. Owning and working Coffee by the Book allowed her to take the part-time librarian position and still live comfortably. She had explained it, but he still couldn't grasp that she'd choose a small town and a small career to go with it.

The doors to the library swung open, and a girl came in. She shot Annie a nervous smile and picked a seat at one of the tables in the far corner. She was wearing the school's uniform and carrying a large book bag on her shoulder which she left at her feet as she sat. Her blond hair was pulled back from her face by a black headband. Just like *Alice in Wonderland,* which was apt since she must be lost. Convocation was about to start, and Annie didn't think any students were exempt from attending.

It took a minute, but Annie remembered her name—Olivia Davis. Annie didn't know every student, but she knew her frequent fliers, those kids who were avid readers and checked out multiple books every other week. Olivia was a freshman, and she seemed to spend every spare moment in the library.

Annie's 'trouble' radar had been pinging the last few times she'd seen the girl. Olivia was never with a friend, and she talked to no one.

Annie opened her laptop and ran through her emails; she also checked the daily schedule. There it was, the high school had convocation today in the gym, and it had started two minutes ago. Dread pooled in Annie's stomach as she realized she'd have to confront the teen. The only way to check for sure was to ask her for a pass. Annie hated confrontation. Even with students. She didn't want to bust Olivia for skipping. That would mean she'd get written up. No big deal if you're the average student, but Olivia was not. She was the foster-daughter of Dr. Katherine MacAlister, the director of the school. Annie found Katherine intimidating already, and the idea of writing up her daughter was nearly panic-inducing.

Slowly she rose from her chair, smoothed down her skirt, and walked over to where Olivia sat. The girl looked up at her under her lashes, and Annie could tell she knew she was busted. "Hey, do you have a pass? I only ask because I thought there was a convocation today, which means this is not a free period for a freshman."

"Oh really?" Olivia's mouth fell open in what looked a whole lot like a feigned surprise. "I totally forgot." She got up and shoved the book in front of her into her bag.

"You'll be marked tardy." Annie pointed out. She saw Olivia's hands shake a little as she clasped her bag.

"Yeah, I guess I will. That's not a big deal though, right?"

"Well..." Annie knew it was probably a bigger deal than Olivia was thinking. She'd end up having to explain herself to a teacher, and if that explanation sounded spurious, it was a trip to the office. "The list of tardy students goes to the office."

Olivia's shoulders sank. "Dr. MacAlister sees those?"

"Yes, she does."

"Is there..." Olivia turned to Annie, her expression a mix of fear and hope. "Would it be possible for you to write me a pass since I was here and not like, doing something bad?"

Annie's allegiances were pulled in six different directions at once. She'd been in Olivia's shoes before, but that didn't trump the rules, or her responsibility for enforcing them. Taking a deep breath, she debated her options as quickly as she could. "I think we both know that you didn't really forget that today was convocation." A stab of sympathy passed through Annie as she watched Olivia bite her lip, eyes on her hands tangled in the strap of her bag. She was gripping it so hard she was cutting off the blood flow to her fingertips. "But I will send an email to verify that you were here and that you went to convocation when I reminded you."

"Will that make it okay?"

"I think it will help." Annie needed to be sure this girl understood where the lines were. "But this isn't the kind of school where you can skip anything, classes or convocation. I know this is your first year here, so it's understandable that you might not realize how things work."

"Yeah, public school was way better, but whatever. I guess it's okay." There was bitterness in her words.

"Okay? It's way better than public school." Annie gave her a smile. "You get to wear a very smart uniform and hang out in this gorgeous library."

Olivia's lips quirked, a near-miss of a smile. "I like the library."

"I noticed. Why don't you come back during your free period when you can be here without the stress of knowing you really need to be someplace else?"

Olivia nodded and shouldered her bag. "Thanks, Ms. Caldwell."

"You're welcome. Anytime, Olivia." She reached out and

gave the girl's arm what she hoped was an encouraging pat. "I mean that."

Hours later Annie sat at her desk staring at the email she was composing, second-guessing every word. "This is stupid." She deleted what she'd written and started over. "Hi, Katherine. I wanted to let you know that Olivia was here at the library at the start of convocation. She seemed..." Annie growled in frustration. "Your daughter is not transitioning well." Annie wrote and then deleted it. "When I let her know where she was supposed to be she left right away." Weak, but it got the job done. She added her signature and sent it off. Too bad there wasn't a polite, professional way to say, 'I was once—sort of—in her shoes, and I can tell she's struggling,' but Annie was not close to Katherine in any way. They went to the same church, but Annie stuck to the balcony and didn't stay for the coffee hour, so it's not like they'd chatted.

Looking up at the clock she saw it was quarter to four, which meant that she'd be going home shortly. Dr. MacAlister tended to stay later. Annie often saw her picking her foster kids up when the after-school sports and activities ended. Olivia had younger twin brothers that also attended the school and two younger siblings who weren't old enough yet. Annie had met the two little ones when she'd volunteered for childcare duty at church, a precocious five-year-old girl, and a sweet three-year-old boy. That was one of the many things that Annie found admirable, therefore intimidating, about Katherine. She and her husband, who were newly married, agreed to foster five kids orphaned when their parents died in a car accident. It was a foster-to-adopt situation which was often difficult, therefore even more admirable.

An alert pinged on her laptop. Annie groaned out loud as she saw the email from Katherine asking her to drop by the office before she went home. "Might as well get it over with." Her voice sounded strange in the empty room. School had ended, and no one seemed to be staying late today. She closed up for the night, locking the doors as she left. The wing with the library was opposite that of administration, so she had plenty of time on the walk there through mostly empty corridors to contemplate what felt like waiting doom in the director's office. What did Katherine want to talk about? Was she angry that Annie had interfered? Had she interfered?

When she pushed through the doors into the admin office Elaine, the school secretary, was still at her post. "Hey, look who it is." She sing-songed. "I feel like I never see you." Elaine came out from behind the reception desk and gave Annie a hug. She had a butterfly barrette in her short gray hair, its wings bobbing as she spoke. "You need to come to our staff lunches, Annie. You've been here for almost a year, and no one has had the chance to get to know you."

"Oh, well. I'm a part-timer. I didn't want anyone to think I was presuming—"

"What? That's so silly. Nobody cares about that. Everyone on staff is welcome. Even the janitor comes. We have a great time."

"I'll be sure to attend the next one."

"Do, because it's a great way to meet people." Elaine's eyes wandered Annie's face for a moment. "I know it's hard to be the new girl and being so much younger than some of us might make you feel like you're not a part, but you definitely are."

Annie blinked rapidly to save herself from the embarrassment of tears. Elaine had always come off as the consummate school admin. She knew everybody and everybody's business, but it appeared she was also sharp. Had she spotted Annie's eagerness to belong? Immediately, Annie worried that she was projecting it, like a lost kitten. "That's so kind, Elaine." She managed the words around the lump in her throat. "Thank you."

"Annie, if you have a minute?" Katherine was standing in the doorway to her office, a polite smile on her face.

"Yes, I'll be right there." Annie gave Elaine an awkward wave, and she ducked away and into Katherine's office. Her boss was already seated, her arms folded casually on her desk. Annie shut the door and took the seat on the opposite side of the desk, trying to quell the tremors in her stomach.

"Thanks for taking the time to meet with me."

"No worries." Annie answered, her voice pitched high.

Katherine smiled. "This isn't an ambush. I'm not calling you on the carpet if that's what you're worried about?"

"Ah." Annie let out a nervous titter of laughter. "Well, a call from one's superior is almost always a cause for anxiety."

"Not here." Katherine's voice was level and her tone serious. "We're a Christian school, and the 'Christian' part doesn't stop at the door of this office. If you ever need to talk to me, about anything, please feel free." Katherine sat back, her elbows on the arms of her chair, her fingers tented in front of her. "Not today though. Today we get to be awkward because I have to ask you for details about Olivia's tardiness to convocation. I would really rather not. I'd rather talk about anything else, but I'm asking as a mom." Her eyes lifted to pin Annie's. "Did I detect a subtext in your email?"

"Yes." Annie sat forward as well, praying quickly for the right words to come. Katherine needed to know why Annie, of all people, might understand what Olivia was going through. It might be the wrong thing, to share about her life, but it felt right. "Did you know I grew up living with an aunt and not my parents?"

Katherine frowned slightly. "I believe I saw in your CV that you attended schools in England."

"Right. I was there because my parents didn't want me traveling with them. They wanted me to have a degree of stability, so I was sent to live with an aunt. When I was old enough, I was enrolled in a boarding school."

"How old were you when you were left with your aunt?"

"Eight."

Katherine's eyes widened, and she dropped her hands to her lap, sitting up. "Eight?"

"So, with that in mind, please take what I say next in the best way possible." She swallowed and gathered her courage. "Olivia is not transitioning well."

Katherine closed her eyes and nodded. "Unfortunately, you're not telling me anything I don't know." She sighed, a sound both frustrated and sad. "She's the oldest. It might be why she's having trouble accepting us. Actually, it's accepting me. I'm pretty sure she's fine with Mac, my husband." Katherine added. She didn't need to since Annie knew of him. Katherine and Mac's story was legendary among the locals. "What do you think would help?"

"I don't know Olivia well enough, but I do know that she loves spending time in the library. In part, I think she's hiding out, but she's also an avid reader. Maybe times when she's feeling anxious or stressed she could use a special pass to come to the library. I have no counseling background, so I'm not suggesting she come to speak to me, more that she has a place where she can feel safe. A neutral place." Annie added, hoping that Katherine would understand.

"Ah, because having her foster mother run her new school is complicating things?"

"Maybe?" Annie lifted a shoulder in a shrug.

"I really appreciate this, Annie. And I'll think about your

suggestion. She can't get special treatment because of me, but if this is something she needs as a student, we should accommodate that."

"I honestly think it is. She...I don't think she's made friends yet."

"Unfortunately, you're right about that too, but how did you know?"

"She comes to the library during lunch. Usually kids do that when they have no one to sit with, or they're being bullied. Since she doesn't talk to anyone and no one seems to talk to her, but they do smile and wave to her, I get the sense it's the former and not the latter."

"You're very observant."

Annie let herself bask in Katherine's compliment for a moment before she corrected it. "I've learned by personal experience."

"And I've been in hundreds of schools over the length of my career, but *I* didn't catch that. Don't sell yourself short."

Annie's cheeks grew hot, and she stumbled out, "...thanks."

Katherine stood and opened the door. "For now, if you could let me know if you notice anything else that triggers a concern—anything—I'd be grateful."

Annie stood and gathered up her bag and coat. "Of course. I'm happy to help."

Annie headed out of the office, and Katherine followed, stopping to lean against the reception desk. "Elaine, remind me, how many days until break?"

"Tough day?" Elaine leaned over the counter and patted Katherine's shoulder.

"Tough season. I'm looking forward to Christmas stockings, hot cocoa by the fire, and everyone being home, in one place. A whole two weeks in which I do not have to drive my children around or wait for Mac to get home from a late shift."

"He's not working the holiday?"

"Nope. He's doing a few shifts to help the deputies, but he's promised me that we're all going to be together and home for Christmas. I can't wait."

"Pete and your mom are going to miss you."

"They'll come over the next day. I think it's essential that the seven of us hunker down and get in a bit of bonding time."

Annie smiled as she waved goodbye to the women, imagining Katherine and her husband gathering their kids by the fire. The pang of longing that hit her heart was almost enough to make her stumble. Instead, she pushed through the doors and out the front entry, letting the cold air fill her lungs and freeze out the pain.

CHAPTER THREE

ALEX WHISTLED AND WAITED. HE HEARD the tags jingle first and then Shep appeared, running at full speed. He skidded to a stop in front of Alex, planting his hindquarters in the snow, his floppy ear at half-mast, its brother pointed skyward. "Had fun, did you?" Shep panted, waiting for a command. By the look of him he'd enjoyed running after that rabbit far too much. If Alex were smart, he'd try to break Shep of his attention issues, but the K9 program had already tried and failed. The dog always found his way back from his sidetracks, so Alex had learned to wait rather than go looking.

"Okay, buddy, let's go home." Alex opened the door of the truck, and Shep jumped in. As Alex got in, the dog snuffled his neck with his cold nose, and Alex laughed. "Quit it." On the drive home, Shep watched out the windows, eyes intent on the scenery as they passed. He was an intelligent dog, even if deemed not suitable for police work. He could track anything, anywhere, but he got distracted too easily. Technically, the dog shouldn't be riding with Alex on his patrol, but the patch they had to patrol today was so remote they hadn't seen another human. Tomorrow he'd be closer to town so Shep would stay home. In winter, Alex's primary duties were checking the snowmobile trails and dealing with the inevitable disputes. So much of the land in Maine was privately-owned that, if the wardens didn't keep the peace, the landowners could effectively shut down the trails. No trails, no tourists coming to the smaller towns. Rural Maine was poor enough already.

Alex slowed down as he passed a car on the side of the road. It was white with large patches of rust. One of the back windows was covered in cardboard with a trash bag over it. He pulled over and got out, leaving Shep in the truck. The interior of the car had food wrappers on the floor and a blanket in the back. At least ten years old, if not older, the car had seen better days. Alex went back to the truck to run the plate when he spotted a man approaching from the north side, setting Shep off. Alex raised his voice above the muffled barks coming behind him. "This yours?" He pointed to the car.

As the man nodded in response, his hair flopped forward into his eyes. He didn't try to push it back. His clothes looked like he'd slept in them, and he was giving off a distinct odor. One Alex was all too familiar with. "You been drinking?" The guy shook his head, but despite that and the early hour, Alex knew better. "Can I see your ID?"

"I...don't have it on me." The man patted his pockets.

"Name?"

He stared for a moment and then blurted. "Tom...Moore."

"You sure? Cause you said that like you weren't."

"No, I'm tired. Been walking a while."

"Do you live nearby?" Alex looked through the trees on the side of the road to see if he could spot a cabin or house.

"No. Car broke down, and I walked into town to get a wrecker to come tow it."

"So, where's the wrecker?"

"Ain't coming for a while." The man stuffed his hands in his pockets. "Said they'd get here before dark. That's in what? Another hour?" He looked up at the sky.

"Where's your ID?"

"Uh..." He patted his pockets again. "Maybe it's in the car?" He looked at the car, then back at Alex. "I think I left it at the station. I took it out to pay."

"Did you also stop by the bar?"

The man stared at him, and his internal debate over the benefit of telling the truth played out on his expression.

"Don't lie to me, buddy. It's easy enough to check."

"Yah, fine. I was at the bar. It's a long walk. Figured it would be a warmer one with a drink or two."

Or five, Alex added in his head. "Okay. Is the tow truck actually on its way?"

"Timmy said it was."

"You're local?"

"I work maintenance at the resort. Live in Newington."

"Address?" Alex took it down while the man gave it. "Okay, wait here." He headed back to his truck and an anxious Shep. After getting in, he made a call to check that the tow was on the way. Surprisingly it was. He also called the Smooth Moose to see if 'Tom Moore' had been in. He had, and from what the bartender said, he was topping off a buzz he'd started somewhere else. It wasn't enough evidence to book Moore on OUI, but he was going to be sure the man wasn't near a car anytime soon. Alex checked to see if he was in the system, and no surprise, he was. Moore had an outstanding warrant. Alex put in a call for backup. Shep growled low, and Alex looked up to see Moore standing at his window of the truck looking worried.

Alex raised a finger asking him to hold on. Hearing the answer over the radio that a deputy was available and nearby, Alex got out of the truck. "It looks like you have some matters you need to take care of. You've got two—"

"Aw, c'mon." Moore interrupted. "That stuff is just unpaid fees." Moore balled his fist. "It's a bunch of nonsense. I can't pay the ticket, so they heap a bunch of fees on it? Like that's gonna get them their money?" Moore's stance changed, his back leg shifted, his hip turned. The situation was rapidly deteriorating. Alex knew he could take the guy if he had to, but he didn't want to have to.

He raised his hand and rested it on his belt, a comfortable

distance from the butt of his gun. It was meant to be a subtle sign that he hoped Moore would understand. "I get it. That's rough, but now you have the chance to clear all that. We'll take you to the station and you can—"

"I need to go to work man, not to jail."

"First, we take care of business, then you get to work. The sooner you get this sorted, the sooner you're working." Alex saw the calculation written on the man's face. He was doing that truth benefit analysis again, only now he wasn't deciding if he'd give a fake name or not, he was deciding if he wanted to bolt or throw a punch. Just in time, flashing lights reflected on the snow behind him as a cruiser came into view. Moore finished his calculation, going for bolt and took off. For a rough looking guy who'd been drinking more than he should, he was fast. Alex was faster. They were knee deep in a snow bank when Alex took him to the ground. He had him cuffed when the deputy reached them.

"I got it from here." Deputy Chavez pulled Moore to his feet. He dragged the man out of the snow, knocking most of it off in the process. "Let's go, buddy." Moore didn't put up much of a fight as the deputy put him in the cruiser.

"I didn't get far with him. Told him about the warrant and he saw you coming."

"Okay. You coming?"

"Sure. I'll follow you to the station."

"Sounds good." Chavez hopped into his cruiser.

Alex stood at the sergeant's desk finishing his paperwork. Moore had one ticket he'd failed to pay. It was $100. Not chump change, but not a bank-breaker either. If he had money for booze, he had money to pay a ticket. Now that he'd let it go, then ignored the summons, he had an arrest on his sheet he did not need and was facing fees ten times what he would have had to pay if he'd done the right thing in the first place. It made no sense to Alex. He'd never been so broke he couldn't pay his bills, though, so what did he know?

A large hand clapped his shoulder. "Alex, good to see you."

He turned to see Pete Coleman smiling down at him. The man was almost always smiling. Then again, he was newly married and retired, so he had reasons for his happiness.

"Hey. Are you here for me?"

"Checking on you?" Pete raised an eyebrow. "Do I need to?"

"No, I've been good. No complaints from the community in the last two months. Boss says they're getting used to me."

"They never really had a reason to complain in the first place. I told you it's more about your style than anything else."

Pete had lectured him about his 'authoritarian tendencies' when he'd first started. Game wardens were law enforcement, but not everybody saw it that way. Wardens needed to handle the people they interacted with deftly to be effective. A hunter didn't always have the same respect for a green uniform that he would a blue one. Pete had to show him the way. If he hadn't, Alex wouldn't have lasted a month.

"I'm here for Mac, actually. Taking him to dinner to see how he's doing."

"Pete, you're married to his mother in law, and you live a mile from his house."

"Sure, but he's got five kids now. I never see him." Pete peered into the distance over Alex's shoulder. "Hang on, there he is."

Alex turned and saw Mac, correctly Deputy MacAlister, coming down the hallway of the station. He used to be Captain MacAlister, a pretty much famous, for Maine, detective. He'd given up the top job when he'd married, which to Alex, seemed completely unnecessary.

"There you are." Pete greeted Mac.

"I'm here. I'm dog-tired, but I'm here." Mac, like Pete, was taller than Alex. He was a good deal older too. His hair had enough gray in it that no one would think he was a rookie.

Alex took a closer look and spotted the tell-tale signs of a man in need of more sleep. "Are you on nights these days?"

Mac nodded. "Yup. All this week. Taking over for Miller."

"Right, he's going to Disney for Christmas, isn't he?"

"His wife's family goes every year. This is the first time they can afford to all go together. He says it's a big deal for her. Something about Christmas making extra magic."

Alex shook his head. "That's crazy. If it were me, I'd take the wife to a beach."

Mac smiled, a knowing expression on his face. "You'll think differently when you're married."

"That is not likely." Alex looked back down at his paperwork to be sure he had it so he could file it and then get out of there. He hated the 'when you're married' lecture from the old guys.

"Which part? The married or the think differently?"

Alex looked up at Mac and wondered what prompted the question. Why would Mac care what Alex thought? They'd worked a few calls together, but that was it.

"I'm not looking to get married anytime soon." That seemed a safe response.

"Enjoying your freedom?"

"No." That was the truth. It was weird that it had slipped out, but there was nothing free about his life. "But marriage isn't in the cards for me."

Pete's eyes narrowed, and Alex braced for an interrogation but was saved by the duty sergeant. "Hey, you got that paperwork?"

Alex handed the man his paperwork then backed away from the counter. "Don't let me keep you guys. I'm heading out anyway. See you later." He walked away, feeling their eyes on his back.

At the door, he whistled for Shep who waited patiently, for once, at the bench in the lobby. The drive to his house was a long one, so he had plenty of time for thinking, which stunk since it was the last thing he felt like doing. His thoughts, when left to themselves, had a way of focusing on purple-blue eyes, perfect red lips, and jet-black hair.

He needed to escape his head. A movie might do it, but nothing good was playing. There wasn't a game on either, so no point in hitting the Moose and dealing with the Saturday night crowd to watch it. Nothing was waiting at home to distract him. He had a TV, but no cable, and he'd been through his stack of DVDs about twenty times. There was no Internet there either, but that was a good thing. When he had picked the house, he'd known that with its quiet and peaceful atmosphere he'd be giving up the outside world. It had been a fair trade. He got to avoid losing himself in a glowing screen for hours as well as cheaper rent.

When he finally pulled into the short driveway leading to his house Shep sat up, ears perky, or at least the one that didn't flop over. It wasn't his usual alert. A curl of the nearly constant tension in Alex's gut unfurled. Something was off. His house was set away from the road behind a bank of trees. Granted they were leafless since it was winter, but it was still a pretty dense screen. No one came down his driveway that didn't have business being there. Alex hadn't ordered anything, and he had a PO Box for his mail, so it was a rare event that anyone came here at all. The house was one-story with a high, peaked roof and probably an attic, although Alex had never looked. A short, covered porch hung off the front of the house, and it was there

Shep's attention was focused.

Alex got out of the car and gave Shep a command to keep him close instead of racing to the door. He approached slowly, one hand at his belt. Walking up the steps, he spotted it. Nailed to the door was a white, business-size envelope with his last name in bold writing. He pulled it off the door and looked it over. It had nothing else on the exterior, only his name.

He moved his focus to the door, checking that it was still locked. The porch looked untouched as well. Nothing else was out of place. The nail in the door was a brad nail, the kind used for fine woodwork like picture frames. Nobody was going to get a print off that, so he left it where it was. Handling the envelope carefully he unlocked the door and checked the house with Shep still at his side. Once he'd cleared each room, he fed Shep and refilled his water fountain. Sitting at his kitchen table, he got out the print kit he'd picked up when the first envelope had landed in his PO Box. He dusted this one for prints and came up with nothing, just like the others. Opening it carefully with his penknife, he pulled out a folded sheet of paper. It was just five words. I KNOW WHERE YOU LIVE written in block letters with black marker.

He brought the paper to his nose and inhaled. It had an odd fragrance. Like soot or smoke, but he couldn't place it. Carefully dusting it for prints, he came up empty again. The tension in his gut became dread. He hadn't received a letter in a while, and he'd hoped that meant they were done with him, that whoever it was had considered the job done when he'd left Lewiston, his hometown. He got out his file of letters and laid them out, all six of them, this one making seven. The first had been delivered to his parents' house and it had read 'ALEX MORETTI IS GUILTY AND WE ALL KNOW IT.' The second came after the news ran a story on the 'hero cop of Lewiston' and read 'I KNOW THE TRUTH AND SOON EVERYONE WILL.' The third came right after he quit the force and, like the fourth which arrived at his new PO Box, it threatened 'JUSTICE IS COMING.' They took a break and didn't show up again until after he'd graduated game warden training and appeared with the rest of the new recruits in the paper, but always to the PO Box. He didn't think anybody knew exactly where he was living. As much as he thought the writer was probably harmless, the fact that they hadn't stopped was bugging him. It wasn't enough to make him report the harassment, but it was enough to worry him. Reporting it would jeopardize a job he needed. Not that the boss would fire him, but he might limit his duties. He didn't need anyone seeing him as damaged goods.

Alex wondered if the writer set a Google alert for Alex's name. Sweet River had a town blog, the *Sweet River Lowdown*. Alex had appeared in it a few weeks ago since he'd officially taken over the district from Pete and Pete had finally retired. That could be how he or she kept finding him. Not that he was hiding. Not really. Alex carefully put the letter away and thought about who it could be for what had to be the hundredth time. Who could nurse a burning hatred of him for this long? It had been two years since she'd died. Even the people back home were over it, according to his mom, anyway. This letter was an escalation. This person, whoever they were, had been to Alex's home. It was a reminder that he'd never be free of it. Never. The letter was also a reminder of why, as much as he wanted to, he couldn't let Annie into his life. For her own good. Everyone he cared about ended up hurt—or worse.

CHAPTER FOUR

THE SOUND OF CLINKING CUPS AND teenage-girl laughter wafted up through the heating duct, and Annie smiled. It was convenient that the HVAC duct carried the noise from the back room of the shop downstairs up two floors to her apartment. She could keep an ear on things so to speak. Not that she needed to. Bethany and Chantal, her Saturday crew, might be a bit silly at times, but they were hard workers. Annie snuggled down in her reading chair by the front windows and focused on the book she'd been trying to read. The sun was streaming in through the window, the heat making her sleepy. It didn't help that her chair was a velvet-covered wingback, a hug in furniture form. She'd promised herself she'd catch up on her 'to be read' pile today, but it was looking less likely. Her brain was too distract-able.

A low rumble came from the floor, and then an orange ball of fur jumped into her lap. "Shoo, Hobbes." But the tabby cat didn't move. Instead, he flicked his tail, so it ran under her nose before curling up in her lap, blocking her book. "I give up." She chucked the book on the table beside her and spoke to her cat. "It was terrible anyway. The heroine let the hero walk all over her and then she'd cried about it to her best friend whose advice was to make him jealous. I don't know about you, but I'm inclined to think that any love you need deceit to secure is probably not the kind that lasts. And if it doesn't last, what's the point?"

She scooped Hobbes onto the floor and then stood. He scampered away, jumping onto the kitchen counter. A moment later she heard the tell-tale sound of crinkling paper and knew he was at the wrapped package of cookies she'd left there.

"No, you don't. I spent an hour on that parcel." She sprinted to the counter as he nudged it off the edge with a paw. She managed to catch it on the way down. Annie examined the package, surprised that it survived intact. It was the gingerbread men she'd promised to Alex. He hadn't come back in yesterday even though he'd left his scarf behind, but that might not mean anything. He could have been busy, and it was just a scarf. She'd spotted it at the end of the day, still hanging, and brought it upstairs to be sure no one mistook it for theirs.

As Annie turned the package over in her hands she thought about how she and Alex were stalled, stuck at friendly, not even real friends. Although they talked more days than they didn't, and he knew things about her that no one else did, it was from a distance. They were safe in their routine. Was she brave enough to break it? She knew that Saturdays were his day off. It would be a friendly gesture for her to run the cookies and his scarf by his place. Wouldn't it? He might not even be home, and she could leave them on his porch. He'd told her all about his house and where he lived, right near the river. She could find it easy enough.

She tightened the twine holding the Christmas tag—the one that she carefully made yesterday—to the package. She'd drawn holly leaves and written 'To Alex From Annie—Merry Christmas' with colored pens, so it looked special, but not girly. Although she liked sparkly sweaters, dresses, and heels, she assumed a man who wore flannel and jeans when not in uniform wouldn't be likely to appreciate overtly feminine touches.

Before she had a chance to think it through, she was at the coat rack taking down her winter coat. It was part of a wardrobe that was a relic of her internship at her father's business in New York. Black, princess-seamed, and cashmere, it was far more flattering than the parka she typically wore when running errands. Grabbing her keys and the cookies, she took Alex's scarf down from the rack as well. A gentle scent wafted up to her as she folded it. It still smelled like him, and a wave of doubt rushed over her. What if he was home and got angry that she invaded his privacy? What if he wasn't, but still found her dropping by his place to be an invasion? Was she out of her mind to do this?

No. This was Christmas-time. A friend would show up on another's doorstep with a gift or to return something. Even an acquaintance would do that. Would she mind if it was the other way around? Not if it was Alex—yes if it was someone she didn't know well. But Alex did know her, so this was okay.

That decided, she said goodbye to Hobbes and headed downstairs. Her apartment was on the third floor of the building. The second floor she'd rented out to Claire and Erin Sullivan for their craft business. One of the beautiful things about owning the whole building outright was that she could offer a friend a great rate on space and ensure that the stores in her home were ones she liked. Her father's voice rose up in her mind, scolding her for throwing away the inheritance from her grandfather. She remembered how he had grimaced and derided her plans, saying she was squandering her degree. 'You have disappointed me, Anne.' Those words had hurt.

Annie stopped in her tracks. She'd made it outside, and the air was cold, but the sun was shining brightly. With light reflecting on the snow all around her and the blue sky overhead she took a deep breath and let the beauty of the day clear her mind. The train of thought she was on ended in only one place, regret, and on the way, it would stop at the stations of insecurity, anger, sadness, and loneliness. None of which she needed. Closing her eyes, she let the sun bathe her face, recharging her spirit like a solar battery. When she opened them, Claire and Erin were standing in front of her with matching, indulgent smiles on their faces.

"Soaking up the rays?" Claire shifted a box of what looked

like craft supplies from one arm to another to give her a hug.

"Yes. Sort of." Annie hugged her back and smiled at Erin whose arms were also full of supplies. "Are you guys teaching classes today?"

"Yup." Erin moved her box a bit to take out her keys to their shared back door. "Last-minute gifts for parents. We're expecting a bevy of kids today from noon to four. You'll probably hear them tromping up and down the steps."

Claire pointed down at the scarf and wrapped parcel in Annie's hands. "I bet I know who those are for."

"Well, he doesn't come in on the weekends, and I thought he'd need his scarf." Annie hoped this would not be grist for Claire's 'Annie and Alex' mill.

"Tell him I said 'hi.'" Claire took Erin's elbow with her free hand and towed her to the back door. "Don't let us keep you!"

Erin was looking confused, and Annie was grateful for that. If Erin didn't know what they were talking about, that meant Claire had kept it to herself. Annie waved goodbye to them and walked to the parking lot behind the building hoping her car would start. Her Passat didn't love the cold. It didn't like the snow either. Between that and its age she really needed to replace it, but she couldn't afford a new payment quite yet. She wanted to get something bigger to handle the snow better, but not something so big she couldn't get into it. Five-foot-two was a whole two inches taller than her grandmother, but it was still short.

When it came to looks, she'd gotten everything from her father's side of the family. Her mother was tall and thin with a willowy grace. She was short and round with no grace at all. But on days like today, she was glad of it, since she wasn't freezing. Body fat had its uses. The air coming from the car vents grew warm, and she checked the temperature gauge. Seeing that it was finally on the move, she drove to the other side of town. It was the side furthest from the lake and the resort. She'd heard it jokingly called 'the wrong side of the river' instead of the wrong side of the tracks.

Minutes later she was turning down the driveway to Alex's place. It was a long one, and once she'd cleared the trees she saw his rental. It was old, but looked well-kept. Beyond it lay a plain of brown grass mostly covered in snow and then the river in the distance. It looked Nordic in its bare expanse. There was a light mist rising over the water. Despite the bleak scenery, the cabin seemed homey with a plume of smoke rising from its chimney.

Smoke in the chimney. "Uh-oh." Alex was home. His truck was parked off to the side of the house. How was he going to react? Would this be weird? There was no point in thinking about it now since she was here, and he'd probably spotted her already. She parked behind his truck. Getting out, she took a deep breath and tried to give herself a pep-talk. Alex wouldn't think this was a sneak attack. They were friendly. And she wanted to move that to friends. He liked her, and she liked him. It was time one of them did something about it. Since it wasn't going to be him, it had to be her. She marshaled her courage and climbed the front steps to knock on his door. A booming bark sounded from inside.

CHAPTER FIVE

ALEX LOOKED OUT THE SIDE WINDOW to the woman knocking as Shep barked his head off. "Shh, buddy, it's a friend." He gave the dog the command to sit, which he did, but his tail wagged with anticipation. Shep loved company, and they rarely had any. Alex stared at the door wondering what Annie was doing there. All night trying not to think of her and all the morning trying to resolve not to swing by the shop to see if she was in, and now she was on his front step? She knocked again, and he pulled the door open.

"You have a dog!" Annie shouted as Shep bounced around her, still barking. She shoved a scarf and a wrapped package into Alex's hands, freeing her own to pet Shep as he trembled with joy. "You are too cute." Shep leaned into her with his full weight, almost knocking her over. He was as tall as her waist. "What's his name?" She looked up at Alex.

"Shep."

She laughed, a sweet sound, and he found himself smiling. "You named your German Shepherd, 'Shep?'"

"What? Oh, no, I didn't name him." In truth, he thought the name was a bit lame, but that's how he'd arrived and had been trained to it. Alex couldn't change it.

"Where'd you get him?"

"He's a rescue. My sergeant asked me if I could take him in. He'd washed out of K-9 training and bounced around a bit before coming up here."

"Aw, that's too bad. He's such a love."

"He's smart too, but he gets distracted easily. They didn't feel he was suited to work."

"So he has doggie ADD?" She rubbed his sides again, and

Shep licked her face, getting her to laugh.

"Something like that." Alex took a closer look at the stuff in his hands. It *was* his scarf. He must have left it at the shop. "Um...thanks. I guess I left this behind yesterday."

"Yeah, I figured you'd miss it and didn't want it to end up going home with someone else. That, and you forgot your cookies."

"Cookies?"

Annie pointed to the package Alex was holding. He lifted it to his nose and then smiled. Gingerbread. "Thanks." She'd remembered him. That was really thoughtful. Two impulses waged a quick war in his head, the kinder one winning. "Do you want to come in?" He took a step back, and she followed him inside, Shep glued to her side. "I'll put these away." He headed into the kitchen, kicking himself. What was the point of trying to be the good guy and not lead her on when she walked right up to his front door? "Have a seat, um...anywhere, I guess." His place was not furnished, precisely. He had a small couch, a folding table with a chair, one floor lamp, and one armchair next to which was his stack of books. She took a look around the room and sat on the couch. Shep immediately hopped up on the seat next to her and leaned in. She giggled while stroking his ears and head.

"He's such a sweet dog."

"Yah. Sweet." More like 'traitor.' He moved the folding chair at the table closer to the couch and sat down. He had no idea what to say to her. She was still in her coat and hat. He liked the contrast of her white hat and black hair. The coat looked expensive, but not flashy. Like her. She always wore dresses and pretty boots or shoes. Classy, like the way she spoke with a slight accent, and the words she used. He had never met anyone quite like her, and every new detail only made him like her more. Which was a problem. He was a good enough man to know she deserved better, but not so good that he could stay away from her. "Thanks for the cookies. You didn't have to bring them."

"No, but they wouldn't be as good if I'd saved them until Monday." Her expression was worried, probably thinking he meant it as a criticism. "And, I also wanted to remind you of that Christmas concert I was talking about yesterday. It's tomorrow night. At the church." She looked up quickly at him then away again. "Even if you're not like...a churchgoer, I think you'd like it."

"I'm a 'churchgoer.' I haven't been going since moving up here, but—" His cell phone rang. It was his mom's ringtone, and he knew better than to let it go to voicemail. "Sorry, I've got to take this." He moved into the kitchen to answer. "Hi, Mamae."

Without so much as a 'hi,' his mother launched right into it, berating him in rapid-fire Portuguese, interspersed with English. Her main complaint—him not coming home for Christmas. He should have expected this call when he'd left her the message he wouldn't be there. He waited through a full minute of yelling before he tried interrupting again.

She wasn't having it. "Alex, please, your family misses you."

"Mamae, you know why."

"I miss you." Her voice was broken, and the sound of it was a knife in his heart. He had to get her off the phone before he caved.

"I have someone over right now. I don't want to be rude."

"Amiga ou namorada?"

"She's a friend."

"Fine, fine. If you have someone over. You call me later?"

"Of course."

"I love you, anjinho."

"Eu tambem te amo."

When he walked back into the living room, Annie was smiling.

"You speak Portuguese? I couldn't help overhear, and I recognized a few words. I had a friend from Brazil in college."

"My mom grew up in Salvador, right on the coast."

"It must be beautiful there. Have you been?"

"A few times, not for a while though. It's not cheap to get down there. My mom flies down twice a year. I think that's probably the only reason she keeps working." When she looked confused by that, he explained. "She works for an airline."

"That makes sense." She looked him over, and he assumed she was wondering why he didn't look more Brazilian but was too polite to ask.

"I look like my dad. His dad was half Italian, half Irish, and his mom was all French, so he's basically a mutt. I got his coloring. My two older brothers look like my mom, and my youngest brother got all the Irish. Red hair." He pointed at his head. Annie laughed, and he smiled, unable not to. Her laugh was always contagious.

"I look like my father too. The Eastern European wins out over the English. My mom though, she's French all the way through. American though, not like France-French, which, I can tell you is another thing altogether. How did your parents meet?"

"Mom came up here to work at one of the hotels on Old Orchard Beach. Dad was working for the summer on the midway at the amusement park. He saw her from his booth, called her over to try a game and let her win."

"I love stories like that." Annie gave Shep a pat. He'd laid down beside her, his head on her lap. This would typically be the part that she'd talk about how her parents met, but Annie rarely spoke about her family. Alex wondered if maybe things weren't so good for her growing up. The way she avoided the topic he suspected that was the case.

Sure enough, Annie changed the subject. "So, before your

mom called you were talking about going to church, or that you didn't up here, but you had in the past?"

"I grew up Catholic, but we started going to the New Life church when my mom met the pastor there. She liked his sermons. My brothers and I got baptized there. It's...different. Charismatic. I've heard Pastor Connors speak before. He's good, though a little more subdued."

"I think you'd get used to it at Calvary, after a while. It's pretty traditional New England-style, which to you would be a lot more subdued, but the teaching is always good. Pastor Connors is probably a better speaker than a small town like Sweet River usually sees. He used to be a missionary too, so that gives him a different perspective. It helps since sometimes I feel out of step. I'm an American, but I spent most of my life in England and Europe. Sometimes I can't relate."

"You didn't grow up here?"

"Not really. We lived in New York for a while, and then I went to live with my Aunt Delia in England."

"How old were you?"

Annie's expression grew cautious and then sort of shut down. "Eight. It was the right time since my father's career was really taking off, and my mother acted as his assistant. She ran the 'business of him' as he used to call it. They're really brilliant. Even now, Father is in high demand. They're still jetting all over the globe. If he weren't so driven, he'd probably have retired by now since he's nearly seventy, but he's still at it. My mom is a good deal younger, and I think she'd rather travel than settle anywhere. She really prefers the seasonality of their life like New York in the summer and Europe in the..." She trailed off, a blush creeping over her cheeks. "Boy, I went on and on again, didn't I?"

"I like it when you talk to me, Annie." And he did. She didn't hide anything. So quiet with everyone else, but not with him. It made him feel special as if he had a part of her no one else did.

"I'm glad. I mean if you let me, I'll talk the ear right off your head."

"I don't think there's any danger of that."

"You'd be surprised." She began to fidget, and Shep bumped her hand with his head. Smiling, she returned to petting him. "Such a good boy." He gave a happy groan, closing his eyes as she rubbed his ears.

"You're going to spoil him."

"It's not possible to spoil any creature with love." Annie was looking down at Shep, a sweet expression on her face.

"No, I guess it's not." He began to understand that she was talking about more than his dog. He could fill in the blanks of what she wasn't saying. Left with an aunt at eight, sent to boarding schools? From what she'd said she would be spending Christmas alone, not for the first time. That was a kick to his gut. Someone as kind and loving as Annie should be surrounded by people to care for her, but she had no one. He wanted to be the one. But it would all go wrong. If he gave in to the temptation, if he allowed himself to care for her he'd only disappoint her in the end. He cared too much for her to risk it.

"So, do you think you'll go?"

He shook his head to clear it but spotted her frown. She thought he was saying no, but he'd forgotten she'd asked about the concert. "Maybe. I'll try." He answered quickly, eager to erase the look of disappointment on her face. If he were smart, he wouldn't go anywhere near that concert. That would definitely move them out of the friend zone and into dangerous waters.

"Great! If you want to sit up in the balcony, I can save you a seat. That's where I usually sit. The acoustics are pretty awesome, and it's chairs, not pews."

"You don't like pews?"

"I feel weird taking the end seat when a pew is full of a family, y'know?" She winced. "There's not a lot of single people at Calvary. Most are attached to somebody in some way. It's awkward. People probably think I'm some kind of recluse always sitting by myself up in the balcony."

"You're way too friendly to be a recluse." He kicked himself for how that sounded. Her face fell, and he stumbled over his words trying to explain what he meant. "I didn't mean...I'm not saying you're too friendly. You're exactly the right amount."

"Oh. Okay," She swiped her bangs off her forehead. "Phew, I know I sort of showed up at your house out of the blue today. That wasn't weird?"

"No, it's fine. Seriously." He reached out and held her hand for a second. She looked down at his hand on hers, and he pulled it back. "Thanks for coming by. I'm looking forward to the cookies." He mentally kicked himself since that sounded like he was telling her to get out.

"Good. I'm glad I brought them." She got up, shifting Shep as she did, and he grunted with displeasure. "I should probably go. Got so much stuff to do today." She headed for the door and Shep slid down off the couch and followed her. He sat on his haunches, looking for more attention.

His dog was in love. *Perfect.* He got up and went to open the door for her. "Thanks again, I really appreciate you coming by."

She glanced up at him. "You're welcome. I hope I see you at the concert."

He nodded, knowing better than to promise something he couldn't.

"Okay then. 'Bye." She waved at him from the porch before heading down the steps and out to her car.

He watched through the front window as she backed out of his driveway. Shep whined as she left. "That's not helping, buddy." Alex went into the kitchen thinking he was ready for a cookie. He started to unwrap the package, impressed that it was wax paper folded into a bundle and tied with twine. There was a tag attached with greenery on it. He ran a thumb over the back and felt the pen marks. She'd drawn the details on the card herself. His efforts to keep her at arm's length had apparently failed. No one put this kind of energy into a gift unless their feelings went with it. He prayed for God to help him protect those feelings since he couldn't be what she needed. He was already living the consequences of his own thoughtless actions. Making that same mistake, hurting someone he cared about again, would be more than he could take.

CHAPTER SIX

ANNIE CHECKED HER OUTFIT IN THE mirror. The belted sweater she was wearing was new, and she still wasn't sure about it. Because it was such a haul to get to the mall, she shopped almost exclusively online. That meant some hits and some misses. The sweater was a bit long for her torso, and the color washed her out. She whipped it off and pulled on the cowl-necked sweater she'd tried on first. The soft white was a good color for her, and a nice contrast to her plaid skirt. Her boots were riding boots, not precisely high-style, but they were dressy and had a solid tread so she wouldn't be falling on her face in them. A high priority since she'd slipped twice earlier that day after church. No more heels to church until the snow was gone.

"He's not going to be there, so I don't know why you're bothering," Annie told her reflection in the mirror. She'd been trying to convince herself that disappointment lay ahead, but it wasn't working. Ever since she'd come back from his house, a drive she hardly remembered for the sheer euphoria, she'd been unable to kill the hope that Alex would come to the concert and that it would be the start of something.

The visit to his house had gone far better than she had anticipated. He hadn't shut the door in her face or laughed or looked horrified that she'd shown up on his doorstep. Instead, he'd let her in, and they'd talked. Although he seemed uncomfortable, it was the usual sort of discomfort she felt from him at times, like he wasn't sure what to do. Granted, as soon as she reached her apartment she went about dissecting every sentence she'd uttered and second-guessing every moment. It had been impossible to get him and that day out of her head all night. She'd had three dreams that night all featuring her embarrassing herself in front of him as if her brain wanted to run through every scenario of humiliation so it could exhaust itself.

Church was the perfect antidote. The sermon had banished any thoughts of Alex at all so that when she got home, it was a few hours of peace before she noticed it was time to get ready, and her head filled right back up. Her usual pep talks were not working, neither was imagining all the things that could go wrong and why they wouldn't. There was no help for it. If Alex didn't show, she was going to feel bad. It would be a subtle hint from him that friendly was where they would be staying–there would be no move to friends and certainly no move to anything else. Annie wasn't sure if she was ready for the something else. She had limited experience in that area, but she was ready for him to be a real friend.

Hobbes wound his furry body between her legs with a rumbling purr. "Ack, no." She hopped away. "Orange fur does not go with black tights." He rubbed his face on her leg. "Don't mess with me." She pulled her leg away. "I'll feed you, and you'll leave my tights alone, deal?" He sat down on his haunches and looked up at her. "Stay." She went to the small table she'd set up for his food and water since he never liked to eat off dishes on the floor. He jumped up on the table and allowed her to rub his ears and kiss him before he stuffed his face into his food bowl. "Piglet." She stroked his back as he purred with every bite, eating like she hadn't fed him in days. Which was how he always ate. She wondered if having been abandoned as a kitten in a cardboard box on the side of the road was why he munched like he was worried he'd never get another meal. Maybe childhood trauma followed cats as well as people.

The chimes of a bell tower rang from the vicinity of her purse. It was her phone alarm, and it meant it was time to leave. A mix of anticipation and anxiety hit her stomach, like butterflies, only not as pleasant. For a second, she thought she might be sick. "Stop it!" Annie scolded herself and walked to the coat rack where her purse was hanging. Getting dressed in a coat, hat, and mittens she said goodbye to Hobbes, who ignored her, and she stepped out into the hall. She locked up and stuffed the keys into her pocket since she'd be walking to the church, not driving.

Outside she was hit with a blast of frigid air and told herself it was bracing, not freezing. Halfway to the church, she was regretting her clothing choices as her body fat did not prevent the cold from penetrating her stylish, but not nearly warm enough coat. "Should've worn the blasted parka," she scolded herself as she walked. By the time she'd made it across the snowy town green and up to the church's steps, she was shaking. Standing in the narthex, she stomped her boots on the entry-way carpet, off to the side so that people could still get by her and into the sanctuary. Each time the doors opened, a wave of heat would hit her along with the lights and sounds of the crowd settling in. She waited, hoping he'd appear, knowing he probably wouldn't. Eventually, she went inside and checked to see who had already arrived. Skirting the edge of the room, she looked for familiar faces.

It looked like Christmas, even more so than it had that morning. The ladies of the hospitality committee handled the decorations, and they'd done it up. There were dozens of poinsettias dotting the room with long swags of greenery and candles in lanterns at strategic spots. The pews were about seventy-five percent full. She scanned the room. The MacAlisters were there with the kids, including a sulky-looking Olivia. Annie caught her eye and waved. She gave her a slight smile in return. Erin and her boys were sitting in the front row, as they would since Erin was engaged to Pastor Connors and would be marrying him in the spring. Claire was with her along with her two boys. Annie waved, and they all waved back. No one called her over since they knew she'd be heading up to the balcony. Pete and Lauren came in and chose seats by the MacAlisters, but still no Alex. Annie headed towards the stairs and paused again, a sinking feeling in her stomach. He wasn't going to come.

She waited until the doors closed, her hope dying as they shut. Climbing the stairs, she tried to talk herself into not minding that he wasn't there while fighting off hope he was late but still coming. She sighed. He wasn't going to show. She should have known. The balcony had more people in it than usual, but she'd left a 'reserved' sign on two chairs at the front earlier that day. She felt a bit stupid taking one sign up and sitting down. The seats she'd saved were on the aisle in the front row.

She sat on the interior one so she'd look like she was waiting for someone else to arrive. Taking her coat off, she laid it on the back of the chair, stuffing her hat and mittens into the sleeve. Her hair was probably a fright. With a small move, she slid her hands up into it and fluffed it out. Curly hair could be beastly in the winter, but she kept it on the edge of short, almost medium-length, so she had enough to work with to prevent its worst tendencies.

The couple sitting next to her smiled in a friendly way which she returned. She would've introduced herself, but the opening notes of the first song began. Annie let her eyes close as the music floated up and surrounded her. Calvary Church was lucky enough to have both a pipe organ and an organist to play it. They were making full use of it tonight. The music filled every available space, resounding in her chest until she felt herself part of it. In the balcony the acoustics were incredible. When the choir began to sing, she wondered how anyone could not feel worship as an active, real thing, when music like this played. It was almost other-worldly. What would music be like in heaven if it was this exquisite here?

Deep into the piece, she felt a brush of air against her cheek. She took in a deep breath and caught a familiar scent; pine needles and warm wool. Alex.

CHAPTER SEVEN

ALEX TOOK THE SEAT NEXT TO Annie, swiping the 'reserved' sign off as he sat. She opened her eyes and turned to him. A bright smile slowly dawned on her face. As if in answer, a rush of warmth filled his chest. Based on how happy that one smile made him, this was a bad idea. If he were a better man, he wouldn't have come. That thought didn't stop him from smiling in return. She turned back to the choir, looking far happier than she had when he first arrived. He'd seen her with her eyes closed, lost in the music, with a slightly sad expression on her face. He'd spotted the sign on the chair next to her and had to steel himself against the punch to the gut that simple gesture gave him. She'd had faith in him. More than he generally had in himself.

He tried to lose himself in the music as she had, but it was a struggle. During breaks in the music, they read pieces of Jesus' birth story from the Bible. There wasn't the usual noise and movement of the church he was used to, but the simplicity of the service moved him. It was similar to Jesus' birth itself. One of two of the most critical events in the universe and it happened with little fanfare, in a stable. God did stuff like that all the time, giving the humble the crucial moments, raising up the nobodies. Moses to Mary, He chose the unlikely, the unsuited. It gave Alex a glimmer of hope that God could still use him. When he thought of all that had happened, he felt so far from redemption, and from God. There was a gulf between him and anything good.

He felt a tug on his sleeve. Annie was turned to him looking concerned. His thoughts must be showing on his face. It was hard to pull off the neutral expression he'd perfected around her. She made him feel things.

"You okay?" she whispered under the projected voice of the person reading the scripture.

"Yah, I was..." What was he? He didn't want to lie, but there was no way he was getting into it either. "...thinking. Of stuff."

She leaned closer and whispered in his ear while her light, flowery scent floated up to him. "When your train of thought starts to take you to a bad station, you need to disembark. Failing that, derail it. That's what I do." She pulled back and gave him a sympathetic look. "Derail it." She repeated and then she took his hand in hers and squeezed it tight before letting go. Alex wanted her hand back. He wondered if pulling her into his arms would help. Maybe Annie could derail his thoughts.

A new song started and broke the tension only he seemed to feel between them. It was a carol he knew well. The choir invited them all to join in. Annie did. Her voice surprised him. He thought the sound would be high, like a soprano, but it was a low, smooth alto. She held out the program for him with the printed words to the song, incorrectly assuming he wasn't singing because he didn't know the words. He knew them, and he also knew that he couldn't carry a tune in a bucket. He started singing quietly, holding onto the program with her, impressed when she switched to harmony in the second verse.

The candlelight, the music, and Annie were all soothing his soul. He took in every detail, the way her hair curled around her face, her long dark lashes, the brightness of her eyes, the way her pale skin contrasted to her red lips. He turned his head away. Best not to think about her lips. He didn't want to pass the point they could stay friends and right now, he wasn't feeling friendship. It was more like fascination. She was a magnet, drawing him in against his will. It was everything about her, even the way she dressed. Tonight she was in a snow-white sweater with sparkles that caught the light—it almost created a halo around her. That should remind him that she was good and he was not. He had to kill this feeling before he did something stupid. Looking down at the program he saw they were two songs from the finale. He could make an excuse and slip out now. That would be the safe thing to do. But he didn't move from his seat.

When the singing ended, and the place was full of applause, Annie stood and grabbed her coat as if she was leaving, so he did as well. He led her out of the building and outside before the stairs or the lobby got crowded. "Did you want to stay to say hi to anyone?" He asked over his shoulder.

"Nope. There's a dessert reception in the church basement, but I don't usually stay for stuff like that. It's super-awkward, and I never know what to say, so I don't go." She shrugged. "But you can stay if you want. I mean, it's probably really nice, and there's cake." Her smile was all wrong, and he realized she was ashamed she wasn't good at hobnobbing. He wasn't either, but he hated that she was counting that as some kind of fault.

"Hey, that's fine. How about I walk you home?" He asked as she got into her coat.

Annie's eyes lit up. "I'd like that. It's not far. I live above the shop."

"I think I knew that." Together they walked down the shoveled path and across the town green, covered with a thick blanket of snow. A way had been cleared leading to Main Street and Annie's building along with other paths to the firehouse, the school, and the shops at the other end of the street. There were people dotted here and there, their voices carrying across the space on the mild wind. The path Annie and Alex walked passed through the center of the green where an arch had been constructed and strung with hundreds of Christmas lights.

"It's magical, isn't it?" Annie was looking up as they approached the arch. "Who put this up?"

"I think there's a committee that handles the decorations of the public spaces. They do the town hall too."

"Well, this is a whole lot better than a string of garland on the town hall."

"Beautiful isn't it?" Someone shouted from the other side.

"Elaine?" Annie asked, squinting into the dark. "Fancy meeting you here."

An older woman bundled in a thick coat appeared on the path opposite them. "I missed the singing at the church tonight, but I aim to make it for dessert."

"It ended only a few minutes ago so you should have time," Annie assured her. Elaine's attention seemed to be on Alex. It was as if she was sizing him up.

"Alex, this is Elaine." Annie introduced them. "We work together at the school."

"Good to meet you." Elaine stuck out a gloved hand, and he shook it. "Heard a lot of nice things about you." She threw a look at Annie who rolled her eyes. "I'm glad to see you two are enjoying the lights. We did a fundraiser last spring to put them up. Gorgeous, aren't they?" She looked up at them with a smile of satisfaction. "Oh! Pictures! This would look great on the blog." She stepped away and shoved Alex into Annie. "Get cozy, I need to take this in portrait mode." She took another step back while Annie stood woodenly next to him. "Get closer." Elaine waved emphatically at them, so Alex turned slightly to the side. The expression on Annie's face was mortified, and Alex had to fight the urge to tell Elaine to forget it. He didn't want Annie upset.

Annie looked up at him and then mouthed 'Sorry.'

"Hey, no worries." He smiled down at her.

"That's mistletoe up there." Elaine pointed above them. "Give us a kiss."

"Elaine!" Annie shouted.

"C'mon, it's only a kiss."

Alex turned Annie towards him and lowered his lips to her forehead, kissing her there while the flash went off and a shutter sounded about ten times. He leaned away, and Annie tipped her face up to him. There was a softness to the look she was giving him.

"Did you get that?" He asked Elaine, his eyes still on Annie.

"I sure did. Thank you. Now I'll be on my way. Don't let me intrude." She shuffled off down the path.

"Intrude? Oh, not at all." Annie laughed nervously. "I'm so sorry. Elaine is too much. I cannot believe she made you kiss me. You must be annoyed. Really, she is out of hand. I'm going to tell her on Monday that it is beyond the pale to ask something like that. I know you and I are only acquaintances, and I'm sure you're mortified by having to kiss me. On camera! It's too terrible. If you want I can tell her that she needs to delete those. I'm sure you don't want anyone seeing—"

Alex kissed her lips while they were still moving. Everything she was saying was wrong. Kissing her was sweet and perfect, and he didn't want her saying it wasn't good and right. It was her nervous habit, her words got away from her. Then again, he might be kissing her because he wanted to—or— was it the look on her face that had done it? As if she doubted that he thought she was worthy of a kiss. He needed to change her mind.

Someone coughed nearby. Alex looked up and spotted a deputy passing by them. It was Chavez.

He tipped his hat, a big smile on his face. "Evening, Alex. Ma'am." He walked past them and was yards away before Alex realized he'd pulled Annie into his arms and was still holding her. He let her go. There was a puzzled, almost dazed expression on her face, and it matched his mixed-up emotions. He was confused himself. After being so careful not to lead her on, to promise something with his actions that he couldn't give her with his heart, he'd kissed her? Since when had he been so impulsive?

The damage was done. He needed to figure out where to go from here. He should talk to her. Explain what was in his head. Looking at her he couldn't think of the right words to say. Instead, he took her hand, turned around, and walked down the path towards her building. He was waiting for her to ask what he thought he was doing. She must have a dozen questions. If she did, she kept them to herself, and she also left her hand in his. They walked in quiet as the occasional car passed them and the voices of people echoed to them across the green. When they reached her building, she motioned to the alley and walked him around to the rear entrance. A glass door and a plaque next to it listed a craft business on the second floor and deliveries for Coffee by the Book on the first.

"I live on the third floor." She explained, unnecessarily since Alex could tell from the exterior that there were three levels. Basic deduction meant she'd have to be on the top floor. But he didn't think she said it to explain anything. He could feel how incredibly awkward the silence had become and somebody had to fill it. It sure wasn't him. His brain was in panic mode, rejecting script after script, desperate to find something to say to make sense of his actions tonight.

"It's not that late. If you wanted to come up, I've got cocoa and cookies. We could talk."

Oh, they could, but that was the last thing Alex wanted to do. Escape was all he was thinking of. Was it too late to apologize? Yes, he should have done that right off. Now that window of opportunity was closed and locked. She had to have felt it, how much he liked her, in that kiss. He'd never be able to move them back to only being friendly. He'd completely blown it. Part of him wanted to take her up on cookies and cocoa and explain that he liked her, a lot—that if she was willing to put up with a man haunted by mistakes that couldn't be fixed, sins beyond redemption, then... what? They'd end up happily ever after? He'd find the person harassing him and get them to stop? He'd be able to go home again? He'd take her to meet his family? None of that was likely to happen.

"Annie I...I've got a real early morning tomorrow. I should go." He watched her face fall. "But, thank you. Tonight was great. You were right, I really liked it. The whole night was beautiful." He tried to get her to see what he meant, that she was beautiful and that kiss, though it might have been stupid, was beautiful too.

"Oh, well... I'll see you tomorrow then."

"Yeah. Tomorrow." He felt the panic in his gut. Tomorrow they'd go back to normal?

"Goodnight then." She rolled up on her toes and kissed his cheek. It was such a sweet gesture. He stood there as though he were a statue. She seemed confused, and he was forced to fumble out a goodbye before turning and leaving. At the mouth of the alleyway, he looked back and waved. She disappeared into her building, and he heard the door shut and lock. Only then did he walk back to his truck, wondering how he'd ever be able to fix this.

CHAPTER EIGHT

ANNIE JUGGLED HER KEYS AND PURSE as she wrestled open the door to the shop. She was operating in a less-than-ideal condition. It had been a week since the night of the concert. An entirely Alex-free week. A week that had started out with a busy Christmas Eve at the shop passed through a quiet Christmas alone with a phone call from her father. That event had not lifted her mood. The week ended with a Sunday dinner alone at Maria's diner. Pathetically, she had dragged her time there out past all sense hoping that Alex would appear. He hadn't. He hadn't appeared anywhere. In fact, he had disappeared. She'd been ghosted. That incredibly annoying facet of modern life where someone you thought you had started a relationship with goes incommunicado. At least she had a word for it, much good as it did her.

She could have asked Pete and Lauren for his number, but that was a step, unlike swinging by his house, that would cross the line between natural concern and pathetic loser-ville. She knew Alex was alive and well—she'd run into Lauren who had mentioned having him over at Christmas. Alex had put her on 'avoid' status. Apparently, a grown adult man *could* be a big baby. She wanted him to come to her. She wanted him to explain what he had been thinking that night, but her life was now 100% Alex Moretti free.

And it wasn't only because he'd taken up residence in her head. He was a wish she'd been afraid to make, only to have it come true for one precious moment before disappearing in a poof. She hadn't reached for that metaphorical cookie. Alex had handed it to her and then slapped her hand away as she'd closed her fist around it. The jerk.

The regular early-morning crowd began to arrive minus one. Again, no Alex. Annie stuck a smile on her face and served her customers, trying not to feel his absence. When Claire pushed through the door at seven, she gave Annie a pointed look before hanging up her coat and unraveling her scarf. Coming around the counter, Claire pulled her phone out of her pocket. "Now I get it. You've been moody, and I didn't know why. Then I saw this." She stabbed at the screen with her finger and then thrust it in Annie's face. "What's up with this?"

It was a web page, the Sweet River Lowdown. Annie squinted at it and spotted a familiar face—hers. It was the picture Elaine had taken of Alex kissing Annie on her forehead. The photo looked almost professional. Elaine had managed to get them and the twinkling lights all around them with the snow sparkling in the low background. His eyes were closed, one hand gently cupping her cheek. She didn't even remember that part. Her eyes were closed. It was a beautiful picture. And it hurt. A lot.

"Honestly, Claire? I have no idea what's up with that picture." She left the counter and walked into the back room, hoping Claire would not follow. She should have known better.

"Honey. This is kind of a big deal." Claire grabbed hold of her arm and turned Annie to face her. "If you were walking on air, I'd know what this was. But you're not. You went from jumpy, to confused, to sad. What happened?"

"He kissed me. Not just there." She pointed at Claire's phone. "After Elaine left I tried to apologize for her coercing him into kissing me for that picture, and then he gave me a real kiss. Like, toe-curling, the real deal, movie-quality kiss. Somebody came along and said hi, and he let me go. Without a word of explanation, he shut down on me. He walked me home. And then he ghosted on me."

Claire pulled in a deep breath. "I had noticed he wasn't

around, but I wasn't sure what the deal was."

"Yes. And it's fine. Because it's not like we were anything to each other. It was probably a pity kiss, and now he wants to be sure I don't get the wrong idea. Which is a good move on his part, because I sure *did* get the wrong idea. I thought he liked me. I thought we were going from friendly to friends and then he kissed me, and I thought we were going to something else. Then he ghosted me and now we've gone from something to nothing, showing that I don't know how to make friends after all. And I sure don't know how to be anything at all to any man, and I never should have started this and—"

Claire took hold of her arms and shook her. "Stop that."

"Ow."

"Did I hurt you?" Claire's brow wrinkled, her voice concerned.

"No, it was jarring though."

"Good. I hope it knocked all that nonsense out of you. You were right. He did like you. I saw it myself. I don't know where his head is at, but it's not your fault. He kissed you, not the other way around."

"Yeah, what's up with that?"

"Men." She shook her head. "Some of them don't know what they want. They're confused, and they act like jerks because of it."

"You think that's what's going on with Alex?"

"If I had to hazard a guess, I'd say he doesn't know what he wants, or he does, and it's confusing him. Annie, you are not the problem here. I'm sorry he treated you this way. I thought he was a better man."

"So did I." That terrible feeling settled in her gut again, the one that made her feel worthless. She had a deep suspicion that Alex's actions were his subtle way of saying she wasn't worth his notice. She'd been tortured for a week thinking that he'd been avoiding her because he didn't want anything to do with her. She'd assumed that kiss had been some kind of pity or mistake on his part. That feeling washed away every good memory she had of their conversations. It swamped any charitable thought of what his true feelings might be.

"Hey, I can take over the shop from here." Claire offered. "Since school is out for the Christmas break, you should take at least today off. Have a real day for yourself. Why don't you go upstairs and lay down for a while? Take a nap. You look terrible."

"Great." She rolled her eyes. "Thanks, Claire."

"You're welcome. We girls need to stick together. Speaking of which, clear your calendar for Friday night. We'll make it a girls' night."

"We?"

"Erin and I will come over, we'll get some food, and sort you out."

"Um, okay. I guess." She didn't know Erin all that well, but she was definitely open to a girls' night. Especially one that could sort things out since they seemed horribly mixed up at the moment.

Annie headed out the back, but not to climb the stairs to her apartment. She needed something to distract her, something besides a new book. She got into her car and started it up, wondering where to go. Having free time was such an oddity she didn't know what to do with it. Eventually, she drove up onto the highway and to the nearest mall. It was a long drive, but it felt good to be going somewhere. There she found a craft store and picked up a kit that was supposed to quickly teach her how to knit a hat. It was quite lovely, two large needles and soft white yarn with a skein of pink, as well, for the bauble on the top.

On the way home, she was feeling peckish, so she stopped

at Maria's. *Not,* she told herself, to see if Alex was there. She was done wondering where he was. Forget him. Sitting at the counter, she ordered a tuna melt, a sandwich that was American comfort food at its best. It was definitely comfort she was seeking. She felt the brush of someone taking the stool beside her and looked up with her heart in her throat. Olivia's cautious smile greeted her, and she had to hide the disappointment flooding through her. "Well, hello there. On your own?"

"Yeah. Mrs. MacAlister said I can wait here while the twins have their violin lessons. I can't take the noise."

Annie laughed, although she didn't miss that Olivia still called her foster mother 'Mrs. MacAlister.'

"Tuna, huh?" Olivia was looking down at Annie's lunch.

"I love it. I can't make it at home because Hobbes becomes almost violent at the smell of it."

"Hobbes?"

"My cat. I'm convinced he's simply a small tiger."

"That's hilarious. I wish I had a cat. There are horses and goats at the MacAlister's, but they're not pets."

"You don't care for horses?"

"Not really. They're huge, and one of them bites if you're not careful. That and the smell."

"I can see that. Maybe you can ask your, um...folks if you can have a cat."

"I doubt they'd say yes." Olivia's expression grew morose. "We used to have a cat. Had to give it away when, y' know."

Annie had no trouble filling in the blanks. She wondered what else the children had lost when their parents died. They must not have had close relatives since they ended up in care rather than living with a relation. They probably lost friends, their old teachers, coaches? Their house, their neighborhood, even their church. Everything was all ripped away from them, a kick when they were already down. Life was cruel.

"How are you enjoying your break?" Annie thought it best to change the subject.

Olivia shrugged. "It's okay I guess. I got through *The Fellowship of the Ring* finally. You were right, it really slows down through the Tom part, but it picks up after that."

"Great! Not everyone has the sort of stuff to stick with it. Have you moved on to *Two Towers* yet?"

"Yes. I love Eowyn. She seems so cool, but I'm not liking the unrequited love thing with Aragon. He's about to break her heart."

"Well," Annie knew how that felt. "Wait until the end. Eowyn's story is one of my favorites. Honestly, they could do a whole movie on her alone."

"Sweet, because as good as these books are, it's the boys that seem to have all the fun."

"Well, boys wrote them. That's generally how it works. I have some other books you can read. There are a few fantasy series that feature great female characters."

"Sure. Although I'm not sure how much time I'm going to have to read. I'm trying to get a job after school."

"A job? Can you work at your age?"

"Limited hours, yes. I really need the cash."

That seemed odd to Annie. The MacAlister's were not hurting for money and were generous by nature, so she doubted the kids needed money. Maybe what she needed was control. When Annie was young, having a few pounds in her pocket made her feel both independent and free. That feeling would be appealing to someone like Olivia too.

"If you're only looking for a few hours I could probably use help in the afternoons. Do you think you'd like working at Coffee by the Book?"

"Are you kidding?" Olivia almost yelled it. "I would love it. I can ask if it would be okay and then could I start right away?"

"Sure." Annie stifled a laugh. "How about Wednesday?"

"Oh, I will be there. This is so exciting." She clapped her hands together. A warmth filled Annie's chest, a happy kind of glow and it did a whole lot more than a tuna melt to dispel heartache.

As soon as she was through the door at home, Hobbes attacked her ankle and then sprinted away. "Beast!" she shouted after him. She went right to the kitty table and pulled out his bowl. He launched himself from the floor half into her, and half onto his bowl.

"Hey!" She filled it and stepped back, letting him attack it. Going into the bedroom, she got changed into her PJs. Sure, it was only four, but whatever, she wanted to be comfortable. Not like it mattered what she wore. No one was likely to drop by. She made herself a cup of tea and then opened her laptop and sent Katherine an email letting her know she'd offered Olivia a part-time job.

When she was done, she checked her email and then surfed around a bit. It was probably a bad idea, but she eventually pulled up the *Sweet River Lowdown*. There, right on the landing page, was the picture. The caption below read 'local residents enjoy the Christmas magic'. "Pfft." But she couldn't deny the beauty of that picture. Alex was ridiculously handsome. Looking at his face made her chest ache. She slapped the laptop shut.

She wanted to believe that he didn't have any feelings for her and was just a jerk, but she knew otherwise. Claire, who did not lie to make people feel better, quite the reverse, told her she'd seen how Alex looked at Annie. Now Annie had seen it for herself in that picture. So what had gone wrong?

She sat back from her desk, putting distance between herself and any trains of thought that would be headed to self-loathing. Rejection hurt. A lot. Even more so from Alex who had been the one to take that step from friends to something else in the first place. She'd been ecstatic he'd walked her home. She didn't need his kiss. The first one might have been for Elaine, but he took the second one for himself. Well, forget him.

Taking the cup of tea and a book, she sat in her comfy chair by the window and turned off all the lamps, save the reading lamp next to her chair. It was dim enough that she could watch the snow falling gently outside. It wasn't supposed to accumulate much, but it would cover all the slushy brown and gray with a new topcoat of white. Main Street was a thing of beauty in the summer with its rows of two-and-three-story brick buildings fronted by shops with overflowing window boxes. The trees surrounding the town green put on a show in the fall, but winter was her favorite so far. Every building owner had decked their halls with twinkling lights, bright red bows, and greenery. At night it was downright magical. The living room of her apartment faced the street, so she had a front-row seat. After New Years it would all come down, so she wanted to soak it all in while she could.

Tonight, it didn't feel quite like magic. Her book wasn't as engaging, and after a while, it fell into her lap as her train of thought started back up and chugged right to sadness. She felt a cry coming on, good or bad. A rumble sounded near her shoulder as Hobbes, purring loudly, rubbed her cheek with his head. She scratched his chin and adjusted so he could curl up on her shoulder and cuddle against her neck. He'd been doing that since he was a kitten, although not often. He was spare with his affection but seemed to have an instinct for when she needed it most.

"I really liked him," she told Hobbes. "In fact, I think maybe a bit of me might have fallen for him." A tear formed and fell down her cheek and, as she rested her head against the back of the chair, Hobbes snuggled close.

Alex sat in his idling truck looking up at the dimly-lit figure of Annie seated by the window. She shouldn't do that. Who knows what kind of creep could see her. She should frost those windows or pull the blinds. "Idiot." He muttered aloud. "You're the creep staring at her." Shep, along for the ride, took that moment to lick his ear. "Quit it." He nudged the dog aside. Like last night and the night before it, he'd found himself watching to be sure she got home, then sat in the dark talking himself out of going up to her apartment and trying to offer some kind of reason for his behavior. If there were awards for class-A fool, he'd win hands down.

Flicking on his headlights, he pulled out of the spot where he'd parked and drove down the road. There was a word for what he was feeling, but he'd only heard it from his mom, *saudade*. It was like a longing for something that can't be, and it was filling his heart. That and guilt. Lots of it. Annie was better off without him. He knew it, but in the moment, he'd forgotten that. All he'd thought about was what he wanted, and as always, it had gone wrong. Even now he wasn't sure he was doing the right thing. Shep whined as they passed her building. "I know buddy. I'm sorry."

CHAPTER NINE

ALEX SAT AT PETE'S KITCHEN ISLAND while the man read the folder of letters, his expression darkening after each one. Finally, he set them down. "He's escalating."

"Yeah, that's what I thought. That last one arrived today. It's different from the others." The letter had arrived at his PO Box, and instead of an outright threat, it was almost like a comment on his life. Alex had trouble sleeping last night. Today he'd finally decided that somebody had to know what was going on. Pete seemed the best option. The old man was sharper than a drawer of knives.

Pete read aloud. "Get used to being alone. You brought it on yourself."

"I think it's a reference to Christmas." Alex shrugged. "I didn't go home. First time for that. My parents were upset. Might have talked about it."

"So you're pretty sure it's someone from Lewiston." Pete stated it more than asked. "Do you have a list of possibilities?"

Alex considered his answer. The answer was both yes and no. "By the time I left, people would have lined up to take a shot at me. It's why I left. They were shunning my parents. My dad's an electrician, and he couldn't get work in his own town. My brothers were showing up at dinner with black eyes and bloody fists." Alex shook his head. "All that stopped a few months after I left, but that's when this started." He pointed at the letters. "It's got to be the same guy writing these. The wording, the way they've appeared. There's a big break which makes me wonder if he was put away for a time or something. I don't know, but it definitely seems like a guy."

"I'd agree with you on that. As for the break, could be

anything. Might have had a job out of state. Could've been busy, who knows."

"That article in the paper seems like the trigger that got it all going again."

"The graduation announcement?" He picked up the newspaper clipping with Alex's name listed among the graduates. "That's the likely source, yes. Son, do you mind if I share these with Mac? He's the best detective I know, and this stuff is up his alley. He used to train people in investigation."

Alex sighed as he thought it over. Letting in Pete was natural, they were close. He'd been honest when Pete had asked him why he'd left the force and joined the wardens. But he didn't really know Mac. Then again, even if the story got around, it didn't matter anymore. There was only one person's opinion he cared about, and he'd already ruined that. "Yeah, I guess that's the smart move, but only if he can do it off the books. I'm not ready to make this official yet. They might suspend me for my own safety and right now I need to work."

"I'll talk to him. He'll want to know everything though, you understand?"

"Okay by me. He might want to start with Eric Michaud, the brother. He took a swing at me when I showed up to the wake. I heard he'd shipped out though, the second tour to someplace sandy. Didn't hear anything about him after that."

"Would he hold a grudge like this?"

"We used to be friends before he enlisted." Alex looked down at his hands, letting the familiar mix of grief and guilt rush through him.

"Good friends?" Pete asked it gently like he already suspected the answer.

"Brother from another mother. Lost touch when I broke up with his sister. He got it, but he didn't like it." Alex's head was a mess. Talking about this, any of it, was incredibly difficult. If it weren't Pete, he probably wouldn't have done it. "It was Eric who asked me to call her, talk to her about Logan. He was worried she'd meet a nasty end because of that guy. Ironic." He looked over Pete's shoulder, out the sliding glass doors to the yard. It was all snow with bits of brush sticking up here and there. The meadow was something else in the summer. Alex had gotten a glimpse of it when he first moved up. Now under all that frozen moisture lay seeds and dirt, waiting to go at it again. "After she died, Eric told me to stay away. I couldn't." Alex shook his head. "Went to the wake and he dragged me out. Took a swing and missed. My brothers rushed him and pulled him off." He didn't bother telling Pete the rest, how Eric had cried and cursed him out in front of a crowd of people or how Alex left, feeling like the devil himself.

"Okay." Pete broke the silence. "I think that moves him to the top of the list. Who else?"

"I guess Logan's crew. Most of them are in jail, but some might be out. Still, I don't see one of those guys caring that much. It's not like they came up together. Logan recruited from his customers."

"He was popular though, wasn't he?"

"Charismatic. Everybody knew he was a user and that he was probably dealing, but nobody cared. They loved his Prince of the People act. Working at the shelter was a total front, but no one would believe it. Samantha…" He hadn't said her name out loud for so long it was a shock to hear it. Even though Pete knew the story, it's not like they'd talked about it. Alex steadied himself and finished his thought. "She believed in him and honestly thought she could save him."

"Of course she did."

"She said he had an artist's soul. That he'd dump the drugs." Alex rubbed his chin. "She had no idea how dangerous he was. He had her snowed. Sam really did assume the best about people, even when they proved her wrong over and over."

"Love can make you stupid."

"That's for sure." Alex hated talking about this, but telling it to Pete seemed safe, as safe as anything was. From the moment he'd moved here Pete had done nothing but support him, give him wisdom, tell him how to handle the locals. Alex hoped the man knew exactly how grateful he was. He should say the words, but somehow, they never came.

"Well, we'll get Mac in on this and see what we can find." Pete pushed the folder aside and rested his hands on the counter. "Now, there's another thing I need to talk to you about. It's a nicer subject for sure. That would be our Annie."

Alex closed his eyes, wishing a hole in the floor would open and drop him in it. "What about Annie?"

"Rumor has reached my wife that you started something with that girl and then walked away."

Alex hated to admit it, but it was a pretty good description of what he'd done. He was ashamed, and like a kid, wanted to hide. There was no hiding from Pete though. "I like Annie, a lot. But I am not the man for her. She needs someone who doesn't have my baggage. Her life..." He trailed off because it was not his to say. He wouldn't betray any confidence she'd placed in him.

"I can see she's a love-starved little thing," Pete said into the sudden silence.

"What?"

"Love-starved. Like a stray kitten."

Alex couldn't believe Pete was dismissing her like that. She wasn't panting after him, begging to be loved. It was him who went into her shop every day. She didn't deserve the way Pete was talking about her.

"I can see from your clenched fists and that scowl that you misunderstood me."

Alex looked down at his hands in surprise. He hadn't realized he'd balled his fists.

"I don't say that as a criticism. What I mean to say is that I can guess what her life was like before she got here, because when she did, she reached out. Unlike you, I might add. She reached out to people. Church people, school people, you. She's putting down roots, building a community, making a family. It seems pretty clear that she doesn't have one in any meaningful sense."

"Her parents travel a lot."

"I don't doubt it. They're also terrible parents. Doesn't take a detective to see that one." Pete slapped a palm on the counter. "That's why I don't believe you could reel her in and then toss her back."

"Hey! If you're trying to say that I took advantage of her—"

"No. I know you better than that. It's her heart you reeled in. That's what you tossed back. What I don't understand is why?"

Alex picked up a letter. "This. Read these, and you know why."

"Alex. You do not have blood on your hands."

"What about Logan's death?"

"You were doing your job."

"If I had been more careful. I wouldn't have needed to—"

"That's enough!" Pete roared.

Alex sat back, surprised by Pete's anger.

"You cannot take that on, boy. There are no what ifs that can raise the dead." He shoved up the sleeve of his shirt and showed Alex the inside of his arm. Tattooed on his skin was a series of black hash-marks, as if counting out a score. Alex saw they added up to twelve. "I stopped counting after the first month. Six years in Vietnam, and if I'd continued counting the men who died, this arm would be covered."

"Pete, those men, that wasn't the—"

"No, it wasn't the same, but in some ways, it was. If I let myself think about the mistakes that got them there, the mistakes that led to the bullets and the bombs, I'd go crazy. Instead, I remember they were there to do their jobs to the best of their ability, and I was there to do mine. None of us is omniscient. You deal with what you have in front of you at the time you have it. Logan made his choice. You did your job. That's the end of it."

"Okay, Pete." Alex gave in. He'd never seen the man that upset.

"I'm not sure where your head is at, but I don't like it." He took a deep breath.

Alex slumped in his seat, his stomach churning with a mix of guilt, anxiety, and what felt like grief. "I'm sorry, Pete. You've been nothing but good to me, and I'm unloading this all on you when you don't need it."

"No, I'm glad you brought this to me. I was bored anyway. Now, Annie, that's a different matter."

"There's no matter. She probably hates me now, and she should."

Pete rolled his eyes. "Let's start here. I think you need to talk to someone who can work you through this. I'm—" He gave him a half smile. "I see too much of myself in you." Pete clapped him on the shoulder.

A warmth spread through Alex's chest. There was no higher compliment as far as he was concerned.

Pete shook his head, maybe seeing where Alex's thoughts had gone. "That's not a good thing. Talk to Dan Connors. He's the one to unwind the knot you're in. He's been in many himself."

"Um. I'll think about it."

"Boy," Pete's tone was impatient. "That sounds like a no."

"It's a no."

"Alex—"

"I'll make it a not yet, okay?"

Pete nodded, and Alex was glad he left it there but was stuck with feeling like he'd failed his friend. It added to the weight already in his gut. Every fiber of his being was telling him to run to Annie, explain why he'd avoided her, and beg her for forgiveness. He wasn't going to do that, but it took almost all of his energy to fight doing exactly that. He wasn't good company right now. Even Shep was giving him a wide berth.

"Is it safe to come back in?" Lauren stood in the doorway, a cautious smile on her face.

"Yes. Sorry, love. The shouting is all done." Pete got off his stool and greeted his wife with a kiss. "Thanks for giving us the time."

"Always, darling."

"Hey, Lauren." Alex waved.

"I'm not talking to you." She came over to him all the same and gave him a hug. She raised her hand and laid it against his cheek, her eyes searching his face in a way that only a mom could. She shook her head. "Such a smart man and yet, still so very, very stupid."

"Hey. Don't make me feel bad. Pete already did. I'm not sure I could take it if you did too." He was kidding, but not, all the same.

"Oh, Alex, you silly man. I'm not going to make you feel bad, but I am worried about you."

"Why? I'm fine."

"Hmm...." She walked into the kitchen and took out a bottle of water. "You're coming to our New Year's party, right?"

"Of course. I wouldn't miss it."

"You better not." She pointed at him with the bottle before taking a sip and then turning to Pete. "Since you've set him straight about our girl, it's okay that I invited her, right?"

"Uh." Pete's eyes widened. "I didn't quite get that worked out."

"Men," Lauren whispered before leaving the room. "I'm going to paint." She called over her shoulder and disappeared down the hall.

Pete pinned him with a look. "Do not ditch the party."

"I won't." Alex held his hands up. That was going to be one awkward party.

The police scanner in the corner of the room crackled out a message, and Pete ran to turn it down.

"You've got a scanner?"

Pete made a face. "You're gonna say something here that's bound to annoy me, so don't."

Alex smiled. "Like even when you're retired, you still can't hang up the badge."

"Maybe. It makes me feel better to know what's up."

"What does Lauren think of it?"

"She knows what I need and tolerates it. That's what people who love you do. They give you what they know you need, but not always what you want. There's a profound difference in that."

CHAPTER TEN

OLIVIA HELPED ANNIE STACK THE CHAIRS on the tables so they could sweep the floors before locking up. The girl fit in perfectly with the rest of her staff. Not a surprise, since most of them were only a few years older than Olivia, and all of them were nice. She'd picked up the basics quickly, learning how to operate the various coffee makers, the register, even the funky machine they used for cards and electronic purchases. The espresso machine was next. Annie didn't allow anyone new to touch it since it was complicated and cost a mint. The weekly greenery was another matter. Annie ordered a big batch of herbs and various greens at the beginning of the week and put them into bud vases at each table. Olivia had a knack for creating the arrangements. There was a trick to making them look like little pieces of art and not a bunch of weeds stuffed in a jar. The girl seemed to have the soul of an artist, so Annie handed the task over to her.

Today had been steady with a rush that afternoon, which was not a surprise. Sunday was New Year's Day and Main Street would be closed. Today and tomorrow would both be busy with shoppers snapping up whatever post-Christmas sales were left. Even her shop had a promotion, offering a two-for-one book sale. The shelves were starting to look thin, a good thing since that meant she could buy more of her faves to restock the shelves. She and Olivia had discussed *The Fellowship of the Ring* at length, and now Annie wanted to stock her shop with more copies of the series and a few others like it.

"Hey, I think we're all set."

"Did you say you'd need me tomorrow as well?"

"Yup. I'm going to Bangor for a book signing. The writer is someone I knew at Princeton, and I'm hoping to talk him into doing a signing here in the spring."

"Cool." Olivia's eyes lit up. "Who is he?"

"Brian Daniels. You may know him. He wrote the Crown series."

"I love those books!" Olivia almost shouted. "I read the first three cover to cover in about a week. Is the fourth one out yet?"

"Next week. The signing tomorrow is a special one for a bookstore that he used to work at. You know he's a Maine native, right?"

"I did, yeah. That's why he's even cooler. I totally want to write books like his when I'm an adult."

"Great. When your mom comes, be sure to check with her that an extra shift is okay."

Olivia's whole aspect changed. Her eyes grew misty and her body tight, like she was about to stomp off in a huff or throw a punch. Annie could feel the emotion rolling off her like a wave and wasn't sure what to make of it. Then Olivia spoke. "She's not my mom."

Annie realized her mistake. "That's at the heart of it, isn't it?" Annie braced for an angry reaction, but Olivia didn't flip any tables or storm out. Annie reached out and took her hand. "It's okay to miss your mom and get to know your foster mom all at the same time. Your heart is big enough."

"You don't get it." Olivia pulled her hand back. "My mom is dead. She's always going to be dead. It's...this wasn't supposed to happen. I'm not supposed to be here. We got dumped in the middle of nowhere with strangers. Nothing anyone can say will ever make that better. The MacAlisters aren't our parents, and they never will be. They're babysitters the state hired to take care of us."

"That's not quite true. They're adopting you all."

"They only want the little ones. They don't care about me or the twins."

"Have you talked to the twins about how they feel?"

Olivia nodded. "They agree." She lifted her chin but didn't make eye contact, and Annie wondered if they did agree. She'd seen the twins with Katherine enough to know that they didn't feel the way Olivia did. She communicated her unhappiness in every gesture, every word. Most of the time she seemed a little hesitant, but not hostile.

"I don't know the whole story, but I do know that Katherine waited a long time to be a mom. I can't think she put an age limit on that. I think she'd be as happy to have a toddler as she would a teenager."

"I had a mom." Olivia's lower lip quivered, but her words were clear. "She loved me better than anyone ever could. Now she's dead."

"Dear girl..." Annie pulled Olivia over to the bar-counter along the wall and drew out a stool for her. By the time they were both seated Olivia seemed to have recovered her composure. Annie had hoped a good cry might help break through the iron around her heart. It was going to take more than compassion. This girl needed words of wisdom, but Annie wasn't sure if she was the right woman for the job. She was there though, and she felt the Spirit more than nudging her to speak. "I can't imagine what you've lost." She took in a breath, hoping that sharing her own pain might lead to understanding. "I quite literally can't imagine it."

"What do you mean?" Olivia was properly perplexed.

Annie wasn't sure how to describe what was between her and her mother or what wasn't. "My mother never planned to have children. She married an older man and looked forward to being his hostess, his assistant, and traveling the world with him. When she became pregnant he was thrilled. She was not."

"Oh my gosh, you can't be serious."

"Not every woman wants to be a mother. My mother tried,

but by the time I was eight, she knew it wasn't working, and she got my dad to agree to send me to live with my Aunt in England with the understanding that I would attend a boarding school when appropriate."

Olivia's mouth dropped open. "I can't believe they'd send you away at eight!"

"It had a happy ending. I arrived in London, and my aunt turned out to be kind, not scary. And she didn't ship me off to school at the end of the summer. She enrolled me in a school nearby, and I lived with her until I was fourteen—a much better age to start boarding school. I went to her for the holidays too. Christmas at her house was fairy-tale perfect. The house was a proper stone cottage with the most amazing gardens. Summer holidays were wonderful. We'd putter about with her flowers or visit her friends in London. I had a charmed life with her."

"But...your parents left you there?"

Annie nodded. "I missed them. At first, it was tough to live with Auntie Delia. She was strict, her house was full of interesting but breakable things she was constantly hassling me about not touching, and I didn't like the food. It smelled weird. There was only one TV, and she never let me watch anything on it. The kids at school made fun of my accent and called me fat. There were no girls my age in the neighborhood. My bedroom was tiny. Actually, the whole house was, and there were no pets because my aunt was allergic. The closest thing to a pet was a neighbor's goat, and I got told off for trying to take it in."

Olivia made a face. "Goats eat everything. Mac has a goat. It's not my idea of a pet."

"I was desperate." Annie smiled. "It was a rough time. Until it wasn't. I started to like the food. I realized that Auntie Delia wasn't strict so much as making sure I knew how to get along in another culture. The kids were still kids, so they didn't improve, but I made a friend who I still keep in touch with now. After a while, my room was cozy instead of tiny. I loved the diamond-shaped windowpanes and found a hidden cupboard in a wall that was like a mini closet, and I kept my dolls in there. Later, I kept my diary in there. Do you know what made the difference?"

Olivia rolled her eyes. "You're about to say something sappy, aren't you?"

"I guess you can decide that for yourself." Annie was a bit frustrated with Olivia's attitude, but she wasn't going to give up. "I started to trust my aunt. I saw all she was doing for me and that it wasn't out of obligation or duty. It was her loving me with her actions. We built a bond from there."

"That's really nice." Olivia got down from the stool. "But I can't do that. My heart" —she pointed to her chest–"in there are bits that are broken, and bits that are angry. None of them is ready to build any bonds." She pulled her coat off the hook by the front entry. "I've got a plan. I'm in the ninth grade now. That means I have three more years after this one. After graduation, I'm going to get a job and an apartment. Then the twins can come live with me when they're ready, and if the littles need to come to me, they can too. We can be a family again. That's what I'm building."

Annie stood as well and was about to tell the stubborn girl not to waste her future like that when the shop bells rang and Katherine appeared, red-cheeked and wind-blown.

"Hi! It is so cold out there!" Katherine gave Olivia a bright smile, hope in her eyes. That hope seemed to die as Olivia glowered back and shouldered her backpack. "Better get bundled up tight before we go. I had to park down the street, so we've got a bit of a walk." Katherine reached out as if to button Olivia's coat, and the girl leaned away, stuffing her hat on her head.

"See ya, Annie." Olivia brushed by her foster-mom and

pushed open the door. "I'll be in the car."

"Sure thing," Katherine said to the door as it shut in her face. "No worries, honey. Wouldn't want to inflict my presence on you for longer than necessary." She turned around to face Annie. "Sorry about that. Needless to say, Olivia has not warmed up to me. More like built a wall of ice and sharp, pointy bits between us."

"I'm so sorry, Katherine. I wish there were some advice I could give you other than to keep trying."

Katherine nodded. "I will. We do." Her lips quirked like she was trying to smile but couldn't manage it.

"We talked a bit before you got here. That might have been the reason for her need to go sit in a cold car."

Katherine raised her eyebrows in surprise.

"I was sharing with her what it was like for me when I went to live with my aunt and some of the struggles I had. She talked about her plans for the future and some of what she's been feeling." Annie left it there, not wanting to betray any confidence. Katherine seemed to catch on.

"Don't worry, whatever she shared with you she's likely shouted at me at some point in the last few weeks. We've gone from having her silently and begrudgingly comply to open defiance and attitude. I actually prefer the shouting. Then I know what she's thinking. With God's grace, I can hope that it will eventually become a two-way conversation."

"Oh, in case she forgets, I offered her a few hours tomorrow. I'm away, and I'd like my weekend staff to have a little support in case it's busy."

"Sure. I'll ask her what hours and give her a lift. That's a forced twenty-minutes in the car with me. Who knows what will happen. Maybe she'll say three civil words." Katherine managed a smile this time.

CHAPTER ELEVEN

"Yes, I'm at Sid's now," Annie told Claire over the phone as she pulled her wallet out of her purse, preparing to pay for what would be her contribution to Girls' Night, Chicken Parmigiana and salad. Sid's made the best Italian food anywhere around, but they did not deliver. It was worth the trip since the smell alone, a magic combination of garlic, spice, and tomatoes that hit her in a whoosh when she'd opened the door, was almost too heavenly for this earth. That would be enough to drag anyone through the cold to their door. It seemed like half the town had the same idea since the restaurant's small offering of tables and booths were almost full. "I'll be there soon. You know where I keep the spare key, so feel free to let yourself in."

"Got it," Claire answered from the other end of the call. "Erin has arrived, so we'll lock up and head upstairs. See you soon."

Annie dropped her phone into her pocket and waited for the guy behind the counter to return with her order. Behind her, the door opened again. She turned around and her stomach dropped. Alex stood in the entry with the door open, half in, half out. Of course, it would be Alex. So many emotions rushed through her at once that she had no idea what she was actually feeling. He looked good, scruffier than usual, but good. He was in uniform, so she guessed he must be getting dinner after his shift.

A taller, older man pushed him in and then budged past him saying "You're gonna let all that nice, warm air out."

Annie knew that voice. "Hey, Pete." She waved.

"Hey, yourself. Getting dinner?" Pete's dark green parka was covered with a light dusting of snow as was his gray hair.

The wind was probably blowing around what had already fallen that day. He had a buffalo-check flannel scarf wrapped around his throat and pink cheeks. He looked every inch the mountain-man-turned-grandpa that he was.

"Is Lauren with you tonight?"

"Nope. It's just the boys tonight. Lauren has Olivia out on a 'Grammy' date. She has a way with that girl. I think it's because the kids didn't grow up with grandparents, so she's sort of neutral."

Annie nodded. It made sense that Olivia would see her as a bonus rather than a minus. Something she gained instead of something she lost. Pete moved aside so another patron could squeeze down the narrow hallway to the bathrooms. Alex shifted behind him, leaning against the wall as if this was all too normal. Annie prayed that the guy with her order would hurry up already. This wasn't normal. It was uncomfortable. Alex hadn't even acknowledged her presence.

"Speaking of Olivia," Pete caught her attention again. "She was going on non-stop about some author you're friendly with. A guy that you're driving out to see tomorrow." Behind Pete, Alex stood away from the wall. Annie made a point of ignoring him, or at least she tried.

"Yes. I'm going to his signing tomorrow and then out for coffee to catch up. I'm hoping to have him do a signing with us this spring." Annie tried to keep her eyes on Pete, but they kept flicking to Alex, as if by their own will. For his part, Alex seemed to be pretending that she didn't exist, staring at a point over her shoulder. That was fine with her. She needed to get used to these awkward meetings. They shared a social circle after all.

"This author must be a good friend of yours."

"We were at Princeton together and kept in touch after. Kindred spirits. We both love books."

"Well, I hope you have a nice trip. Bangor is a haul, and

we're expecting you at our party. Don't forget it's New Year's Eve."

"Of course. I wouldn't miss it for the world." She heard her name called and turned around to see the man at the counter finally had her order ready. "Gotta go."

"We'll get our table." Pete pointed to the booths. "Good seeing you."

As he left, she took the cash out to pay for her order. The man handed her a paper bag, the top of which was folded down and stapled. She grabbed it up. He tried to hand her the seventy-five cents change, but she didn't have a free hand. "Keep the change. Thank you!" As she turned to leave she found Alex standing in her way, wearing a thunderous expression. The breath caught in her chest. Her skin prickled, and she tried not to feel any of it. She didn't want to be affected by him anymore. Why did her heart have to pound in his presence? Why couldn't she kill her attraction to him? He was standing so close she could see the flecks of brown in his hazel eyes.

"Bangor is a long way from home. Do you have anybody going with you?" His voice was low, and it rumbled over her, setting off more fireworks in her senses.

She put them all out, remembering that he was nothing to her now. "Why?"

His eyes widened as if he didn't expect her to question him. "You haven't seen this guy in a while. People change. It isn't safe."

"I think I can handle myself."

"It would be better if you took a friend, Claire or somebody, just in case this guy gets ideas."

Her eyes narrowed. "Why do you care?"

Alex lurched back, a look of surprise on his face. How could he be shocked that she'd ask that? He'd ghosted on her, shouting to the world that she was a stranger, nobody to him, and definitely no one special, not worthy of his time or attention.

"Seriously?" His voice was barely above a whisper.

"I don't know what you're about with this sudden concern for my wellbeing, but it's not welcome or necessary." She pushed past him and headed for the door.

"Annie."

She turned around, but Alex didn't seem to have anything else to say. He was staring at her, emotions she didn't understand flitting across his face.

"I'll be fine. Not that it matters to you." She pushed open the door and stepped out into the cold.

The drive home didn't help to quell the war going on inside. Her head told her that she'd been rude and blown any chance of finding a way back to being friends with Alex. Her heart told her he deserved every word she'd said. A kind of self-righteous anger was still singing through her veins, telling her she was right. When she reached her building and climbed the stairs, she couldn't help stomping on each riser thinking of another reason to be angry at Alex. Being angry helped, since a wave of regret and loss was making its way to her heart, and she didn't want it to take over.

Her apartment door swung open, and Claire peeked out. "What's with the stomping?"

Annie sighed. There was probably no way she'd be able to get out of this one. "Alex." The anger was still there, but it was getting washed out by the sadness. If she had to go into the details, she might burst into tears, and no one needed to see that.

"So what did he do now?" Claire threw the door wide and backed up so Annie could come in.

Annie set the bag of food on the counter and got out of her coat, hat, and mittens. She hung them up on the hook in a far more orderly fashion than usual, as if she was getting graded on her effort. She opened the paper bag and began to pull out the food when Claire cleared her throat.

"You're stalling."

"You're pushing." Annie snapped and almost immediately regretted it. Claire didn't deserve her attitude. Yes, she was pushing, but it was because she cared. Friends cared. *You moved here for this.* She'd wanted people in her life, caring about her, and yes, getting in her face sometimes. This was what it was like to be connected to people, and she didn't want to ruin that. She sat on one of the stools at the island. "Alex was at Sid's with Pete."

Claire winced and then gave Erin a pointed look. Erin sat too, an expression of sympathy on her face.

"He told me I shouldn't go to Bangor tomorrow for that signing. He'd heard Pete asking me about it. Alex said that I shouldn't go alone as if my friend would end up jumping me or something. So ridiculous."

"Law enforcement sees the bad in everything. Occupational hazard." Erin took her long, blond hair and tied it up in a knot on her head, securing it with an elastic band. She was still in her gym clothes. Erin typically wore something similar when she took spin-classes at the Y. The woman must have come over right after work. Something about that was endearing as if spending time with Annie was important enough to skip going home and changing first.

"Thanks for coming over, you two," Annie told them. "I'm not the best of company, and I'm sorry. I wanted tonight to be fun, and already I'm a drag."

Erin reached across the island and grabbed Annie's hand, giving it a squeeze before letting go. "All of us need to vent from time to time. You're not the first woman to be confused by a man's behavior. I'm a good deal older than both of you, and I still have trouble understanding why my fiancé does some of the things he does. It's okay to reach out to friends when stuff doesn't make sense."

"So, he objected to you seeing this guy alone or did he object to you seeing a guy at all?" Claire cocked her head to the side and waggled her brows at Annie until she laughed.

"He waited until after I had paid and was leaving then sort of stood in my way, telling me that I shouldn't go. I asked him why he cared, and he acted surprised. He said 'seriously'?" She said it in her best Alex-voice. "I said he didn't need to worry about me, and then I left. The author I'm going to see tomorrow is an old college chum, not a threat by any stretch of the imagination or a potential boyfriend for that matter."

"Ah, but Alex does not know that."

"You think he's not worried about my safety so much as me with another man? That makes no sense."

Erin shrugged and began to unload the food, passing out the paper plates, napkins, and forks that Annie had left out for them on the counter along with a few bottles of seltzer and ice tea. Claire sat silently, but her expression was thoughtful.

"Some men, actually a lot of them," Erin said as she dished out the food, "grew up believing that emotions were for women. That a grown man should insulate himself from feeling things too deeply."

"Toxic masculinity." Claire unscrewed the cap off a bottle of seltzer.

Erin rolled her eyes. "While that's a bit much, it's close to the mark. I mean, think about it. Men have been given an impossible role model to follow. They have to be strong, tough, and in charge. Never doubting, or hurting, or anything that's seen as weak, like being loving or gentle. I think it isolates them, makes them feel alone." She picked up a fork and knife and began sawing into her chicken parm. "I wish we could popularize Jesus as the role model instead. Humble, loving, steadfast, dedicated to God."

"Aw, like your Dan." Claire gave her a dreamy look.

Erin wiped her mouth with her napkin. "He has his moments." She turned to face Annie. "I don't get the sense that Alex is macho, though. I think he's hiding pain. He's not close to anyone but Pete. He never dates that I've seen, never even flirts. And I've noticed how he looks at you too, Annie." Erin shared a smile with Claire. "The whole town could probably tell he was into you."

Annie found that hard to believe. Considering how he was acting now, that was highly unlikely.

"It's almost like he views you as a temptation, and he's trying to stay away." Erin's brow furrowed. "I can't imagine why."

"Does it matter though? I mean, he acts like he's done with me."

"Then why does he care about you going to Bangor?" Erin tilted her head to the side. "He either cares or he doesn't, right?"

"Yeah..." Annie trailed off, her brain hopping a train of thought headed to hope.

"Better to keep your heart safely intact than let a man stomp on it." Claire pointed at her with a fork. "Not that I'm usually one to give up, but if he's that confused he's better off alone. Why drag a person down with you? Right? Don't worry, Annie. You're adorable. Someone will come along who doesn't inflict damage, someone who feeds your soul instead of shredding it." She stabbed angrily at her salad, and Annie could guess that the heat in her words wasn't about the situation at hand.

Erin seemed to agree since she pivoted on her stool to look at Claire. "Troubles with the ex again?"

Claire nodded. "I don't know what his game is. Weeks of no contact and then all of a sudden he wants a regular schedule with the boys. He's dropping by all the time, and he insisted on spending Christmas with them. Not taking them to his house but coming over and spending it at the apartment." She threw her hands out in a frustrated gesture. "He and the new girl supposedly have a huge house but can't have the boys over for Christmas? Does that sound kosher? Uh, no. He's playing games again."

"Are you sure?" Erin asked. "Is there a chance this is him realizing that he misses his sons and wants more time with them?"

"I will be the first to get my pom poms out and cheer if this means that he's finally woken up to how much his boys need him, but I don't know if this is on the level." She pointed at Erin. "You remember how nasty he can be. He left us with rent we couldn't pay, no car, no TV, cleaned out the good furniture. I was served with papers before I knew what hit me." Claire was talking with her hands, one of which still had her fork. A round, cherry tomato flew off the end of it, landing on the floor. Hobbes pounced on it and batted it between his paws until it rolled under the fridge. "Sorry."

Annie shook her head. "Don't worry about it. I have to pull the fridge out once a week and retrieve his toys from under or behind it. He has terrible aim."

Claire smiled, but it was tinged with sadness. "It really stinks that I can't be happy that he's spending more time with the boys. Instead, I have to worry that this is some ploy, and that he'll break their little hearts."

And your own heart, Annie added in her head. Claire deserved a man who loved her with no reserve, not a man so easily tempted to leave. She was gorgeous, by any standard. With her beautiful hair, bright smile and a body that most women work towards and never achieve. And all of that was second to her sense of humor, her *joie de vivre*. She was a joy to be around, making even the most mundane task fun. How could any man walk away from her, never mind one who had promised before God and her family never to do that? "Men are stupid."

"Annie." Erin's tone was gently scolding. "They aren't any more stupid than we are. It's the human heart. It's desperately wicked. We want all the wrong stuff, the silliest things. Y'know how people in movies always tell you to trust your heart?"

Annie and Claire both nodded.

"That's massively misguided. Your heart is what's stupid. It will run after all the wrong things, get hung up on petty disagreements, lead you to do the dumbest stuff. If there is one thing you should mistrust, it's your heart."

"Okay, so if I can't follow my heart, what do I do?" Claire folded her hands in her lap.

"Square everything that comes your way with God."

Claire rolled her eyes and huffed out a sigh.

"Now c'mon. Let me explain before you dismiss it. When I have a decision to make, I pray about it, but I also take my choices and consider them regarding whether they line up with what I know are God's priorities, not mine. Not like, what would Jesus do, but what does God want for me, and is this something that's going to take away from that or add to it."

"It sounds a bit like running the pros and cons." Annie was all too familiar with that. "Auntie Delia helped me buy this place." She waved at the room around them. "We spent months considering every decision carefully, writing pages of pros and cons. We researched places, real estate companies, businesses. It was endless. She'd always say prayer was important, but that we still had to do our homework."

"Kind of like that. It's the same way with relationships. Your heart might be a mess, but your conscience rarely is. The Holy Spirit inside you knows the right way to go. Listen to Him. That's why you have to take Bible-reading seriously. You have to know the Word inside and out. That's the compass I'm navigating my life with. Not my heart." Erin pointed at her own. "Y'know what it wants most of the time?" She sighed. "An empty house and a nap."

Claire gave her a sympathetic look. "Is Linda driving you crazy with wedding planning?"

"Linda?" Annie searched her memory. "Is that your step-mom?"

"Yes and she is, God love her, driving me crazy. Dan is immune. He does whatever she wants. Keeps telling me to be glad that we have her help. I should be glad since planning this wedding has been a ton of work. She keeps telling Dan all he has to do is show up with 'his handsome self.'" Erin bent her fingers in air quotes. "I'm not sure if it's her that's got him wrapped around her finger or the other way around."

Annie wondered if their quick bond had more to do with his recent loss. It was only a few months since the death of his mom, and by all accounts, he had been devastated by it. She didn't know Dan well enough to say for sure. To her, he was very much Pastor Connors, not a friend. But she knew what it was like to lose someone who loved you like a mother. Auntie Delia had given her that when her own mother couldn't. "Could that be because he misses his mom?"

Erin's eyes widened. "Of course." Her voice was almost a whisper. "I'm such an idiot. All this time and I should have known. Linda's been cooking for him, pressing his shirts, she even went to his place and cleaned it." Her face softened. "They were sitting together on the couch last night, looking at picture albums. She was telling him stories about me as a teenager. Nothing hair-raising, the funny stuff. You should have seen his face." Erin pressed her lips together while her eyes got bright. "His mom was pretty much all he had left for family. Other than a few distant cousins he's on his own." She blinked quickly. "I bet she spotted that. It should be impossible considering I already love my step-mom, but I think I love her a little bit more for that."

"My auntie was like that. She had a sixth sense for when someone needed mothering. Our Christmas dinners were never lonely. We always had guests she called her 'holiday orphans,' people that didn't have anyone to go home to. She used to say that if life didn't give you a family that loved you, go find your own. If you didn't have a home, build one."

Claire and Erin exchanged another of their pointed glances. Erin was at least five years older than Claire, but they communicated like twins at times. A look could communicate some shared understanding. At times it had made Annie a bit uncomfortable since she wasn't as close to either of them, but tonight she had a feeling they were thinking of her, not about her.

"That's why I'm here. In Sweet River." Annie clarified. "I wanted a place to call home. I knew I wanted to live somewhere in the northeast because I love the change of seasons. It had to be rural, but close to tourism so I could run a business, but not too crowded or commercial. When I researched Maine, I found the blog, *The Lowdown,* and I fell in love with this town. That was it."

Claire leaned towards her. "Can I ask what is probably a nosy question?"

"Sure."

"How did you manage it? You bought the business and the building, and you're what, twenty-six?"

"Claire!" Erin tossed a balled-up napkin at her.

"I don't mind the question." Annie smiled at them. "Trust fund. My grandfather left me a tidy sum. Auntie Delia taught me that money is a tool, not a goal. She suggested I find my own place in the world." Annie felt the prickle of tears start, but ignored them. "I think she knew she was dying. Not a word was said to me, but she seemed really intent on me finding my way. I had an internship at my father's business right out of college, but it was a bit of a disaster." Annie laughed. "I was not suited to the pressures of a New York arbitration firm. Delia pestered me to come back to England for a visit, and when I did, she encouraged me to invest in something that could take care of me."

"Does it?" Claire dodged Erin's attempt to cover her mouth. "I'm asking as a friend. Sheesh. Yankees, so weird about money."

"I own the building and the business outright, so that's a head start. It's too early yet, but eventually, I want a manager to take over the day-to-day for me." She turned to Claire. "Someone who knows the business." It didn't seem that Claire was getting the hint she was dropping. "After that, I can focus on my work at the school. I plan to save up for a house and rent out the top apartment, but that's years away."

"That and you might get married. That would change things. He might have a house already." Claire suggested.

"And little, pink piggies may fly." Annie knew her sarcastic tone was unnecessary, but she couldn't stop herself.

"Why not?" Claire seemed genuinely confused.

"I'm not the sort of person...I don't inspire that kind of feeling in people."

"What are you talking about?"

"People don't feel deep things for me." Annie's chest grew tight. This was not a topic she wanted to discuss.

"Where did you get that idea?" Erin was staring at her like she had eight heads, but it was because they didn't know how accurate it was. Other than Delia, Annie had no one. Claire and now Erin were friends. Pete and Lauren were friends too, in an almost grandparent sort of way, but none of them knew her well enough to be her people. When things got tricky, would they stick around? Would Claire and Erin want anything to do with her if she were hard to deal with? If she weren't friendly and kind, if she had too many bad days? Annie made it a point to be easy to work with, easy to befriend. If she weren't, she'd be alone in a heartbeat.

"Annie." Claire reached out and rubbed her arm. This was dangerous since Annie didn't get a lot of human contact. When she did, it touched a part of her heart that longed for intimacy, to be close to someone. It wasn't about wanting a man. She wanted to be close to people, to feel free in calling on them if she needed to, not always having to rely on herself alone. She was worried that if she gave in to that longing, she'd be lost to it.

"Your parents are terrible people." Claire pulled her into a sideways hug.

"What?"

"I know you don't like talking about this stuff. You've got ninja-level skills in avoiding it, but you deserve love." She sat back. "Between what you've said, what you haven't, and the simple fact that they don't visit, I'm guessing things aren't great with your folks."

"It's complex," Annie said. Oh, what it would be to have a typical story to share, but Annie didn't want their pity. She wanted their friendship. "It is what it is."

"That's a good attitude to have." Erin reached out and put her hand over Annie's and gave it a squeeze. "Sometimes we are born into a great family, sometimes we build our own."

"And friends can be family." Claire offered. "There's nothing wrong with building a family with friends who love you. I'm still holding out hope that you find a man who falls madly in love with you, but you're doing the right thing, reaching out to people, making connections even when one doesn't work out. I'm pretty happy you picked me, for starters."

"Thanks," Annie spoke around the lump in her throat. "I

moved here hoping I'd find friends like you. Despite all the drama with Alex, I still love it here. I wanted to belong to someplace. Without Auntie Delia, I don't belong to England. Without my parents, I don't belong to New York. When I found this place, I knew I wanted to belong."

Claire raised an eyebrow. "You thought that even after reading *The Lowdown*?"

Annie laughed out loud.

CHAPTER TWELVE

ANNIE PEERED THROUGH THE WINDSHIELD INTO the gathering dark wishing she'd left Bangor an hour earlier. Brian had been so interesting to talk to that she forgot all about her drive back to Sweet River. He'd been engaging and funny, and they'd run through two refills and three hours before a chirp from her phone reminded her that she was due at a New Year's Eve party tonight. There wasn't going to be time to stop at her house to change, but the dress she was wearing wasn't too bad. It was one of her favorites—thick, black cotton with folklore embroidery all over the hem and down the sleeves. Granted, black wool tights and boots were for the weather, not fashion, but the party wasn't posh, it was at Pete's. She'd do as is.

The driving was dicey as a storm had rolled in bringing freezing rain. She was white-knuckled for miles, going thirty-five on the interstate to keep from skidding off it. That put her further behind when she finally pulled off the highway. The roads were smaller now, and the sleet and freezing ice had turned into snow. It wasn't the fluffy sort, it was wet and clung to her wipers as she drove. It would probably be smarter to head for home and forget about the party. But when the turnoff arrived, she didn't take it. Instead, she headed up the mountain. Calling and canceling at this late hour would make her look like a wimp. She wanted to be a local, unafraid of a bit of snow.

After this trip though, she was going to bite the bullet and replace the car. She could pull enough out of the rainy-day fund to buy a used SUV and then she wouldn't have to drive like a granny every time it snowed. As the snow grew less wet and fluffier, she began to relax and pick up speed. The blowy-stuff was always better to drive in, although it made it harder to see.

Her headlights formed two cones of swirling snow in the dark. It wasn't much further. The bridge over the river was coming up, and then it was ten minutes to Pete's house.

She hit a rut and the car began to skid. Annie pulled the wheel too hard, over-correcting. The car went into a full spin, hit the guardrail, but instead of stopping, flipped up and over, plunging nose-first to the riverbed below.

Alex stood with his back against the wall, watching the room of people talking, laughing, and generally having a good time. He couldn't relax. With every knock at the door, his gut twisted waiting for Annie to walk in and give him the cold shoulder. He'd barely recovered from last night. The look on her face shattered his heart into about a million pieces. When he'd sat down in the booth with Pete the first thing out of the man's mouth had been 'You're not skipping the party' as if he had seen her knock Alex to his metaphorical knees. He knew better than to argue, so he'd come, but he'd gotten into his uniform first, hoping that he'd be able to use a call as an excuse to leave. He was about ready to fake one at this point. The tension was killing him.

When he had seen her at Sid's all he'd wanted to do was take her into his arms and beg for forgiveness. He'd been angry when he'd heard Pete talking about her driving down to Bangor alone to see some guy. If he was such a great friend, why couldn't he come up here to see her where she'd be surrounded by her friends? What kind of man puts a friend out like that? Annie had taken his own concern the wrong way and then ripped his heart out. It didn't help to consider he might have hurt her, as well. Alex wished he could stop feeling anything, ever. What was the point?

"Hey, Alex, how's it going?"

Dan Connors was holding his hand out. Alex shook it, trying to twist his features into something resembling a welcoming expression. "Pastor Connors, good to see you." Alex had noticed him when he arrived. The man had been standing with his fiancée, Erin, and her two boys. They were mostly good kids, but like boys, they were also trouble. He'd had to tell them off for trying to put a float into the river, then again for fishing without licenses, and then another time when he suspected they were hunting rabbits. He'd come across them last week on a snowmobile trail near the MacAlister place, but at least they had their registration and permits in order. Maybe Dan was a calming influence on them.

"You can call me Dan. No need for titles." The man had a genuine, welcoming smile. "You see the game last night?"

It took him a second, but Alex figured Dan meant the Celtics. "Nope. I don't have cable. If I want to watch a game, I usually head to the Moose, but Friday it was crazy."

"Next time give me a call. Half the time I'm not home to see them anyway. You're more than welcome to my TV. Granted it's small, but it beats the Moose."

"Thanks for the offer. I'll think about it."

"Speaking of which, you should swing by the office sometime. I'd love to pick your brain for fishing spots. I've got one, but you probably know a few more. I'd like to find a good place to take the boys to get them started."

"Fly fishing?"

Dan nodded. "I'm going to take them ice fishing in a few weeks, but I'm not sure if that's the best fit for two active boys."

"It's typically a good fit for a middle-age guy and his case of beer." Alex smiled, although dealing with drunk fishermen was his least favorite winter activity.

"Right. The boys need something with a bit more moving

around. We'll see how they do and then maybe I'll save fishing for the spring. I'm not much of a hunter. I suppose you are?"

"Not really, no."

"A game warden who's not a hunter?"

"Didn't start off as a warden. Besides, the woods might be filled with game, but their only purpose isn't to become food. I feel like I'm there to make sure they get what they need and that the public is safe out there. Everybody has to play by the rules."

"Sure. I hike a lot. I love the peace you can find in nature. The world can be too noisy to think at times." Dan gave him a searching look. Alex began to suspect that he was chasing the next topic to keep the conversation going. "I suppose you get a lot of quiet, in your job?"

"Dan. Can I ask you a question?"

"Of course." He didn't seem too unhappy to have the subject changed.

"Did Pete ask you to talk to me?"

Dan smiled. "Was I too obvious or are you that smart?"

"Probably a mix of both." Alex chuckled. "I'd be happy to come to your office and discuss fishing spots. I do know of a couple that would knock your waders off, but if you're feeling obligated—"

"Not a bit. I think of Sweet River as my parish, so whether you attend Calvary or not, you're my parishioner. Pete didn't betray any confidences if you're worried about that. He said you'd benefit from having someone besides him to talk to, that you had some stuff you were dealing with. I don't know what you've got going on, but stop by sometime, and we can talk fishing, the Celtics, or whatever. I can't cook, but I make a mean cup of coffee, or tea if that's your thing."

"Definitely not a tea guy, but I'll—"

"Think about it." Dan echoed him, but he did it with a wink. "I know that probably amounts to a no, and that's completely okay. When you're ready, my door will be open. It isn't easy living in a small town, having everyone in your business. I should know." He ran a hand through his unruly blond hair and laughed. "I had a full-on meltdown in full view of anyone caring to watch. But I survived, and I managed to get Erin in the bargain." He looked across the room to the woman who would be his wife, and he raised his glass to her. She squinted at him as if she didn't know what he was doing, but raised hers too, then shook her head and mouthed the word 'dork.' Dan laughed.

"I don't know Erin well, but she seems really great."

"That she is." Dan was still smiling at his fiancée.

Alex liked Dan. He seemed to be a good guy. In other circumstances he'd probably like talking to him about fishing or whatever, but he'd had about enough of the sappy, in-love version of the man. Alex was inventing excuses, planning on calling in to work to see if he was needed tonight. The weather had really turned, and he'd heard the roads further south were a mess. The roads Annie would be driving home on. The tension he had felt all night began to ratchet up. Why wasn't Annie here yet? She had to have left Bangor hours ago. He pulled the cell out of his pocket and checked the time. It was eight. He started to do the math on when she was likely to have left, whether she'd stop at her place first, how slowly she'd drive in this weather.

Excusing himself he searched the room until he found Pete. The man's face looked a bit like Alex felt, worried. Pete and Lauren were huddled together, talking in quiet voices. "I left that message hours ago. She should have been here by now," Lauren was saying as Alex approached.

"Annie's late?" Alex slowed to a halt, and Lauren nodded. Like her daughter, Katherine, Lauren was tall, but she was also graceful. She practically floated as she walked. Right now she looked shrunken, her shoulders bowed, her hands knotted together. She looked up at Pete and his lips pressed together into a firm, thin line.

"Alex, I need you to get in your truck. We've got to look for her."

"Do you know the route she'd use?"

"We're gonna need to split up. If Annie headed here after stopping at her place, she'd take Mill Road. If she was coming straight from Bangor, that's route eleven. It goes over a few bridges, more than one spot to get into trouble. I figure we drive both ways. I'll check her apartment and then meet you at the highway. If we haven't found her, we call the state police."

"Got it." Alex was already moving to the door when Pete grabbed his arm.

"Get that dog of yours."

"Shep? You think we'll need to search?"

"I don't think she's gone off the road on the highway. If she had, we'd have heard by now."

"You're right. Someone would've seen, called it in. I'll keep an eye out on the way and get Shep, then I'll restart from route eleven and call you when I get to the highway." Alex pushed his way through the door and jogged to his truck. As it started, he pulled out his phone and called Deputy Chavez. "Hey, you on duty tonight?"

"Unfortunately. Been nothing but drunks and spin-outs all night. You clocking in?"

"No, I've got a friend missing. Annie Caldwell. Pete Coleman and I are looking now. You get any calls in the last few hours about a single female in a crash or calling for assistance?"

"No, but I'll call it in and see if anybody else has. Give me a shout if you need help."

"Will do." Alex disconnected the call and drove down the road praying that Annie was okay, wherever she was.

CHAPTER THIRTEEN

ANNIE WAS BEGINNING TO THINK GETTING out of the car was a mistake. The water wasn't that deep, as she suspected, but it was seeping into her boots which turned out not to be exactly waterproof. The cold wasn't so bad, it was the water. It had soaked the lining of her boots, and they were like lead weights on her feet. Every step was a struggle.

She looked back at the car. No help there. The front of her Passat was smashed, the interior covered in glass. She was lucky in the way that it fell. All she'd had to do was open the door and hop out. It was just too bad she hadn't been able to find her phone. Looking up over the banks of the river, she searched for lights of any kind, house or street, anything to tell her where she was. The woods were too thick, she couldn't see any breaks in the trees that might be paths or a driveway. Getting back up to the road was the only option. Once there she'd have to decide if it was better to walk back toward the highway or ahead toward Pete's house.

The route she was on wasn't well-populated and bypassed town entirely. She tried to remember how far up the mountain it started to pass houses, but she hadn't been paying attention to distance. It was too dark, too snowy to get her bearings. A twinge of panic hit her stomach, but she fought it off. She took a deep breath and gently exhaled. "There is no point in getting upset. It will only make this worse." That was all too true. She needed her wits about her. The river bed she was in was mostly dry, but the banks were high. She'd have to climb out.

She looked up into the snow, falling steadily, her eyes blinking as the flakes landed on her face. There was a faint bit of moonlight coming through the clouds, enough for her to see a few yards in front of her. The bank on either side of the river was smooth with snow, but ahead it looked rougher. She trudged on, her feet wet and cold, until she found a section of the bank where roots and branches stuck out through the snow. With something to hang onto, she should be able to pull herself up. Grabbing onto one long, ragged looking branch, she tugged. It held. She shoved her boot into the side of the bank and hauled on the root with all her might, swinging her arm higher, searching for another branch. Her hands hit something that felt thick enough, and she hoisted herself up again. It broke in her hand, sending her sprawling backward. Waving her arms in the air, she managed to keep on her feet.

"Blast it!" Annie cried out in frustration and tried again. The first root held, but she couldn't find anything above it to use. The snow was heavy and wet, compressing and making the bank slippery. She clawed at the top for a hand-hold, a small sob escaping her throat as she failed and fell back again. A wave of despair filled her. It was too much, too hard. Her whole body began to tremble. Her feet were completely numb now. She couldn't feel the skin of her legs. Her mittens were soaked through, and her fingers were stiff. "Hold yourself together." She shouted aloud.

Annie threw off her mittens and attacked the bank again. The root was slippery and cold under her bare fingers, the snow even more frozen, but she hauled herself up, planting her toes into the soil as deep as she could. Grunting with the effort she flopped herself forwards and up, using her elbows to dig into the snow and solid earth, propelling her further. Inches. She was inches from the top. "Please!" She half screamed, half prayed as she hauled herself up. The ground held. She got her feet under her again and crawled up to the top, throwing herself onto the undisturbed snow. Panting, she got to her knees and then to her feet. There was nothing but trees and snow in either direction.

If only she knew which way to go. Back the way she came there were a few houses, but not for at least a mile, if not more. She wasn't sure she could walk that far. What if nobody came along? Her feet were already freezing. Ahead she had no idea how close the nearest help might be. Pete's place was too distant to shoot for. It was probably smartest to go back the way she'd come. She could walk along the edge of the road where it was mostly cleared and flag down any car that passed. If they didn't see her, she'd only have a few feet to jump out of the way. Better to risk getting whacked by a car than stand in the snow and freeze, though.

She trudged her way through the snow, back to the bridge, and then out onto the road. There was no sign of life in either direction, so she set out the way she'd come. Trying not to think about the fact that she couldn't feel her toes, she walked on in the gently falling snow. In any other circumstances, it would be beautiful. If she were back at home, sitting in her chair by the front window under a blanket, it would be downright cheerful. Right now, it was like puffy, white evil. "Next time put your phone in your pocket." She kept walking—not that it helped. The cold seeped in through her heavy coat. The walk should be warming her up, but it wasn't.

The road narrowed a bit, the trees closing in. Without the faint moonlight overhead, it was dark enough that Annie wasn't sure she should go on. Maybe it would be better to get off the road? But then no one would see her if they drove by. She kept walking, fatigue and fear taking turns trying to overwhelm her. Annie made herself keep walking as dark thoughts began to invade. What if no one comes? How long can I last in this? I could die out here.

That last one was true, much as she wished it wasn't. People died in conditions like this. She tried to push those thoughts away as she grew tired. Her muscles ached, her feet, although numb, also seemed to hurt. The wind wasn't too bad, but it was freezing her face all the same. She tried to hunker down in her coat, but the collar wasn't high enough to block the wind. Around the next bend, the road started to widen again. Ahead she spotted a tree down and another leaning beside it. They made a sort of lean-to. Maybe she could take a break there for a minute, get her face warmed up. She'd be able to see the road and run to the edge if anyone came by. Trudging over the snowbank and into the woods she climbed on top of the downed tree and up against the trunk of the other. Finally out of the wind she prayed for a plow, a neighbor, anyone to come by.

As Alex drove toward his house, he scanned the roadsides ahead of him for any sign of a car. It was all so thickly wooded that no car could be there that wouldn't still be sticking out. All he could think about was getting home. He skidded to a stop in his snowy drive and jumped out of the truck. He opened his front door and called for Shep who was sitting on the couch. The dog immediately sensed Alex's mood. He vaulted over the back of the couch and came running. He was up in the truck and sitting at attention as if waiting for a command. Alex got in and rubbed Shep's neck. "Good boy." He backed out and hit his lights, headed back up to route eleven, driving as fast as it was safe to go.

When he reached the turnoff, he took it slow, using his searchlight to check the sides of the road for any indication a car had skidded off. The conditions weren't great. The temperature gauge on his dash read eighteen degrees. They needed to find her quickly. He knew this route pretty well. There were two spots where a car could run off the road and not hit a tree. One, and he didn't like to think about it, was at the bridge over the

Sweet. The river was deep there. A car would go right through the ice and be buried. But, that section was closer to the highway and better traveled. The other spot was the bridge over the West. That river had been as big as the Sweet years ago, but the Army Corp of Engineers had diverted most of it for an irrigation project. What was left was a trickle of water, lots of rock, and a steep river bed. Decision made, he shut off his spot light, hit his lights and siren, and sped off for the West River overpass.

In minutes he was approaching the bridge. Slowing down, he spotted something as he crossed over. A faint red glow a few yards from the road. He flicked the spot light on and pulled off into the snow as close to the edge of the river bank as he dared to go. The car was nose-first in the creek. He got out and ran towards it, his chest tight, his mind trying not to think about what he might find. Shep was on his heels. The dog plunged over the side of the bank and up to the open door of the car. As Alex followed him down, he could see it was empty. He took out his cell and called dispatch.

"This is Warden Alex Moretti. I'm at the West River overpass on route eleven, and I have a 10-55. The car is a Volkswagen Passat. The plate is," he sprinted to the back and read it off. "No occupant." Alex added as he took out his flashlight and lit up the interior. The windshield was smashed, but there was no blood, no center hit to indicate she'd been thrown against it. The window was intact and had no blood either. The airbag wasn't deployed either, which meant the force of the crash wasn't nearly as bad as it looked. This was all good. He was half-listening as dispatch was talking. "Can you repeat, please?"

"Vehicle is registered to Caldwell, Anne Elizabeth."

He'd known they were going to come back with her name, but it still tore through him. He had to take a breath, to find his calm. "Copy that. I'm going to search for her now. I'm leaving my vehicle at the scene and proceeding on foot. Give the deputies my cell." He started climbing out where he'd slid down, but Shep was running ahead to another spot and whining. He knew that sound. "You got her scent?" He stuffed his phone into his pocket and climbed up the bank. Jogging over to the spot Shep was sniffing he got the dog's attention. "Find her. Find Annie." Shep took off.

CHAPTER FOURTEEN

ANNIE LAID HER HEAD AGAINST THE bark of the tree trunk knowing she should get up. All the stories she'd read of people surviving these sorts of things involved them not sitting still. She was making what was probably the single, worst mistake she could, but her body felt frozen. She wasn't sure she could move. Maybe someone had seen her car? And they'd come find her? Slim chance of that. She had to get to her feet. Right now she was huddled up, wet and colder than she'd ever been in her life. All her energy was gone. Stopping had probably been a mistake.

Pray, she thought. That was a good start. She looked at the sky and the flakes of snow floating down in their haphazard way. They were beautiful, even if they were trying to kill her. Why couldn't she keep her thoughts on track? *Dear God, send someone, because I don't think I can move.* Her eyes closed as the snow fell and covered her. She told herself to get up, but her body wasn't listening. Her ears still worked though. She could hear a jingling approaching. It was a cheerful sound and reminded her of something. It was a good association, but she couldn't put it together. The noise grew louder and then she heard light footfalls, like an animal running. Something wet touched her face. She reached out her hands and opened her eyes.

Shep barked in her face, wagging his tail so hard his whole body wiggled. Between happy barks he licked her face from chin to forehead. "Shep." Holding his face still she tried to get him to stop licking her. She was confused for a minute. "How did you get here?"

"Annie!" She knew that voice. Alex had come for her. She almost burst into tears as a wave of relief swept through her.

Trying to call out to him, her throat seized up. She pushed up and away from the tree as Shep bounded away and then returned to nuzzle her again. He ran back and forth between them until Alex came into view, his breath steaming in the cold.

"Annie." He said it brokenly as he fell to his knees in front of her, running his hands over her limbs. "Are you in any pain? Did you hit your head?" He pulled her knit hat off and looked at her forehead.

"No." She pushed his hands away. "I'm only cold. Can you take me home?"

He slid his hands over her arms and legs again. "Does anything hurt? Did you feel any pain after the car crashed?"

"No. Didn't hit my head. Take me home, please?"

"I'm going to get you out of here and checked out." He rummaged through a pocket and took out his phone. "First, I'm going to call Pete. He's probably freaking out. I forgot to call him when I found your car."

"Oh no, I didn't think about worrying them."

"I found her." He spoke into the phone. "She's cold, but okay. Her car's off the road, and she was walking the road a while." Alex paused. "No, I've called it in. I'm going to get her into my truck, and we'll wait for EMS there. I'll keep you updated." He paused again. "Yes, I know. Okay." He disconnected the call and handed her the phone. "Hold that." He scooped her up in his arms and struggled to his feet.

"Alex! I'm too heavy."

"Hold onto me."

She raised her arms and linked them around his neck.

"It's a bit of a walk, but we'll be okay." He adjusted his hold on her and started to walk out onto the road. "Can you go into my contacts and hit the one that says 'dispatch'?"

Annie let go of him for a second to touch the buttons.

"Hold the phone up to my ear."

Annie engaged the call and then held it against his ear. She heard someone answer. "This is Moretti. I found the driver on that 10-55 I called in." Alex had to be a lot stronger than he looked since he barely seemed breathless. He ended the call quickly. "Okay, you can take the phone back."

She disconnected the call and held the phone with one hand and onto him with the other. He shifted his grip on her again. "I have an inside pocket, you can put the phone there." He gestured with his chin to his chest. She pulled open the edge of his coat and slid the phone into the pocket. The warmth radiating from him was tempting. She had to resist slipping her cold hand inside his jacket.

"Your hand is freezing. Put it in my coat."

He didn't need to ask twice. She stuffed her hand inside and then leaned against him, trying to absorb every bit of heat. Shep ran ahead of them as they walked. Alex whistled to him anytime he got too far ahead, and he'd come running back.

"You should put me down."

"No."

"Seriously, I'm too heavy."

"I've trained to carry someone twice your size. Relax."

"But I'm heavy for my size."

He laughed. "I'm not sure your understanding of physics is quite all there. You're perfect. Hush."

She wasn't sure how she felt about him telling her to shut up, even if it was done nicely, but she was too tired to go on arguing. She laid her head against his shoulder and shut her eyes. *Thank you*, she prayed.

Alex's biceps were screaming by the time they reached his truck. He didn't care. He was so glad he'd found Annie that he couldn't do anything *but* carry her back. Even now, it was hard letting go. He had to put her on her feet so he could open the door of the truck. Shep hopped in onto the seat first and then into the back. Alex tried to pick Annie up again, but she batted his hands away and climbed in on her own. When he was in, he started the truck up and turned up the heat. Annie put her fingers over the air vents. "Oh, that feels so good."

"Careful, you might have frostbite."

"Not on my fingers, but my toes are another matter."

Alex reached down and took her legs, pulling them up onto the seat.

"Hey, what are you doing?"

"We need to get your boots off." He undid the laces and managed to get one off. The sock underneath was wet. "Those boots are useless." Going to work on the other one he had it off and was tugging on what he thought was her sock when she smacked his hands away.

"I'm wearing tights."

"Oh." Warmth flooded his cheeks. "You probably want to take those off on your own."

"Yes. Look away, please."

"I can cut them. That would be quicker and easier."

"Just look away." She spun in the seat. He turned his face away, looking out the window. A moment later she spoke. "Done."

He pulled his first aid kit out from under Shep who was happily licking her face again. "Quit it, buddy." Shep sat back. Alex pulled two heat packs out of the bag and crushed each, activating the chemicals inside. He felt around in the backseat again and pulled out the bag he kept a change of clothes in. He'd fallen in mud or stepped in it enough times that he now kept multiple pairs of clean socks. He took out a pair. "Don't worry, these are clean."

She raised her feet so he could put the socks on. He slid one on her foot, and she pulled it up from there.

"Um. Thanks."

Her feet were tiny in comparison to his, and the socks looked ridiculous. They did the job though. He placed a heat compress over each of them. "We need to be sure these don't get too hot. Your toes didn't look frostbitten to me, but the EMTs will be able to tell for sure. They'll also have my head if I make things worse with too much heat."

"I trust you."

"Do you?" He watched her face, looking for some sign that she might forgive him for being a complete fool. Because he was. Staying away from her to keep her safe was the stupidest idea he'd ever had.

"Are we having that talk?"

"What talk?"

"The one we would have had the morning after the concert if you'd showed up at the shop."

Guilt flooded his gut. He deserved whatever she was going to say. "Yes."

"Can you tell me what's been going on with you? Not some stupid excuse, but the truth."

"Annie I—" He was interrupted by the sound of a siren. Flashing lights shone into the cab of the truck. "Perfect timing." He gave her a smile while she rolled her eyes. "Let's get you checked out." He got out of the truck and went around to her side. "Wait, let me help you." He reached out his arms, but she ignored them.

"I don't need you to carry me. I can walk."

"You're in socks. Please, let me." He looked into her eyes, hoping she'd see what he couldn't say. That he needed to help her because he'd been imagining the worst for the last hour. He needed to hold her close, to feel her breath, a tangible reminder that she was alive and okay. He stretched out his arms to her again. Her eyes flicked down to his hands and back up to his face. He wondered what she was looking for. Not for the first time, he was speechless, lost in her eyes, waiting for her to save him.

She slid her arm around his shoulder, and he picked her up. The EMTs had pulled up right next to his truck. They had the back of the ambulance open already, the light streaming out. "This is Anne Caldwell." He told them as he carried her to the stretcher in the back. "I got her boots off, and her feet look okay, but they did get wet, and she had no feeling when I first found her."

"We got it from here." They all but pushed Alex out of the back of the van. He could hear Annie immediately refuse to be taken to the hospital. He hoped they could talk her into it, but she was stubborn. He felt a hand on his shoulder and turned to see Pete. "Hey, I didn't even hear you pull up. I told you I'd keep you updated."

Pete waved at Annie before turning to Alex. "Wanted to see for myself she was all right. Lauren wouldn't sleep well tonight if I couldn't tell her I'd seen Annie was okay with my own eyes."

"Well, she's okay enough to hassle me about waiting for the ambulance, so there's that. She wanted me to take her right home."

"Sounds like her." Pete looked Alex over. "How are you?"

"I lost about a decade of my life when I saw her car in the creek. Other than that, I'm fine."

Pete chuckled and clapped him on the back. "Wrecker coming?"

"Yeah. The car is likely a total loss. I told them to drive it to the station's lot rather than back to her place. Her building doesn't have its own lot. They have to park in the municipal one, and I didn't want her getting grief from the town about it sitting there."

One of the EMTs walked over to them. "Which one of you is in charge?"

Alex stepped forward. "That's me. How is she?"

"She's lucky. Missed hypothermia by that much." He held his hand up with his finger and thumb almost touching. "Much longer and she would definitely have had frostbite. Smart move with the socks and heat packs. But she's refusing transport. Are you going to take responsibility for her?"

"Yes." And for more than tonight. He'd decided something after picking her up out of the snow, feeling her frozen against him for the entire walk back to his truck. He'd have to fix what he'd broken, but he wanted to at least try to be the man she needed him to be. He wanted a real relationship with her. When he thought she might be dead, that she might be out of his life forever, it had nearly broken him. For better or worse, he planned to make Annie Caldwell his friend again. If she'd let him be more, he'd take that too.

He followed the EMT to the ambulance and insisted on carrying Annie again since she still didn't have dry boots for her feet. He was taking her back to his truck when Pete tried to divert him.

"Put her in mine. I'm taking her to my house. Lauren would rather have her with us in case she needs anything. We can help her with anything that might come up."

"No. I can get her home and make sure she's okay."

"I'd really feel better if she was with us."

"*She's* right here." Annie pointed to herself. "And she's perfectly capable of saying where she's going."

"Honey, you've had a bad night. You're probably shaken up." Pete gently patted her hand.

Annie pointed to Alex's truck. "Please let me sit."

Alex took her over to the truck and set her down. "In all

honesty, you should've let the EMTs take you to the hospital. Any time you're in a car crash, even if you don't immediately seem to have an injury—"

"Oh, my giddy aunt!" Annie shouted. "Stop treating me like a child." She pointed at Pete. "Both of you. Your offer is very kind. Please be sure to tell Lauren I appreciate the invitation to stay with you tonight, but I want to go home. And I'll be honest, this night wasn't fun, but it barely makes my top ten list of all-time bad experiences. I'm fine. The paramedics said the same thing."

"If you're sure," Pete asked her, a look of concern still on his face.

"Totally. Hobbes needs to be fed, I need to get out of these clothes, and call my insurance company. Not that anyone will be there considering the holiday. That's a shame. But it doesn't matter." She watched as the wrecker slowed to a stop, its driver hopping out. "I was going to buy a bigger car anyway. Something that handles snow better so I don't end up in any more river beds."

Alex left her where she was and approached the driver. "It's front-wheel drive. The bank is slick so be careful. Let me know if you need any help."

"Been doing it all night." He looked over to the ambulance packing up and Annie sitting in the truck. "Looks like this one had a happy ending at least." He walked away, lifting his chin to Pete's greeting. Alex's gut grew tight thinking about the may-have-beens. For many families tonight, it wasn't going to be a happy ending. He didn't envy any police officer on duty right now. Those calls were gut-wrenching. Especially the ones with little kids. He sent up a quick prayer of thanks adding to the dozen he'd already prayed. Annie didn't know how close of a call she'd had.

He approached the truck in time to hear Pete say, "Okay, I'll stop the lecture there, but you know you can call us anytime? I don't mean that in the way people say it because it's the thing you're supposed to say. I'm saying it in the way you can count on it being real. You're not alone here. You have Lauren and me and apparently,"—he gave Alex a look he couldn't quite decipher—"you've got this guy too."

"You do." Alex immediately echoed and fervently hoped she believed it.

She slid her legs into the truck. "Thanks, Pete." Her voice was quiet, and she wasn't looking at Alex. Not the best sign. Alex gave her a smile as he shut the door.

Pete followed him to the other side. "She has you, doesn't she?"

"Yes. I just said so."

"That's not what I meant." Pete was giving him a hard stare as if he could see through to Alex's thoughts. "Are you hers?"

Alex nodded. "She has me." He looked at her huddled up on the front seat of his truck, and a rush of warmth filled his chest. "I'm not sure what to do about that."

"When a man truly loves a woman—I know that sounds like the start of a bad pop song." Pete chuckled. "But when you're at that spot where she has your heart, then you need to stop thinking about you and what you want from her, and start thinking about what she needs. If you focus on who she needs you to be, what struggles she's facing, then it will all fall into place. I'm not saying it will get easy. Considering you are who you are." Pete left it there, but his point was made. "But you will see your way clear."

"I hope you're right."

"Do right by her, think of her first, and you'll be surprised how easy it is."

Alex nodded and then waved goodbye to Pete who got into his SUV and drove away. The wrecker had Annie's car out of the creek, so Alex walked over to be sure they were all set. As it was driving away, he finally got into his truck. At some point, Annie must have started it up again since it was running and warm.

"I love Shep." Annie began. "But I had to start your truck to get the air moving again and deal with his um...breath."

Alex laughed out loud. "Yeah, it can get deadly."

Shep, sitting in the back seat, licked her face all over again. She laughed. It sounded like music to his ears.

"Cut it out." She smiled and patted Shep's neck, pushing him back into his seat.

It was a quiet drive back to town. They didn't restart the conversation that had been interrupted earlier. Alex knew there were things to be said, but Annie was tired and maybe tonight wasn't the time. He stopped in front of her building and came around to her side. "I know you're going to argue with me, but do you really want to walk through that snow in socks?"

She looked at the alleyway to the rear of the building and shook her head. "Maybe my boots are dry?" She picked them up from the floor of the car. To Alex's eyes, they looked ruined. Annie frowned at them and then sighed. "Okay. One last time." Alex picked her up. Shep tried to follow, but she pushed the door shut. "Sorry, but he's got to stay down here. Hobbes will lose his mind if I let a dog in the apartment."

"I'm guessing Hobbes is a cat?"

"Yes, and a rather ferocious one."

Alex smiled, thinking that it was unlikely there was a cat that could scare Shep, but it was probably for the best. Shep would likely chase it around the apartment and end up breaking something. When they reached the shop, he put her down long enough to open it. "Do you have your keys? I didn't even think of that."

She reached up a hand with them dangling from her fingers. "I took them out of the ignition when I got out of the car." She opened the back door, and he started to come inside, but she stopped him. "Y'know, you probably don't need to come up. I've got it from here."

"No, you don't."

"I don't need you to help me up the stairs." She gestured up the flight behind her.

"I'm responsible for you. I need to see you safely inside your residence." He waited while she rolled her eyes, but she let him in. Once they were at her apartment door, he was afraid she'd leave him there, but she opened it and held it for him. It definitely looked like a place Annie would call home. The kitchen was large and airy, the living room gracefully furnished, a wingback chair right in front of a large window overlooking the street. He could smell the faint echo of her perfume.

"I'm all set now. You can go." She had put her things down on the counter.

"I'd like to talk, Annie."

"Well, I'd like to call it a night."

"I suppose I'm a jerk for wanting more of your time." He meant that honestly, but from the expression on her face, she thought he was being sarcastic. "I meant that I shouldn't ask you for anything right now. You survived a car crash, had to climb up a frozen river bank, then walk a mile through the snow. If Shep hadn't found you..." He shook his head. "I'm trying not to think about that."

"I like Shep."

"I'd like to get back to the place where you liked me as well."

Annie frowned. "Alex, it took a lot for me to reach out to you, to invite you to that concert and then you—"

"I messed up. Let me make it up to you. I'm so sorry for hurting you. I never meant to. Please, give me another chance?" He was lost in her eyes again, waiting for her to decide he was worth the risk. "I wish I knew what you were thinking."

She shrugged. "I do like Shep, so I suppose I'll need to give you that chance if I expect to see him again."

Relief washed through him. "I'm glad his obsession with you has paid off."

"Nice." She pushed his shoulder, and he rocked back on his heels before tilting towards her again. He raised his hand to brush the bangs off her forehead and stopped himself, turning it into an awkward wave.

"I should get going." He was at the door when an orange ball of fur attacked his ankles.

"Oh, I forgot about Hobbes." Annie sprinted toward him and grabbed the thing clawing at his ankle.

"Hobbes, no." She wrestled the large orange cat into the closet and shut the door. "I am so sorry. I should have realized he'd attack you. He didn't recognize you, or he would've launched himself right off. He thinks it's funny. Or at least I assume he does, since there's no other reason for it. It's why I renamed him, Hobbes. From Calvin and Hobbes, y'know that cartoon with the little boy and the pretend tiger who becomes a real tiger in his imagination. Anyway he always attacks Calvin when he comes home, and when I brought Hobbes home from the shelter they called him Michael, which is a stupid name for a cat, so I was thinking of a new name and after three days straight of him attacking my ankles when I got home from work I lit on Hobbes, and it's been his name ever since. I think it's accurate, I mean, it seems accurate and—"

Alex leaned down and kissed her lips. He pulled back almost immediately. "Sorry, I can't help myself. When you get going, it's the only way to stop you."

Her long, black lashes fluttered for a moment, and then she fixed him with a hard stare. "Is that why you kissed me that night?"

"Yes, well...not really. I kissed you because you were

beautiful, and you were saying terrible, wrong things about yourself. I couldn't think of the right words to show you were wrong. I wanted you to know that none of what you were saying matched what I thought or felt."

"But we weren't… Did you had feelings for me before?"

He nodded.

She shook her head, the curls around her face swaying with the motion. "You're going to confuse me Alex, and the confusion I've already felt was rather painful. I'd rather not repeat the experience."

"You deserve better than me. I kept telling myself I need to do the right thing and let you find that better man."

"You are a good man, Alex."

"I've already proved otherwise."

She waved her hand. "That's true, but not all the same. You didn't set out to hurt me."

"But I did hurt you."

"Yes, you did. How about we start over and you don't do it this time?"

He nodded, knowing that he was making a promise he probably shouldn't.

"Okay then." She paused long enough for him to wonder what she was thinking. "Thank you. For tonight, I mean, and I was kidding about Shep."

"You would've been fine. You're a fighter."

She squinted up at him as if she didn't believe it. "All the same, for what you did, you have my thanks."

"Anything for you, Annie." The words had rushed out of him, but he meant each one. "I'll go so you can rest. Tomorrow's the holiday, so no excuse not to put your feet up and stay warm."

"I will."

"I'll see you soon." He reached out and stroked her cheek. "Goodnight, Annie."

CHAPTER FIFTEEN

ANNIE OPENED HER EYES TO SUNSHINE, which was odd. She felt around for her phone and then remembered it was at the bottom of the riverbed...or that's where she assumed it ended up when the car crashed. Clock. She needed a clock, but there was none in the bedroom. Heading out into the living room, she looked around and found the one on the mantle. She stared at it until her eyes adjusted and she could read it. Then she reread it. It was ten. How? "What's today?" Her brain chased her thoughts around until she remembered it was Tuesday, and she'd taken the day off to deal with the hassle from the accident. Per the doctor's or rather the EMT's orders she'd laid low over New Year's Day to recover. They'd warned her that although she wasn't hurt in the accident, her body was bashed about, and she'd be sore. Boy were they right.

She sighed, wondering what to do first. It was probably time to think about coffee and breakfast, and that meant changing out of her flannel PJs to go downstairs or make her own. She was deciding which she had the energy for when there was a knock on the door. She looked out the peephole and saw Alex, to-go coffee in his hands. She ran to the bathroom, grabbed her robe, tied it around her, and opened the door. "What are you doing here?"

"Hoping you'd be up." He lifted the to-go cup. "I have coffee. It's good because I got it at this place downstairs. They're fantastic."

She smiled. "Yes, I think I heard they were good." For a moment she was occupied by how utterly handsome he was. He was dashing in uniform, but dressed casually, like now, he took her breath away. The Carhartt coat he was wearing didn't look new, and his jeans and boots weren't, but they spoke of his character. He was the kind of man who knew how to fix a car, chop wood, build things. These were all traits she found wildly attractive. Knowing that he was also kind and intelligent made it better. The one sticky wicket was that she didn't know his heart well enough to tell what kind of man he was.

"Annie?"

She realized he was still standing in her doorway. "Sorry, my thoughts were...elsewhere. Do you want to come in?"

"Yeah, I brought breakfast. Your girls made something blueberry. I forget what they're called. They smell good anyway."

"Oh, it's scones." She led him over to the island and set down the coffee and the bag of food. Hobbes took that moment to launch himself at Alex's ankles again.

He yelped, but then looked down and laughed. "Nice try tiger, but those are steel toe and thick leather. You make it through that, and I'll be impressed." Hobbes bit his boot a few more times before taking off for the other side of the apartment. "I like your cat."

"He can be quite sweet, but mostly he's barmy." She unpacked the scones and offered him one on a plate. "I'm sorry I don't have clotted cream to offer with this, but I do have jam and butter."

"Nah, I'll take it as is." He took a big bite. "They're good. Softer than I expected. Your girls have talent."

"I have a secret." She leaned over the counter. "They didn't bake them. Even *I* don't make them. I do the special stuff, but day to day it's a wholesale bakery who makes most of what we sell."

"Really?"

"They deliver it at the crack of dawn. I usually do the special, like the gingerbread or cinnamon rolls. When I did up my business plan that was the first thing Auntie Del had nixed. She said it would be too much trying to run the place myself and make it all by hand. I had no training for starters and would've had to apprentice at a bakery. She was right of course. It was enough of a challenge to get the hours in as a barista."

"You worked at a coffee shop first?"

"Yes, while I finished my masters. It was the only way to get enough experience. There's only so much you can read up on."

"That makes sense, but why open a business at all? I mean, if you've got a graduate degree in something you love, why take the risk of opening a business?"

"Part of it was to please my aunt. She was worried about my future. Towards the end of her life, that's all we seemed to talk about. She wanted me to have financial security, and my field doesn't often provide that. Librarians are usually the first to go when budget cuts start. That and she wanted me to find a place I could call home, and be able to stay there, even if I lost my job. We did a lot of research and decided a coffee and bookshop was the best idea. I found Sweet River Christian Academy and then this building, and the rest is history."

"That's pretty brave. I mean, moving to somewhere you know no one and investing everything you have hoping it will work out."

She shrugged her shoulders. "I prayed about it a lot, and I had Delia's blessing. She had done the same thing herself, really. She'd taken her inheritance and put it into a high street shop selling home goods and custom cabinetry. She made a pile."

"Did you inherit from her?"

"No, all her money went to a charity helping orphans and children in need. Which was perfect. She left them her house but allowed me to take anything that was special to me. The rest was sold. The charity got a nice check out of it."

"I can imagine the cause was close to her heart." Alex was

giving her a gentle sort of look. She liked that almost as much as his smiles.

"Yes, it was." She had to say it around the lump in her throat. Annie turned away to get two napkins from the cabinet over the sink and gave one to Alex. She was thinking of a way to change the subject when he did it for her.

"I was going to offer to take you car shopping today. I have the day off. The nearest dealerships are in Bangor, so I figured you'd need help."

"You must be psychic. I did a bit of online shopping last night. I found what I think is the perfect car, but the dealership is in Portland. It's a good deal further."

"I can take you there and help you buy it."

"I don't need help."

"Okay, then I'll be company."

"You don't need to do that." Annie dismissed his offer immediately, almost by reflex.

"What if I want to do that?" He threw the words out like they were a challenge. When she failed to respond his mouth tightened, and he looked down at the remains of his scone, a muscle ticking in his cheek. "You don't trust me." He told the crumbs.

"It's not that, Alex. It's that I don't know what to do with where we are. What am I to you? Are you helping me because you feel bad about what happened to me, or are you helping because I'm something to you?"

He got up and came around the island, but she looked at the ground, uncomfortable with the conversation and her mixed feelings. He stood in front of her, and she could smell pine and bergamot again. It was strangely comforting. Slowly he reached out and took her face in his hands. She looked up into his eyes which searched her face.

"You are something to me. You must feel it too, the way

we're connected to each other. From the first moment I met you, I felt it. I didn't know what to do with it, and I've done a bad job with it so far, but I care about you."

"Oh, well–that's good." Her heart started beating faster. Was he saying what she thought he was? She moved her face out of his hands. "And now we're going to take what might have been a perfectly friendly relationship and turn it into something else?" She wanted to think that was possible, but thus far it had been a disaster. "Are we about to make a mess of things?"

He leaned back on the counter and crossed his arms. "I don't know, to be honest. But I don't think we can go back to where we were before. I can't pretend that I don't feel something for you, that you're just a friend. I don't want to go to your shop every morning and watch you from afar wishing we could be something to each other. I also don't want to avoid you so it doesn't hurt."

She tried to read him, but what she saw was a mix of emotions, frustration and confusion chief among them. He was a mess. Then again, her own feelings weren't exactly sure. She cared for Alex, a great deal, but he'd hurt her. Would he do it again? Was being with him worth the risk of getting wounded the next time he changed his mind? "I hated you avoiding me, so yes, let's not go back to that."

He nodded. "Can we draw a line under all of it?" He swept his hand like he was pushing it all away. "If you can forgive me, then maybe we can go from here. Forget all that and start from here." He leaned forward and stuck out his hand. "Hi, I'm Alex Moretti."

She chuckled and shook his hand. "Annie Caldwell."

"Would you like to get dinner sometime? How about tonight, after I drive you to Portland and back?"

She wanted to believe that was possible, that she could trust that he knew what he wanted. Right now, he seemed confident in everything he said, but she suspected he didn't know himself as well as he thought. Who does though? Did she? She knew that what she felt for him was strong, and she suspected it could very quickly become love. She didn't want to give up on that, on him. This was a risk, but if this were the only way to keep him in her life, she'd do it. "Okay. I would like that." The answering smile on his face warmed her from the inside out.

Having Alex at the dealership was handier than she'd thought it would be. The salesman was much less unctuous in his presence. Annie had come armed of course. She'd spotted the car she wanted on their website, a lightly-used Subaru Forester. She knew they had it overpriced, so she came in with what she wanted to pay and held firm. Other than the hassle of getting a certified check to the dealer once the funds were transferred to her bank and having to get a ride back to Portland to finish the deal and pick up the car, the thing was a matter of a few hours work. As they drove back, Alex suggested dinner at Maria's.

"You know that means going on the record, so to speak."

Alex's eyes were on the road, but she could see that he was working through what she had said.

"Going to Maria's together is the Sweet River equivalent of a courtship announcement. I only say it because—"

"Because I gave you a reason to doubt that I really want to be seen with you, which is on me."

"That's not what I meant."

"Maybe not, but would you have mentioned it if we had a different start?" He glanced at her before turning back to the road ahead. "I think the answer to that is no. And I bought that."

"Alex, you take too much on yourself."

"It's not me taking it on, it's me acknowledging the

consequences of my actions. I mistreated you and burned you. You don't trust me. I'm going to need to earn it, and I plan to do exactly that." He glanced at her quickly and gave her a soft smile. It reminded her how much she loved his smile. He rarely shared it which made it all the more precious. The truth was that she didn't trust him, but she wanted to. It might be different if she had more experience in relationships. As a teenager she'd formed a few close friendships, but nothing romantic. Her one, brief relationship in college had taught her to be cautious, but not how to build real trust.

When they pulled into the parking lot at Maria's, Annie almost called it off. Judging by the steamy windows, the diner was packed. Alex got out of the truck, and Annie followed, feeling less confident the closer they got to the front door.

Alex chuckled. "Are you going to run for it?"

"What?"

"You look about to bolt." He opened the door. "Nobody's going to look twice at us. It's wicked crowded in there. We'll blend in."

"Ha." She walked in ahead of him into the little lobby, conscious of his hand at the small of her back, wondering if the gesture was solicitous or preventative. He pulled open the interior door, and a wall of warmth and sound hit her. "Once more unto the breach." She quoted under her breath. Spotting an open booth at the back of the restaurant, Annie made a bee-line for it, eyes forward, ignoring the other booths packed with people, some with familiar faces. She slid into the booth and immediately pulled out a menu, burying her face in it. "So what do you like here?"

"You're going to give me a complex." Alex's eyes were full of mirth, belying his words. He leaned forward and whispered, "Maybe it's you who doesn't want to be seen with me."

"Stop it, you know that's not true."

"Then don't worry about it, Annie. So the town knows we're dating. It's no big deal."

"We're dating?"

"Yeah." He pointed to her and back to himself. "You and I having dinner. Date."

She put her menu down. "I'll be honest. This is all new to me."

"I got that."

"What do you mean?"

"Relax." He reached out and took her hands in his. "I get that you haven't dated a lot. You're shy, it totally makes sense."

"I'm not actually that shy. Men don't usually... I mean I'm not conventionally what a guy looks for. I'm too short, too fat, too whatever. I get looked over, and that's totally fine because I don't want some guy who's all about physical appearances anyway, and if that's their stumbling block, then so be it. Uh, this is humiliating." She closed her eyes, so she didn't have to see his reaction to her rambling. Maybe she could duck under the table and stay there for perhaps the next year. Why did she let her mouth get away from her like that? A rush of air tickled her cheek, and her eyes flew open in time to watch as he took her hand and brought it to his lips, kissing the back of it, before letting it go.

His expression heated. "Here's the deal. Every time you say something bad about yourself I'm going to kiss you. No matter where we are or who is watching."

Heat crept over her cheeks. "Alex." She tried to find the words to both thank him for the gesture and to tell him to cut it out.

"Nope, that's the deal. You talk yourself down, I will kiss those words off your lips because they're not true. I don't tell people polite lies about who they are. In fact, I usually do the opposite. I don't know who convinced you that you're not worth loving, but they lied to you."

She bit her lip and looked down at the table as the telltale sting of tears hit her. Maybe Alex spotted that she was about to blubber since he deftly changed the subject.

"You know what's really good here?" He let go of her hands and picked up the menu. "The pot roast. Sounds boring, but it's good. But if you're not into meat and potatoes, the tomato soup and grilled cheese rocks."

"I quite like their shepherd's pie. It's almost as good as the English version, although they never seem to use lamb, only ground beef."

"I gotta say, it surprises me you eat baby sheep."

Annie shrugged. "Compartmentalization is an essential skill if you're going to be a successful omnivore. If I thought about how cute cows, pigs, and even chickens are, I'd be a vegetarian in a heartbeat."

"Good to know. I was thinking, if you're free Friday night, you could come over to my place, and I could attempt to impress you with my cooking."

A broad smile broke out on her lips. "I'd love that."

Alex walked her up to her door and waited while she unlocked it.

"I wish it wasn't so late. I'd invite you in to watch a movie."

"I've got to be on patrol pretty early so..." He shrugged.

"Then I'll say goodnight and thanks. I really appreciated your help today."

"It was my pleasure. I mean that. I like spending time with you, even when it's running errands." He was standing close, looking down at her, and she felt a kind of pleasant tension between them. Her stomach was fluttery, and her heart was beating fast. She watched in fascination as he slowly pulled her to him and leaned down until his lips were almost brushing hers. She closed her eyes, and he kissed her. It was much lovelier this time. All the awkward was gone. She might not know what she was doing, but he did so she followed his lead. When he lifted his head, she was surprised to find she had rolled up on her toes, her lips following his. She laughed a little and stood back on her heels.

"Goodnight, Annie." His words were low and soft, for her alone. She shut the door feeling far better than when she'd first opened it that morning.

CHAPTER SIXTEEN

ALEX STOOD AT THE WALL OF post office boxes and found his own, using his key to open it. He hadn't been here in a while, so it was stuffed full. He took the pile over to the counter by the display of shipping boxes and started sorting through it, most of it landing in the trash. There were a few bills, but most of it was junk. There was a manila envelope that gave him pause. It had been mailed from a nearby town but had no return address. He looked around to be sure he was on his own and pulled out a pair of gloves from his pocket. Once he had them on, he opened the envelope carefully with his penknife. Inside was a single sheet of paper, but this time there was a picture to go with the words. It was from the *Sweet River Lowdown*, the town blog. The image was of him kissing Annie on the forehead. The words underneath read, 'Does she know what you did?'

He had to get this to Mac. Sliding it back into the envelope he gathered up the rest of his mail, put away his knife, and headed out. In his truck, he stowed the threat in the glovebox. The exterior would have been handled by a dozen people, but they might still get a usable print if another could be found on the inside or under the flap. He took out his cell and called Mac, but only got his voicemail. "Call me when you get this if you can. I've received another letter, and this guy has included someone else in the threat. Thanks."

When he arrived home, he got out his printing kit and dusted the letter. As usual, no prints. He was feeling frustrated more than worried, but he knew this meant a conversation with Annie. He was going to have to have a talk with her about safety. She was too trusting. She thought Sweet River was an idyllic small town, but between the tourists coming through and the county in economic distress, it was all an illusion. The drug trade was alive and well in the woods and remote corners of the county. Sure, crime was low generally, but that didn't make it safe. He didn't want to worry her, but he wanted her to start paying attention to her surroundings. He'd probably need to talk to his boss as well. He hadn't said anything about the threats because he didn't want to make it a bigger deal than it was. Maybe Mac could give him guidance there. He didn't need anything else to convince the sergeant that he was trouble.

His phone rang, and he answered. "Moretti."

"Alex, I got your call." It sounded like Mac was calling him from his vehicle.

"Picked up my mail and with it was another of those letters. Can I bring it to you?"

"I can free myself up. Where you at?"

"At home. Can you meet me at Maria's?"

"Be there in twenty." The call disconnected.

Alex left the house and drove into town. Pulling into a parking spot outside the restaurant he headed in and nabbed a booth at the very back, hoping no one sat near them so they wouldn't be overheard. He'd put in his order when Mac joined him in the booth.

The waitress turned her attention to Mac. For Alex, she'd been all business, but Mac got a bright smile and a hair flick. "Can I get you anything, hon?"

Alex managed not to roll his eyes. The waitresses didn't like him much. Maybe because he didn't talk to them when they tried to flirt. He knew they didn't really mean anything by it, but it made him uncomfortable. He'd never been good at the natural charm some guys dished out or the professional friendliness Pete had mastered. Even Mac, as stoic as the man could be, managed the friendly banter with the waitress. He was careful not to let her think it was anything other than it was, but he probably got better service than Alex usually did. When she left, Alex slid the manila envelope across the table to Mac.

Mac looked down at it and then up at Alex. "No prints?"

"No. I dusted the whole thing while I was waiting for you to call me back. The paper is clean, the envelope has several prints, but only on the exterior in places you'd expect from normal handling. Nothing under the flap, nothing inside."

"Does the handwriting on the address look familiar?"

"Only in that it matches the other letters. It looks like someone deliberately using block letters to mask their writing style."

Mac nodded in agreement and looked the sheet over again. "Did you talk to her about this?"

Alex shook his head. "She doesn't know about the threats. I haven't had one in weeks. I was hoping the guy had given up. Should've known better. I'll need to tell her, but I don't want to freak her out with too much information."

"He may try to contact her, may send her something." Mac seemed to be considering the options. "If this guy wanted you dead, I think you'd be dead by now."

"Great."

Mac grimaced. "Sorry, being honest. What that means, or at least I hope it does, is that if he wanted to hurt her, he'd have done it already. I think he wants you to be paranoid. He wants you looking over your shoulder. He wants you uncomfortable. I'd say he wants to ruin your life, not end it. It's almost like he enjoys knowing you're suffering. Have you talked to your sergeant about this?"

"No, I wanted to keep it unofficial. They already know my story. They don't know about the recent threats, but they know why I left the force, why I came up here."

"If it were me, I'd consider the loss of privacy a small price to pay for having another set of eyes watching my back. Who knows what avenue this guy will take? I think he sent this because you looked too happy." Mac gave him a smile. "Although it's nice to see you happy. Olivia will be thrilled. She 'ships' you and Annie, whatever that means."

Alex smirked. "It's a pop culture thing. A play off the word relationship. It's usually a book or movie thing like you hope those two characters end up together."

"Whatever." Mac waved a hand in the air as if dismissing it. "Half of what she says I don't understand, but at least she talks to me. More than can be said for the average teenager. But you should talk to Annie. She needs to be aware of her surroundings, locking her car, paying attention as she walks to work, the basics. You should get her pepper spray and train her how to use it, too. You don't have to go into the history of what happened if you're not ready for that, she doesn't need to know the details, just that you've got a stalker."

Alex nodded in agreement. She definitely would not be getting the details. Things were finally going well. They were spending most evenings together. He'd even gone to church with her. They were taking it nice and slow, building a solid foundation on the friendship they already had. Something like this, if he didn't handle it the right way, could end it altogether. "If this is Eric, I can't believe he'd hurt her. We might not be friends now, but the man I knew, he's not like that."

"You don't know this Eric. This is the Eric that lost his sister. Loss changes people in unpredictable ways. There are other factors too. If he's here, stateside, that means he's out of the service. My inquiries haven't been answered yet so we don't know for sure. Still, there's a kind of stress in re-entering the civilian world that only vets experience. They've built these instincts, habits, skills to stay alive, and a lot of them don't transfer. They have to find a way to leave them behind. Some can't. If Eric's struggling with that while also trying to process his sister's death, then you're dealing with someone who is in a lot of pain and confusion. That's a recipe for making bad decisions."

The guilt Alex already felt when he thought of Eric was compounded by empathy for what his friend was likely going through. It wasn't easy to give up something you'd worked hard to learn, a job that was everything to you, even if it was for a short time. He'd hated leaving the force—it felt like a failure.

Annie's pocket buzzed, and she pulled out her cell. Smiling she read Alex's text. "My place. I made chili. Six?"

"Sounds lovely" She texted back. Stowing her phone away she went into the back and packed chocolate chip cookies she'd made earlier in the day. Alex always cooked, even if it was at her place, but she liked to contribute something other than the drinks. When she returned to the counter a customer was waiting. She looked at the clock. It was a minute until closing. "You're just in time." She smiled, hoping he'd have an easy order. She was closing the shop tonight since Claire was at a meeting. The man looked around the room and then frowned.

"Um...is Claire here?"

Annie took a closer look at the man. He was tall, broad, and probably not much more than thirty-five. She didn't recognize him, and he wasn't a local, judging by his accent. "No, she's off tonight. Did you want to leave a message for her?"

"I'm Paul. Paul Murphy. Her husband." He grimaced. "Her ex-husband. I've been having trouble getting in touch with her."

"Well, Claire's pretty busy."

He nodded. "She does a lot. I know. That PTO talked her into running their fundraising events again. I tried to..." His eyes widened as if he realized he was about to say something he shouldn't. "It's okay. I'll try to catch her another time. Please let her know I came by, that I'm hoping she can call me. Thanks." His lips tipped up into an incomplete smile and he left. Annie pulled out her phone and texted Claire to let her know. Claire called back as Annie was locking up.

"Are you kidding me?"

Annie dropped the keys in her pocket. "Not kidding. He said he had been trying to contact you."

"The nerve."

"He seemed nice."

"He's a snake."

Annie had no idea how to reply to that one. Paul wasn't her ex, he was Claire's. If she thought he was a snake, that was her business. "He mentioned that you were on the fund-raising committee again. He didn't seem pleased about that."

"Why would he care?"

"I might be reading into the few words we exchanged, but he seemed to think you were overworked."

Claire was silent on the other end of the phone.

"But, keep in mind, we spoke for all of two minutes."

"He never cared before, why would he care now?"

"Claire, if I had any advice to give I would. All I can say is that he seemed sincere. He was polite and nice."

"Okay. Thanks. Have a good night."

Annie put her phone back in her pocket and headed out to the parking lot. Her new car waited, and it would be warm since she'd hit the remote start when she'd locked up. Alex had talked her into that feature, and he was right, it was worth it. Getting in she drove to Alex's place, pleased to see that he was already there. Sometimes she beat him to the house and had to wait in the car while Shep barked his head off indoors. The dog was barking now as Annie approached. Alex opened the door, and she was struck by how ordinary this moment had become, a moment she once thought impossible. *Here I am, at my boyfriend's house. That is so weird.*

He let her in, and Shep danced around until she set her purse and package of cookies down on the table so that she could pet him. He sat at her feet and leaned into her. "You are so sweet." She stroked his ears and he licked her hand.

"One of these nights he's going to ditch me and go home with you." Alex was in the kitchen, stirring a large pot of what she assumed was chili. "Actually," he put the cover back on. "It might be a good idea for Shep to go over to your place when I'm working a night shift."

"Why?"

"For protection." He leaned a shoulder against the fridge, his arms crossed.

"I live on the third floor. That's two locked doors between me and trouble. I think I'm fine. Besides, I'm not sure what Hobbes might make of him." She leaned down and kissed his snout. "He'd probably shred you, baby dog."

Alex grunted in derision. "He's an eighty-pound German Shepherd. A cat, even yours, is not going to shred him."

"Maybe." Annie took off her coat. "Is dinner ready?"

"Mostly. Have a seat and I'll get it."

Annie sat at the table on the folding chair Alex had added since they'd started dating. He now had a grand total of two chairs for entertaining. He brought out the chili in two bowls, setting it down and then returned with cornbread. Annie said grace and then they tucked in.

"This is incredible. You really do have the knack." Annie managed to say between bites.

"My offer to teach you still stands."

"I've been practicing."

"Really?"

"I got a cookbook which promises to make everything easy,

and so far I've had limited success with a vegetable frittata and a quiche."

"Fancy." He raised an eyebrow. "Friday night, how about you give one of your recipes a whirl? I'm working the next two nights."

"Sure." She was happy to have the chance to cook for him, although now she was nervous. Through the rest of dinner, she was mentally evaluating her menu options and rejecting them. Maybe that roast chicken she saw? That was supposed to be simple. Alex chuckled, and she looked up to see him giving her a knowing look.

"Stop worrying. I'll like whatever you make."

"How do you do that?"

"Do what?"

"Read what's on my mind?"

"Easy. It's usually written on your face."

She sat back, her spoon clattering in her bowl. "Please tell me that all those times at the shop I was thinking about how to approach you and what to say, that you didn't already guess."

"Sorry."

"I may not be able to live this down." She pushed her bowl away and covered her face with her hands. "Ugh, knowing that you knew I liked you all that time and—"

Alex pulled her hands away from her face. He'd gotten up and come around the table without her hearing. "You're very stealthy."

"That's part of the job." He knelt next to her, so they were eye to eye. "I was gone for you from almost the first day we met."

"What?"

"Pete told me Coffee by the Book had the best coffee in town and insisted we stop in. Had to be maybe a month or two after you opened. I walked in and it smelled like heaven. I was looking over at the wall of books when I heard your voice. You were greeting Pete. He stepped aside, and I saw you for the first time." His lips quirked like he wanted to laugh. "I was rendered speechless. You may not know this, but your eyes are an other-worldly color of blue. When I finally made it past them to your hair and to your perfect lips," his eyes dropped to her mouth. "That was it. I think I managed to nod when you said hello."

She remembered that. Pete had joked that his new partner was a stoic man, and they'd laughed. It wasn't until he came back in on his own the next day and the next that she'd noticed he wasn't always so quiet or that he wasn't quiet around her.

"So I shouldn't be embarrassed that it was obvious I liked you?"

"No. It gave me confidence. No really, it did," he added when she made a face. He stood up and held out his hand. "Leave the dishes, come sit with me." He took her over to the couch and sat down, drawing her into a cuddle. This was her all-time favorite thing about being in a relationship. Kissing was nice, toe-curlingly nice, but nothing beat being held.

She laid her head on his shoulder and listened to him explain. "When I got to Sweet River, I wasn't in a great place. I love being a warden, don't get me wrong. Having the woods as my workplace, nothing beats it, but I left my family and everything I knew behind when I took this job. My head was a mess. Then I met you." He kissed her forehead. "You were a bright light in the darkness. To be effective in this job I have to be neutral, to keep people a bit at arm's length, but you never let me stay there. I loved how you'd come to my table. I never knew what you were going to say. It was always the highlight of my day. Still is."

She snuggled closer. "I'm glad. You are the highlight of my day too."

He wrapped her in his arms. "Now, it kills me, but we have

to talk about something a whole lot less pleasant."

She looked up at his face, but his expression was closed as if he was carefully controlling it. "What is it?"

"It's hard to know where to start." He sighed. "Two years ago an incident occurred while I was on duty, and the consequences of that made me decide to leave the police department. I don't want to get into the details if that's okay. It's not really the why, it's the how anyway."

"You're not making a lot of sense."

"Sorry." He sat up and she moved away a bit. Shifting in his seat, he took her hands in his and faced her directly.

"I've got a stalker."

That was not what she was expecting to hear. "What?"

"I've gotten some letters with vague threats, nothing serious, but concerning."

"Oh my gosh, are you serious? Are you in danger?"

"No, probably not. He's likely trying to mess with my head. The reason I'm even telling you is that he sent me a copy of that picture of us from *The Lowdown*. He may try to send you something. If you see anything in your mail that's addressed to you, but has no return address, don't open it until we're together. Okay?"

"Sure. I don't get a lot of mail anyway, but I can watch out for that. Alex, I'm so sorry you have to deal with this."

"There's more. I want you to be aware of your surroundings when you're headed to work, or here, or wherever. It's stuff you probably have heard before. Keep your keys in your hand, don't walk with headphones on, stay on well-lit sidewalks and paths."

"I lived in New York, Alex. I know how to take care of myself."

"I know. I figured you did, but I'd also like you to consider carrying pepper spray. I can show you how to use it and how to make sure it doesn't get used against you."

Annie shivered, unable to shake the idea that this was far more serious than he was making it.

"Hey, it's okay." He pulled her close again. "This is just a precaution. Captain MacAlister, you know him, he's on the case, and so is the department. We'll find the guy and make sure he knows to leave you alone. I don't think he's going to come anywhere near you, but I want to be sure you're safe."

"That's why you wanted Shep with me."

"Yeah, but not if you think he and Hobbes will have a showdown."

"You're really okay? This really isn't that serious?"

"Yes and yes."

"Okay." She laid her head against his shoulder again. "You don't have to worry about the pepper spray. I took a self-defense class. My father insisted. You'd be surprised at my skills."

"Yeah?" He looked down at her, mirth in his eyes. "Well maybe you can come to the gym with me, and we'll spar."

"I may be short, but I'm fierce."

"I believe you."

CHAPTER SEVETEEN

Alex looked down at the remains of what he was sure had been a chicken, at some point, and tried very hard not to laugh. He'd seen the look on Annie's face and knew that she did not find this funny. He could also see from the state of her kitchen that she'd likely been at it for hours. Every inch of the counter was covered with the evidence of her attempt to make dinner. There were vegetable peelings, various spices, and a cookbook lying open covered with more of the same.

He tried to find something encouraging or comforting to say. "Uh..."

"It's a disaster. I know. How could anyone manage to ruin a roast chicken which this supposedly knowledgeable author"—she stabbed a finger at the cookbook—"says is idiot proof. Idiot proof, Alex!" Her voice raised an octave. "How did I ruin something idiot proof?"

He could see where this was all headed. She was going to berate herself for failing and likely end up in tears. "Okay, let's be honest. You can't cook. It's not your thing. Who cares?"

Annie's expression suggested that she cared.

"You bake cookies that could end wars. Your coffee is out of this world. Who cares if you can't cook a chicken?"

"I care."

"Why?"

"It's a girl thing. You wouldn't understand."

"Try me."

"It's part of the womanly arts. I have few enough as it is."

Alex turned her away from the failed dinner and toward him instead. "I don't think the measure of a woman is whether or not she can cook."

"No, but—"

"You own a successful business, you work with kids helping them read, you're kind to everyone you meet, you volunteer at the church. That's the kind of stuff that matters." He pulled her into his arms and dropped a kiss on the top of her head. "And you're cute, too." He chuckled. "It's a nice bonus."

She slid her arms around his waist. "Fine. You'll do the dinners. I'll do the desserts."

"Ah, the balance is restored."

"What?"

"I have to bring something to this relationship."

Annie leaned back and looked up at him. "Don't be daft. You're great at your job, you're unfailingly patient with people when they're mean to you, you save animals, and you're pretty cute too."

Alex smiled down at her upturned face. A ring sounded from the other side of the apartment. "What's that?"

Annie slipped out of his arms and sprinted to her desk by the windows. There was a laptop there and she clicked the mouse, bringing a screen up. "Hi, Daddy."

"Hello, Anne. I assume this is a good time." The voice was low over the computer speakers, but Alex could still hear it. Annie looked over her shoulder at him and then back to the screen. "Um...I have a guest at the moment."

"A guest?"

"Yes, um—"

"Well, I wouldn't want you to be rude to your guest, but I'm not sure when I'll be able to call again."

"Oh, well..."

"I don't mind." Alex half-whispered to her across the space.

Apparently, his voice carried further than he intended since Annie's father answered. "Was that your guest? Do you have a man over?"

She stole a glance at Alex over her shoulder, her cheeks pink. "Yes, Daddy. His name is Alex Moretti, and he's my...boyfriend."

"Oh." The man sounded surprised. "Will you introduce me?"

Annie turned around, and the look on her face said, 'this is your fault,' but she waved him over all the same. "Sure, Daddy. Alex, would you like to meet my father?" Annie pointed Alex to the couch, lifting her laptop and taking it with her.

Alex sat down, and Annie took the seat beside him, balancing the computer between them. In a large window on the screen, Alex saw the image of a man in an office. The background was dim as if it was night where he was as well. He was dressed in a suit and tie, his gray hair curly like Annie's but cut close to his head. He wore glasses with a thin, metal frame, and his complexion was that of a man who spent most of his time indoors.

"I'm pleased to meet you, Mr. Moretti."

"Nice to meet you too, Mr. Caldwell. You can call me Alex if you like."

The man's image smiled. "Certainly, and please feel free to address me as Edward. I'm sorry for interrupting your evening."

"It's no problem at all. We were just fixing dinner."

"Ah, well, I'll let you return to it soon enough. Anne, I was calling to let you know that I received your email and I am glad to hear that the difficulty with the car was sorted out so easily. When Remy told me you'd accessed your fund, I was concerned." He paused. "Naturally."

"Of course. Although—"

"I'm still the executor, Anne. I still see the statements, and I'm not questioning the withdrawal. The size alarmed me and with reason. The fact that you had to replace your car because it ended up in a river is cause for alarm. It's quite rational and natural for a father to be concerned."

"No, Dad, that's not what I was going to say." Annie started, but her father didn't let her finish. Alex felt her shifting on the couch as if she was about to stand.

"What's more, it was...troubling that you didn't contact me when such an event occurred."

"Alex was there." She blurted out. "He found me and got me help. Got the car towed to the police lot for me as well. Did I tell you he's a game warden?" Annie's words were running away with her, but he wasn't about to interrupt them with a kiss in front of her dad. He had a feeling that she'd brought him up as a distraction anyway. "The wardens enforce the state's wildlife laws, I wasn't sure if you knew. He has a lovely German shepherd named Shep of all things. I know you don't like animals, but he's such a nice dog I would—"

"Anne Elizabeth Caldwell." Edward's voice was stern, and it seemed to snap her out of it. "I'm quite sure that Alex is a fine man, and I'm very glad he was there to help you, but I would have liked to have had the opportunity to do that myself."

"What?" Annie sat back, her shoulders slumped. She stared at the image of her father on the screen. "You would have come here?"

"You know it's nearly impossible for me to get away from the office at this time of year, but I would have welcomed the opportunity to help you in other ways, sent someone to help you with the details, arranged for a car to be brought to you. You are so fearsomely independent." The way he said it didn't sound like a compliment. Alex caught his audible sigh over the call as the on-screen image of Edward leaned into the camera. "It's getting late." He looked up to the corner of the screen. "Past midnight here. I should probably let you go."

"How is mother?" Annie asked before he could disconnect.

"Fine. Redecorating the New York apartment again."

"She's back in the states?"

"Ah...yes. I suppose she didn't say." There was a slight frown on his face.

"No. You know she doesn't call." Annie's voice was quiet.

"I had thought she sent a card."

Annie shook her head. Edward's lips thinned, and he sat back from the camera. He didn't seem to be the sort of man who struggled to find an answer to any situation, but here he appeared flummoxed. The silence grew until he broke it. "I'm sure she'll be in touch," he mumbled. "Yes, sometime I'm sure." He picked a paper up off his desk, scanned it, and then put it down. "Well, it's quite late. I should let you go. I hope to talk with you soon. Goodnight, Anne. It was a pleasure to meet you, Alex."

Annie waved at the screen, and the connection ended. She set the laptop down on the couch beside her and slowly closed the cover. Alex wondered if he should ask her if she wanted to talk about it, or if he should pretend he hadn't heard any of the call and offer to order a pizza. He waited, trying to assess her mood, but she wasn't giving anything away. She sat quietly, face forward, hands in her lap. Something was wrong, but he didn't know what.

Her relationship with her parents wasn't typical, she'd said as much, but it seemed like she was floored by her father being upset that she hadn't called when she crashed her car. She was also affected by the news that her mother was in New York. Maybe that was because she hadn't called? Did they call each other at all? Alex had no idea. She rarely talked about her family. It was weird. Not knowing what else to do, he did what usually worked when she seemed upset—he put his arms around her. Annie face-planted into his chest.

"Babe, what's this?" He tried to look her in the eye, but she curled tighter into him. "Do you want to talk about it?"

"Not really." Her voice was muffled by his shirt.

"Would it be okay if I admitted that I want to talk about it?"

"No."

He chuckled. "Okay, then."

Annie pulled away from him and sat up. "It's all..." She waved her hands haphazardly in front of her and then sighed. "My mother isn't interested in being a mom. Something she has communicated to me through neglect since I was old enough to cogitate. I don't know why I expect her to change."

"That's rough." He winced. "Your dad didn't seem to like it either."

"Really?"

"You didn't spot that? He looked angry."

"I guess I didn't. That's odd." She appeared thoughtful for a moment. "What's even odder is the whole idea that he'd care about me having to buy a new car."

"Annie, he didn't care about the car, he cared about you being in a crash."

"Well, I guess."

"There's no guessing. I don't blame him either. If my kid was in a wreck, even if they walked away fine, I'd still want to know." He brushed the curls off her forehead. "It's obvious he cares about you. I'm sorry you think your mom doesn't."

"Know. Not think, know." Annie ran her fingers through her hair and sat back from him, her arms crossed over her chest. "Every time I convince myself that I've accepted it, that she is who she is and I can't change it so I should let it go, that's when something else hits and I can't—" She got up from the couch, snagged her laptop and thumped it back down on the desk. "I'm sorry that I've pretty much ruined our evening." She threw a hand out in the direction of the kitchen. "First, I incinerate dinner, then I take a call from my father. It was rude. I shouldn't have answered and put you on the spot like that. Then you got to hear all about our twisted, mixed-up excuse for family life." She dropped her face into her hands.

Alex stood and slowly approached her, feeling like any sudden movement would send her bolting for the bedroom, locking him out. Not that she'd ever done that. This was a side of her he hadn't seen before. Words weren't tumbling out of her in a confused rush, she wasn't being quiet and thoughtful. He wasn't sure what to do with this Annie, but he knew that getting it out was better than keeping it in. "All families have drama, Annie."

"Not like this. Do you know how humiliating it is to have to explain it? Do you know how sick and tired I am of feeling like an oddity?"

"Hey, lots of people have childhood stuff that's not exactly normal."

"Alex, you have no idea." She squinted her eyes shut. Her hands were balled into fists beside her. "When I talk about how I grew up people look at me like I'm some emotionally-damaged unicorn. Like I shouldn't exist. I'm thoroughly tired of feeling like I don't belong, as if I'm not normal."

Alex reached for her, but she leaned away. "No, this isn't something you can fix. I don't want to hear your reasonable counsel. I don't want to be reasonable at all. I want to call her and tell her that she's a horrible person. I want to hear her say it—that she doesn't love me, that she wishes I hadn't been born at all. Dear heaven, it feels that way." Annie covered her mouth with her hand and Alex could hear the sob she was trying to hide.

He put his arms around her quaking shoulder and pulled her close. "I'm sorry. I'm so sorry." He rubbed her back. "You're right, I have no idea what you've been feeling. I know it's got to hurt."

She wrapped her arms around his waist and laid her cheek against his chest. "It does. It rips right through me. After all this time, why does it do that?"

"Maybe because you think this is about her finding fault with you. It isn't. It can't be. I've known you a few months, and there's nothing about you I don't like. This is her deal—her loss too."

"Thank you for trying to make me feel better."

"You're welcome, but that's not what I'm doing." He let go of her so he could see her face. "I don't know her, but I know she's wrong. Your dad clearly loves you. Everyone who meets you ends up loving you." *I love you.* He couldn't say those words out loud yet, but his heart knew they were true. "This is not about you, it's about whatever her deal is. If she won't share that with you, then you've got to forgive her and move on."

"I thought I had."

"Maybe you can't until you really believe it, believe that you're worth loving and that it's not some fault of yours if the one person on earth you'd expect to automatically love you, doesn't seem to. And Annie, she might be mixed up somehow. Who knows? It's not your problem though."

"It's not my problem."

"Right. Your problem is how you feel, how you act. That's all you can control."

"I get it." She took a deep breath and slowly let it out. "I'm okay now. I'm sorry for all that." She waved a hand in the air, avoiding his eyes. Turning away, she looked around the room. "I guess we should call it a night."

Panic shot through him. "Don't do that."

"What?"

"Get embarrassed and shut me out."

"I wasn't...some things don't involve you, Alex."

"Are we something to each other?" He stood in front of her,

forcing her to look at him. "Because if we are then a call from your dad that tears you up is definitely something that involves me. Watching you take that hit and seeing what it did to you?" He took her hand and laid it against his chest. "It killed me. I can't leave you alone to deal with this. I won't be able to sleep tonight if I leave now." He reached out and gently stroked her cheek. "Besides, I'm wicked hungry. How about a pizza?"

Annie smiled. "I could eat."

"Good. I'll order, and you can put on that show you like." He searched his memory for the title, but it escaped him. "British people, baking stuff." He towed her over to the couch and handed her the remote. "No mushrooms or black olives, right?"

"Or sausage or anchovies. Too greasy."

"Gotcha." Alex ordered a pizza and then took a seat beside Annie. Her program was already on. Alex wondered if she liked it because it was British and she missed home. He shifted to the corner and put his arm around her. She took the hint and laid her head on his shoulder.

"Thank you."

"For what?"

"For being here. It means a lot to me."

"Anytime, Annie." Always. He wanted it to be true. Even if it was far too soon for that, his heart wanted it all the same.

Hours later he pulled into his driveway feeling pleasantly tired. Spending time with Annie, even if it was fraught with emotional stuff, fed his soul like nothing else did. The second his foot hit the stair to his porch he knew something was wrong. He could hear Shep growling, a low and menacing sound, not his usual barked greeting. Spinning around he scanned the yard, but he didn't see a thing, not even a nocturnal animal scurrying away.

The normal sounds of the night came to him, soft and familiar. Alex's heart was pounding all the same. Maybe Shep's instincts were off? As unlikely as that seemed, there was nothing out there that shouldn't be. He turned and climbed up the stairs. There, hanging on the door, was another letter.

CHAPTER EIGHTEEN

Alex sat in the interview room feeling like he was in the Twilight Zone. He'd never been on the victim side of things. He hated that the letters put him there. The chief looked up from the one Alex had found last night and frowned.

"What's this guy gonna get out of writing to the paper about you? That's some crazy stuff right there."

"Honestly, I'm not sure anymore. If this is Eric, Samantha Michaud's brother, then like Mac said, he's got the skills and probably the weaponry to kill me if he wanted to. Maybe writing some kind of tell-all is another way to humiliate me. I don't know what's in his head. We were friends for a long time. Before this, I would have said he doesn't have it in him to do something like this."

"Mac." The chief turned to his deputy. "You find anybody other than Eric Michaud who seemed a likely suspect? What about a friend or family member of the perp who died. Logan something?"

"Logan had a crew, but they were mostly fellow junkies and all but two are incarcerated or dead. There's one guy. Distributor. I caught some rumors, loose stuff, that he'd been planning to use the teen shelter as a front of sorts to cover his operation. Logan's death put an end to that."

"Wait, was this Kevin Pelletier?" Alex was surprised to hear that name.

Mac glanced up from his report. "You know the guy?"

Alex nodded. "He graduated a few years ahead of us. That dude was bad news. A real nasty piece of work, but no kingpin. At least not that I knew. He was a low-life for sure. Always up for whatever might make him money or cause the most chaos.

Bar fights, petty theft, that kind of thing."

The chief rubbed his chin. "Not a huge leap to running drugs."

"But even if he was, why would he care about Samantha? If he was angry, he'd stick a knife in my ribs, not send me letters."

"Right," Mac took the papers in front of him and slid them back into the folder they'd come from. "Which is why I dismissed him."

Alex sighed, thinking of any other motive someone could have for getting involved in this mess. "Who owns the Steeple Street building now?"

"Samantha left the building to Eric." Mac ticked off on a finger. "But he donated it back to the program. I talked to the shelter director, Dorothy Beauchamp. She says he hasn't set foot in the place since Samantha's death. He has no contact with them. A board of directors oversees the whole thing."

Alex sat up a little straighter. Things were making more sense. He knew where the threats were coming from. "The letters are Eric. It was dark enough last night, and he had enough cover that whoever he was, he could've shot me where I stood if he wanted to."."

"We need to draw him out." The chief leaned back in his chair. "Don't worry about the paper. I'll give them a call, ask them to send anything they get up here." He passed the letter back to Mac who added it to the file in front of him. "If he doesn't get what he wants, he'll reach out again. Next time, let the dog get him."

"If I could be sure Eric isn't armed, I would. I don't want to risk Shep's life on the chance that Eric loves dogs more than he hates me."

The chief chuckled. "Whatever you need, the department is here to help. Have you explained this to your girlfriend?"

"Not the details, but that she needs to keep alert. Lock her doors."

"I can increase the patrols in her area for a while."

"Thanks."

On the way out to his car, Mac stopped Alex. "I think you need to sit down with Annie and give her the details. You two have been dating for what? A month now?"

Alex's gut tightened, and he pivoted to face him. "That mean something to you?"

Mac tilted his head a bit, his wide-brimmed deputy's hat exaggerating the gesture. "Y'know it's always interesting to find out what a guy's deal is. Some men, you insult their team, they'll get in your face. For others, it's their truck. For you, anytime someone brings her up you get defensive." Alex tried to argue, but Mac wasn't having it. "You roll out the barbed wire anytime the subject switches to your girl. That's fine. I'd even say it's good if you were serious. If you're playing around with her until something better comes along, then break it off now. Nobody deserves to get sucked into trouble they had nothing to do with making."

Alex closed the distance between them, his face inches away from Mac's. "Who do you think you are to say something like that to me?" He stabbed a finger at Mac's chest. "Do you think I would let any of this touch her?" He fought off the urge to shove the man back a few feet and take a swing to wipe the doubt right off his face.

"Hey, fellas!" An SUV came to a stop near them. The drivers-side window was rolled down, and the woman was waving at them, concern written on her features that didn't match her happy tone. It took a second, but he recognized it was Mac's wife. "You said to pick you up at ten, Mac, and it's only five past." She laughed and turned to Alex. "That's pretty much a record for me. Never on time. This guy though. You could set your watch by him." She pointed a thumb at Mac. Alex had no trouble believing that Mac was as careful with his time as he was with everything else. As his anger faded, he started to feel guilty for telling the man off.

Mac didn't take his eyes off Alex. "I hope, for her sake, that you mean what you say. And I hope you're right about Eric not wanting to hurt her. You fail to handle this the right way, and it's Annie that pays." He looked away and then back to Alex. "I've seen you coming to church with her. If any of *that* means something to you, treat her like it does."

He turned on his heel and headed for his wife's vehicle. "Her safety is in your hands. Don't let your trouble become hers." With that parting shot, he got in and slammed the door.

Katherine's eyes widened. "Okay, I guess that's goodbye. Nice seeing you, Alex." She rolled up the window, and they drove away. The lead weight Alex was carrying around in his gut seemed to get heavier. He respected Mac. Having the guy think he was a fool was rough. Annie didn't need to be dealing with Alex's past while coming to terms with her own. He wasn't going to double her burden to lighten his own.

Annie took care of her last few customers with one eye on Alex in the far corner of the room. He was at his favorite table, a bar-top height cafe table with two stools. It let him sit with his back to the wall of books, but his eyes either on the front counter or out the window. Right now he was staring out the window, his hands wrapped around the coffee all but forgotten in front of him. He'd been like that for long enough that she had started to worry his train of thought was on a cross-country trip to someplace nasty. His shoulders bent forward, and his lips were tipped down, not in a frown, but almost a grimace. He was still in uniform which was odd. Normally he'd go home to change at the end of a shift before he picked her up. Today he'd arrived early, sat down, and hadn't so much as glanced her way since. Olivia had served him a second cup before she left for the day and even she sensed his mood, giving Annie anxious looks as she walked away.

Annie had no idea what the trouble was. Last night had ended in a good place after all the emotional upheaval brought on by her father's call. She'd even slept well, something that rarely happened after a night like that. Having Alex to talk to, to hold her, had made a huge difference. She'd dozed off watching the show, huddled into his side and he hadn't woken her up until he had to leave. His attitude this evening was a concern. She'd given him time to snap out of it, and as he hadn't, it was time to intervene.

Walking to his table, she caught his attention. He looked up at her, and his lips turned up in a small smile. "Hey."

"Hey." She sat down across from him. "Penny for your thoughts?"

He shook his head. "You don't want these."

"Yes, I do. What hurts you hurts me, remember? That goes both ways."

He seemed to blanch as she said that. He closed his eyes and hung his head. As she reached out and covered his hand with hers, he turned it and laced their fingers together. Staring down at their linked hands he shook his head again. The hanging lanterns she had added to the front window to mark the Lunar New Year shone down on him, highlighting the strands of russet in his dark hair. She wasn't surprised one of his brothers had red hair.

"Alex." She didn't want to push it, but she didn't want him

to wall her off. If he was suffering, she wanted to end it.

Slowly, he looked up. "Got a letter last night. It's no big deal, but we should probably talk about it."

"Okay."

"Not here." He let go of her hand and sat back. "Later." He slid off his stool and stood. "I got a thing I need to take care of. I'll come to your place. It might be a while." He turned and walked away.

It took a second for her brain to catch up long enough for her to react. "Wait." She turned, but he was heading for the door, not looking at her.

"I'll call later." Alex nearly collided with Claire as she was grabbing her coat. He caught her before she tripped. "Sorry, Claire." And then he was gone.

"No problem." She frowned as she watched him all but run across the street to his truck. Turning to Annie, her frown only deepened. "What was all that about?"

"I have no ruddy idea." Annie shoved the stool into the table causing it to wobble.

"He was Warden Broody all over again today. Did something happen between you two?"

"Nothing that should have soured his mood. I get the idea this doesn't have anything to do with me. Not that I'd know for sure since that would require actually talking to me, which he didn't." She was shell-shocked. Alex had literally run away from talking to her with no explanation. That wasn't even like the old Alex. What had he been brooding about? She'd assume it was getting another letter from his stalker, but he acted like that was no big deal. "I don't even know. I am utterly confused." She threw her hands out wishing she had Alex there so she could give him a shake. Maybe that would knock some sense into him.

"Well, add my ex into the mix of men who make no sense. Guess who just called and offered to take the boys to practice tomorrow morning. In fact, he says he can take them to practice every day and pick them up so I can have a break."

"Well, that's nice."

Claire's eyes narrowed. "It's suspicious is what it is. I have no idea what his game is, but I'll figure it out." She banged her purse on the counter and slid on her coat. "Anyway, I'll see you tomorrow. Maybe all of mankind will have regained sense and meaning." She waved goodnight and headed out. Annie braced against the rush of frozen air coming in through the door. February was as cold, if not colder than January had been. Claire might complain, but Annie suspected she'd be glad to have her ex-husband picking up the boys and taking them to hockey in the cold tomorrow morning.

Annie sat on the couch with her legs tucked under her, Hobbes in the crook of her lap, his rumbling purr vibrating against her stomach. She'd been there since giving up on dinner an hour ago. After having made a very nice salad for herself, she got about two bites down before her anxiety over what was up with Alex took over her appetite. Hobbes, possibly sensing she needed the cuddle, had hopped up and provided fur therapy. The phone buzzed on the arm of the sofa, and she read off Alex's text. Here. *Just the one word, because being polite is apparently too much to text.*

She was not in the mood to go down and let him in. Spare key in the rock to the right of the door. Pick it up and swivel out the bottom.

Two minutes later she heard a knock on her door.

She turned to the door and shouted, "It's open."

The door swung open and Alex stood in the portal, a thunderous look on his face. He shook his head and then slowly shut the door. He pointedly turned the deadbolt before turning around, his hands on his hips. When he looked up at her his eyes were flashing, his jaw hard, his lips thinned into a flat line. Uh oh. "What did we talk about?" His voice was terribly quiet.

"No idea." She shouldn't bait him. That was dumb, but she couldn't help herself. Something inside her itched for a fight. She wanted a reason to shout.

"There is a man out there who may be dangerous. He's got a grudge against me and that means he might try to hassle you." His voice grew louder, his words clipped. "You are supposed to keep this door locked any time you're home. And you shouldn't be hiding a key right outside your front door." The last word he ground out as if she'd kicked a puppy, not hidden a key.

She jumped to her feet, landing Hobbes on the floor. "Don't be unpleasant. That key is perfectly safe. No one would think to look for it."

"Are you kidding me?" He laughed, but there was no mirth in it. "It's totally obvious. That's not going to fool anybody trying to break into your apartment. As a matter of fact." He walked further into the room, standing a few inches away, his finger pointed at her face. "You need to have a talk with Claire and Erin because half the time I come by, they've got that door propped open for their craft students. I understand it's trouble to have to have one of them go down each time they get a buzz up, but that's the way it has to be. If it's a real problem, then get an intercom on that door and they can buzz people up that way."

"I will not." She straightened to her full height and crossed her arms. "Do you have any idea how that would look to their students? That they're in a secured building? This is Sweet River, not New York. And I need that door open for my bakery deliveries too. There is nothing wrong with it being open during business hours."

Alex made a sound of disbelief and shoved a hand through

his hair. "Do I need to have a cop come up here and explain to you all the reasons you're wrong about that? You act like this town is totally safe, it isn't. Think about how many tourists are in and out of here during the high season. Even when it's quiet, we've got strangers around. This isn't a regular small town. Nobody is watching your back. Nobody is looking out for your business like it's their own. You think the guy in the jewelry place next door is going to notice if somebody that's not supposed to be there is getting in through that back door? No! A guy could get in here and up to this apartment," he pointed at the floor. "Through that door you're not locking," he angrily stabbed at it. "And right now"—he reached out and held her upper arms—"he could get his hands on you before you could even scream." Alex's eyes pinned her with a pained stare. "It's my job to keep you safe. How can I do that when you don't even lock your door?"

"Let go of me." She pulled back and he dropped his hands.

"You're not taking this seriously."

"Maybe it's because you haven't explained it fully. Exactly what are you afraid will happen?"

Alex shook his head. "That's not the point. These are reasonable things you should already be doing as a woman living alone."

"I had the door open because I was expecting you. I don't normally have it unlocked."

"You hid a key in an obvious place. You let people prop open what should be a security door, at all hours. Someone could get in and hide in your maintenance closet until everyone had gone home for the day or even get up here and pick your lock. He could be in your apartment waiting for you." He threw out a hand toward her bedroom. "You'd have no reaction time. No chance to call for help."

Annie wanted him to stop telling her all the horrible things that might happen. He was starting to freak her out. He was probably right about the hide-a-key rock and about the door. She wanted to tell him that, but he kept cutting her off. She was done with being scolded. Her parents had never raised their voices, and Auntie Delia would never have dreamed of it. Alex might be used to loud discussions, but she was not.

"I'm trying to make sure nothing happens to you, and you aren't even helping me with something as straightforward as locking the door." He was yelling at her as if she was stupid and worthless, beneath contempt. It was breaking her heart.

"Stop yelling at me." She started to tremble, and she could feel the tell-tale prickle of tears start. Her stomach tied in knots as he went on.

"I'm not yelling. I'm trying to make sure you understand you can't do that again. A guy could be waiting at your apartment for something other than your purse."

She flinched and drew back, but he kept going.

"You can't float through life, Annie. There are real dangers all around you, but you act as though the whole world is full of good people with good intentions. I hate to break it to you, but it's full of miserable, selfish, cowards looking to take what they can. You cannot assume the best—you have to be prepared for the worst."

That was it, she was done. This wasn't her Alex. This man standing in front of her didn't even like her, much less care for her, and she couldn't take even one more word. "Well, you're certainly showing me your worst. Get out." She pointed at the door.

His head jerked back. "What?"

"Get. Out." She walked to the door and opened it, anger flooding in, pushing the wounded feeling aside for the moment, but she could tell it wouldn't last. It was as though he had shoved a spiked ball down her throat, and her insides were shredded. Knowing herself as well as she did, Alex had to go before all that anger ebbed and the hurt flooded in. She wasn't going to cry in front of him. He wasn't going to take care of her, or go easy on her. He'd shown her what kind of man he was with this tirade, and she wasn't interested.

"Annie." He huffed out a sigh. "Throwing me out isn't going to change the fact that—"

She stood an inch away. "Get out!" She screamed it at him and then the tears started.

Alex seemed to collapse. His shoulders bent forward, and he stooped down, level with her face. "No, please don't...I'm sorry, Annie. Please don't cry. I'm sorry. Man, I really blew it. Please, please." He reached for her and she was going to bat his hands away, but she had her face covered. He scooped her up into his arms and carried her to the couch, sitting down with her in his lap. He grabbed the box of tissues on the table next to the end of the sofa and held it out for her.

"I was a jerk. I was wrong to yell at you. Please forgive me. Please stop crying."

She took a tissue and blew her nose as gracefully as she could. "The way you spoke to me was horrible, Alex. You sounded as if you hated me like I was a worm crawling on the ground. Your tone—"

"I lost it. Mac was riding me today, and I let it get in my head. Between the key and finding your door open... This stuff is getting to me. I don't want any of this to touch you. I thought you weren't keeping yourself safe, and I had to convince you to do it. I am so sorry I sounded that way. Annie, it's as far from the truth as it could be. I don't hate you." He pulled her hands away from her face. "You are the world to me. I'm not making that up so you'll feel better. I don't know what I would do if something happened to you—something because of me."

That guilt again. She could see how it ruled his emotions.

Deep-down she knew he was angry at the situation, not at her, but the way he'd said it… "I *have* been taking care of myself. It's only because I knew it would be you that the door was open. You're right about the rock. I won't use it anymore. I'll make sure Erin and Claire know not to prop the door. Maybe I'll get a camera and the intercom."

"That would be good."

"I can't handle it when you yell at me."

"I…" He didn't finish his thought. His expression was bleak. The silence stretched on as she wiped her eyes, and a tiny seed of doubt sprouted and pushed itself up through the fog in her mind. How could their relationship work if he could gut her so easily? Was she too sensitive? Was he too callous? She didn't think so. It was their circumstances more than their nature. He needed to tell her the whole story of his past so she could better understand what was going on. She tried to think of a way to phrase her request so that he didn't shut her down or avoid answering it.

"Can we make a deal that if you're ever that angry again, you don't yell?"

He shifted her in his arms so that her head rested on his shoulder. "Yes, Annie. That's the least you could ask of me. Please say you forgive me."

"I do." She closed her eyes as he rubbed her back, turning his head to drop a kiss on her cheek. They sat quietly for long enough that she felt some equilibrium return. This was her Alex, kind and caring. He was wound too tight, too worried. She had to find a way to ease the burden for him. Even if he didn't want her to.

"Annie, the last thing I want to do is to hurt you." His voice sounded gruff. He sighed heavily enough that she felt his chest move, so she sat up. "I'm not ready for this. I can't be the man you need right now. If we stay together, I'm going to tear you up no matter how much I try not to."

"What?" He couldn't do this, not now.

"We need to take a break. I've got to sort this stuff out."

She felt the tears start back up. "Don't do this." They were something to each other. He couldn't end things like they were nothing.

"Please, Annie." He closed his eyes. "You're killing me."

"I can't help it. You're breaking up with me."

"No, I'm hitting pause." He slid her off his lap and held her face in his hands. "Look at me." She raised her eyes to his, her tears spilling onto his fingers. He shook his head. "This isn't over, but I can't do right by you while I'm dealing with this threat. I will not let the consequences of my mistakes touch you. You are not going to suffer because of me. No way will I let that happen. I've got to get this settled. I have to fix things and then we can be together."

"But, you said... What hurts me hurts you. You want to solve all my problems, but I can't help you with yours?"

"No, this is different." His eyes had a kind of darkness in them. She didn't understand it. As upset and freaked out as she'd been by him yelling at her, this was almost worse. He needed to get it out, shine a light on it.

"Can you tell me what happened? Why is this man stalking you? What mistakes are you paying for?"

He looked away. She wanted to grab him and shake him, but instead, she sighed. "It feels like you're giving up on us."

"What else can I do? I need to get this settled so that I can treat you the way you should be treated." He jerked his head as if he'd made a decision. "That's what I'm going to do. You were ready to throw me out five minutes ago. And you were right to do it. I was out of control. This thing, it's like a poison in me."

"It sounds like sin to me. God's forgiveness can wipe that away no matter how dark, how serious."

He held his hand over his heart as his eyes pleaded with her. "But I've got to atone. I haven't done that. I have to make it right, and then I can be forgiven."

"Alex, that's not—" He did need help if he was thinking that's how forgiveness works. She didn't doubt that Alex believed, that he had faith, but it seemed like something fundamental in it was twisted around the wrong way. God's grace was bountiful and free, but you had to humble yourself to receive it. Alex acted like he was in control, in full authority, and the boss. He had to repent to be forgiven; he had to acknowledge that there was nothing he could do to receive grace, that it was God alone who granted it. Atonement was what Christ did on the cross. Alex was talking about making amends, and that was dictated by the people he hurt. She didn't know what he had done or who he had harmed. How could she counsel him on what was the right thing to do?

"I've got to get it gone before it poisons everyone around me." He kissed her gently. "So, we hit pause."

"Like it's a magic button."

Alex winced, evidently not missing the sarcasm in her words. "I know this sounds like a harsh way to go about this, but—"

"Devastating, destructive, damaging." She couldn't look at him. Her heart and mind were at war again, one was sad, and the other wanted to start shouting, maybe throwing things, definitely tell him, in full detail, how stupid he was being.

The corners of his mouth tipped up as if he was fighting the urge to smile. "Trust a librarian to be de-scriptive."

"Don't try to be funny when my heart is breaking."

"Annie." He lifted his eyes to the ceiling and then back to her. "This is for the best. You'll be safe. I'll have the time I need to draw this guy out and settle this for good. Then we go right back to where we left off." He held her cheek in the palm of his hand and gently pulled her gaze to his. "You're in my heart. No matter how long we're apart, nothing changes that. Let me do this. Please."

"You're in my heart, too." She took his hand from her cheek and touched his fingertips to her ribs. "And when you leave, right here, is where I'll feel it. I'll be empty. I hate that feeling."

"Baby girl, you will not be empty." He pulled his hand away and held hers together. "I'm leaving you with that piece of mine. And I'm coming back for it. I promise you that." He brushed her lips with the lightest of kisses.

Annie sighed and closed her eyes. There was no swaying him. He was going to do this whether she liked it or not. "What can I do but accept it? It's not like you're giving me a say in this."

"I can't."

Annie saw the intensity of his expression, and the pain too. She would have to trust that God's will for her life meant Alex would be absent from it for now. "If this is the only plan, okay." She expected Alex to look relieved. He didn't. He slowly closed his eyes, his shoulders slumped.

Alex retook her hand. "If it's all right, I'll ask your buddy Elaine to put something in *The Lowdown*." His eyes were on their linked fingers. "Something that will show anybody looking that we're not together."

"Oh, that's great." A pit opened up in her stomach. This was all too real. After she got used to him being in her life now, she was back to alone. The entire town would be looking at her with careful sympathy. 'Poor girl, the hot guy dumped her and what would you expect. Still, she's such a nice thing.' An old doubt began to creep through her, the one that told her she'd never be loved, not for real. Annie was wise enough to know that it was insecurity wrapped up in self-pity, and it stemmed from her mother's rejection, but that didn't lessen its power. Every time she thought she'd beat it…

She shook her head as if she could knock that thought loose; unhitch that engine from the rest of the cars. That wasn't who she wanted to be. She'd spent far too many nights on that circular ride to nowhere, and she wasn't about to let herself go there now. Annie took in a deep breath, her chest constricting when a hint of pine and bergamot hit her senses. He really was going to leave her alone, but it was going to be okay. Whatever happened here with Alex, she needed to remember that she was loved by God. It wasn't arms to hold her or a shoulder to cry on, but something infinitely better and more important. What would her soul be without the love of God? She didn't like to think about it. She wasn't about to make the mistake of hitching her self-worth to the temporary love of a man.

Annie looked up into Alex's eyes. In the soft light of her apartment they were darker than usual. His face was hard to read. She mustered up her courage. "How long?" Maybe he was right about keeping her safe, but her instincts said that wasn't entirely what this was about.

"I don't know, honey." He put an arm around her shoulders. "Is it okay if I hold you for a bit?"

Annie laid her head on his shoulder. "Definitely. It will give me time to get used to the idea that you'll be gone."

"I'd give you everything if I could Annie. Every last thing." He held her close, and she tried to memorize the sensation, his warmth, and his strength. She was going to need it.

CHAPTER NINETEEN

Someone was pounding on her door. Annie listened to the knocks while deciding if she wanted to cross the entire apartment to answer it. There were only two reasonable options for who it was. Annie was in her favorite chair under a blanket, a now cold cup of tea on the table beside her, a book open on her lap. She hadn't read a word. This morning she'd opened the shop and then told Claire she was on her own for the day. Dutifully, she'd had the locksmith fit the door with a new set of locks. She'd also extracted his promise to install a state of the art security door with a programmable electric lock so that Claire and Erin could assign their pottery and craft students a unique code that expired after the class was over. She was even getting a closed-circuit camera. It was an impressive feat. First, because she got the guy out on a Saturday, and second because she was utterly miserable. Her body had a slight ache pretty much everywhere. It felt like someone had died. Only, her love wasn't dead, it was very much alive.

That was the first realization she'd had when she woke up this morning. Despite knowing better, she'd gone and let herself fall in love with Alex Moretti. He might be able to put his heart on pause, but she could not. They might not have broken up, but her heart hurt all the same.

She heard a key scrape in the lock and then Erin say, "I hope you don't have the chain on." The door opened and Erin appeared with a paper bag filled with what looked like groceries. She shut the door and locked it behind her, dropping the bag on the kitchen island. She looked down as if searching for something. "Is that ginger demon in kitty prison?"

"No. He's hiding under the bed. I think you're safe." He was in a snit because the locksmith had been there, and Hobbes hadn't liked the look of him. Now that she thought about it... She squinted at Erin. "How'd you get in here?"

"You gave Claire a new spare key. When she told me the state you were in, she gave me the key and told me to come sort you out."

That was kind. Claire was thoughtful, but a visit from Erin and what was probably going to be a pep talk, was not wanted. "I'm fine."

"Oh, girl, I have seen this before." She pointed to Annie's face. "I have chocolate ice cream. It's not a cure, but it helps with the symptoms."

"Symptoms? I'm not sick."

"Yes you are. Heartsick. It's a real thing." She went to the kitchen counter and began to unload various ice cream pints from the bag she'd brought.

"You're a personal trainer. Shouldn't you be telling me to exercise for endorphins or something?"

"That's stage two. Stage one is comfort. Stage two is running off the rage. Stage three is accepting a new reality with a visit to the salon. But, you've got to be careful not to move to stage three too early or you'll end up cutting off all your hair ala Miley Cyrus and that will haunt you. It takes a long time to recover from bad hair."

"That is so cliché." Annie tucked the blanket tighter around her. She didn't need to follow any rules to feel better. She needed Alex.

"Like all good clichés, it's based on a nugget of truth. Chocolate really does lift your mood. Exercise really does help with emotional angst, and a new 'do really does make you feel confident and cared for. All of this goes a long way to healing a broken heart."

Was she heartbroken? He'd stomped on her heart while at

the same time holding it gently. She'd never been in love, so she didn't know how to measure what she was feeling. What she did know was that she cared deeply for a man who had pried himself out of her life for her own good only it didn't feel like good. It made a sunny, bright morning feel bleak. Her whole being was shouting to her that this was wrong, that separation from him was the exact wrong thing. "He says we're on pause."

"Oh boy." She shook her head, her long blond hair swaying with the movement. "Being on pause is the worst. I know from experience. You can't move on, can't fix what's wrong. Instead, you're stuck having to wait to see if he gets his head together." Erin finished unloading goodies and took a seat on the hassock by Annie's chair. "You and I didn't know each other well last fall, so you missed a good deal of the drama with Dan and me. He was struggling with a spiritual crisis when we first got together. Talk about bad timing." She rolled her eyes, but the smile on her face spoke to the happy ending. "It made for a rough start. I had a lot to learn about trusting God, but Dan was walking through a valley of shadows, some seriously tough stuff. There was a point I had to put some distance between us."

"Wow, you called it off?"

"Had to. I have kids. I had to protect their hearts and my own. What Dan was dealing with, it wasn't something my love for him could help him with. He needed to get right with God. When he did, it all fell into place."

"That's not what Alex is doing. He thinks he can't get right until he atones for something. It's some big awful thing from his past he won't talk about. He has it all mixed up. He thinks that he can fix something and then he'll deserve to be forgiven. I want to help him, but he won't let me. He won't talk to me about what happened to him. I know he left his job with the police and his hometown because of it, but that's all. I can only assume it was bad and somehow public, but he won't talk about it."

"Google him."

Annie's lip curled. It would be a betrayal to poke into his past without his permission. "Isn't that an invasion of his privacy?"

"I don't see how." Erin waved off her objection "You'd be looking at what everyone else already knows, the publicly available stuff."

Annie was still dubious, and it must have shown on her face.

"It's not like you're reading his diary. This would be things that he may assume you already know. It could make you feel better to do something versus wait and hope it all works out. Something proactive." She stood up and shouldered her purse. "Personally, I think Alex is doing the right thing in creating some distance until he has whatever it is sorted out. But I know it has to hurt. Claire and I are here for you. If you want to talk, or don't want to. If you need more ice cream..." She smiled. "Whatever it is. Remember you can reach out. People are right there, hands out, waiting." She headed for the door. "I'll drop by in a week or two and see if you're ready to go running."

"I don't think running is ever something I will be ready for."

"Try it, you'll love it."

Annie shook her head. "Thanks anyway. Goodbye, Erin."

After Erin left Annie got up and looked for Hobbes. He was still under the bed, nursing his snit. She dropped a few crunchies in his dish hoping the sound would bring him out. When he didn't appear, she left a treat on the kitty counter in case he changed his mind. She sat down at her desk and thought again about what Erin had said. She could search for articles about Alex, and that wouldn't be such a big deal. It wasn't like she was creeping his Facebook profile. Actually, she doubted he had one. A man with no cable and no Internet probably didn't do social media. Booting up her laptop, she opened a browser window and searched Alex's full name and a few key search words trying to pull up any actual news items. The first one she found was from

Lewiston, where Alex was from, and it had quite the title.

Hometown Hero Saves Woman

"Police responded to a disturbance at a homeless shelter for teens on Friday night. There were several calls to 911 stating an armed man was holding a woman hostage at A Place Like Home on Steeple Street. A standoff ensued and was only ended when an officer climbed the exterior fire escape to shoot and kill the suspect. The officer is currently on administrative leave which, according to the Lewiston Police spokesperson, is standard procedure in any police-involved shooting.

The suspect died at the scene and has been identified as Logan Miller, a popular local artist who reportedly worked with teens at the shelter as an art therapist. No motive for his actions has been released. Several reports have indicated that the woman held hostage was the shelter's founder, Samantha Michaud, but the police had not confirmed that at press time."

There was a link to a follow-up piece, and she wasn't surprised it had multiple articles. In general, Maine didn't have a lot of violent crime. Lewiston, one of Maine's larger cities, was downright safe compared to most cities. Something like this must have rocked the whole community. She read a few stories that repeated the details she already had, other than the shooting had been ruled justified.

Then she found a profile of Alex. It had a picture of Alex in his police uniform with the hint of a smile on his face. He looked proud. It must have been the first time he was photographed as a cop. He seemed remarkably young. The caption read, *Patrolman Alex Moretti.* The article identified him as the officer who shot and killed Miller. It confirmed he was originally from Lewiston and a graduate of Saint Dominic where he was captain of the basketball team before going to Bates. It painted him as a hometown hero. Included was a picture of Alex as a teenager, crouched with a basketball in his hand as if ready to take a shot.

He was leaner then.

After everything she read, she still didn't understand him. It seemed pretty straightforward, and although it was awful that Alex had to shoot someone and that the man died, if he did it to save someone how was that a bad thing? There had to be something else. She followed a link to related articles and a headline popped up.

Victim of Hostage Taking Found Dead. Annie sat back, her fingers covering her mouth. This must be it. She read on.

"Samantha Michaud, director of A Place Like Home shelter, was found dead by shelter employees. The police are releasing few details, but the death is believed to be a suicide." Annie read the rest with her heart in her throat, waiting to see what link she had to Alex. Other than the incident itself, there was none. Samantha was said to be in a relationship with Logan which made sense. It was a domestic dispute. Maybe that's why she killed herself?

Annie had enough of poking through third-hand accounts of what had happened. She searched and found a Facebook page for Samantha and read through the comments that must have been posted after her death. They were heartbreaking. "I hope you found peace," "The world lost an angel," "Why?" That one got her. Her nose stung with impending tears. Why had she done it? Her profile picture was beautiful and peaceful. There wasn't a sign that she was a troubled woman. She was sitting on a rock ledge overlooking the ocean, her face turned over her shoulder at the person holding the camera. She had long, toffee-colored hair, and it was streaming out behind her as if caught in the wind. Her other pictures were lovely, all of them catching a soft smile. Annie wondered if she'd been shy. The way she seemed to curl into herself in the pictures, never smiling very broad. Was she the reason for Alex's pain?

There were no more articles, no blogs with local reactions for her to read. Nothing productive anyway. The shelter was intriguing though, and she wondered if it had closed after Samantha died. Annie found a very basic site listing their mission and contact information. It looked like the same building but renovated into offices. The About page listed a charity as the people in charge with a program director, Dorothy Beauchamp. From her bio, she'd been there when Samantha ran the place. A plan began to form in Annie's mind. She could drive down there and talk to Dorothy, or whomever else might be there. Maybe they'd have some answers.

The very idea of going to someplace she'd never been and boldly asking questions pretty much filled her with fear, but doing nothing would feed into her anxious thoughts, making everything worse. Taking some kind of action felt right—even if, in the end, it might not be the best action she could take. Maybe she could ask Pete? But she dismissed that thought almost as soon as she had it. If Alex had confided in the man, Pete wouldn't share it, and if he didn't, she might worry him with her questions. There was no good alternative. If she explained to these people at the shelter that she was Alex's friend and he was having difficulty with Samantha's death, wouldn't they want to help him? If she kept it to herself it wouldn't get back to Alex. She didn't want to think about how angry he'd get if he knew she was asking questions in his hometown. She'd have to go carefully. A quick stop at the shelter and that's all. It was worth the risk.

CHAPTER TWENTY

'HOME, HEART, HELP.' ANNIE LOOKED UP at the words scrawled in spray paint across the brick wall of 38 Steeple Street. This building wasn't quite what she expected. It was beautiful. The aged bricks were offset by large Victorian-era windows with bright, white trim. The paint was limited to the side of the building facing an alley, and the words were only a small part of a large mural depicting a table with people of every color, every age sitting around it. Painted on the table was the usual food of Thanksgiving dinners with stylized ribbons labeled with things like 'dignity,' 'love,' and 'peace.' Large letters read 'A Place Like Home.' Annie's one semester of art appreciation gave her enough of an eye to see that the mural was well-done, definitely the work of an artist.

"Pretty, isn't it?"

Annie turned to see an older woman standing at the entrance of the building which was up a short set of steps in the front. The door behind her was still closed, and she had her arms folded, one shoulder leaning against the wall. The woman looked her over. "You with the state?"

"What? Oh no," Annie looked down at her plain black trousers peeking out from beneath her good, black coat and realized she probably did look like a social worker. "No, I'm not. I was hoping to talk to someone about the program. I'm considering a donation." She walked to the steps.

"Really? Okay." She didn't sound like she thought that was okay.

"Yes," Annie held her hand out for the woman. "I'm Annie Caldwell."

The woman seemed to be just the other side of middle-aged.

She was tall and solidly-built, dressed comfortably in a sweater and jeans with a barn coat left open.

"Dorothy." She shook Annie's hand briefly, but she didn't move away from the still-shut door. Annie was going to have to do something to show she was trustworthy or this was going to be a wasted trip.

"I'd like to know more about the program, its history if I could."

Dorothy gave her a top to toes look. "Don't you know how to Google?"

Rats. This was not going well. "I've read your website, but I was hoping for more information."

"Everything you need to know is online." Dorothy's eyes narrowed. "Unless you're lying and you're actually the media. If that's the case, then I'll let you know that horse is dead, and you can quit beating it. There's nothing new to tell." She straightened away from the wall. "And you can get your backside off the property."

"Wait. I'm not the media. I really do plan to donate, but I'm not here because of that."

"You have about a minute left of my time."

"Alex Moretti is a friend of mine. And he's...I need some answers. I need to help him."

Some of the tension seemed to go out of Dorothy, but she still looked wary. "Alex is in trouble?"

"No. Well, I'm not sure. He's... he doesn't talk about all this." She gestured to the building. "But it's eating at him. I don't know how to help him, but he needs help."

"Heard he left. Moved out of state."

Annie climbed a step up toward the landing, the better not to get a crick in her neck from looking up at Dorothy. "No. He's a game warden up north. His territory includes the town my coffee shop is in. That's how we met. He's my friend." She looked up at the building and then back down. "And this is haunting him."

"Yah, well it would." Dorothy turned around and unlocked the door. "Can I assume you know how to make coffee?"

"Um, yeah."

"Okay, I'll make you a deal. I've got to get ready for the morning crew. You make the coffee while I do the rest, and you can ask me questions while I work." She threw the door wide, and Annie stepped inside a dark, cold foyer. "But when I'm done, you go. Understand?"

Annie nodded. The hall they were standing in was long, and once Dorothy flicked the lights on, she could see they were in a typical Colonial layout with two large rooms to either side and a center staircase. The air was still, as if no one had been there for some time. "I thought this was office space."

"No. We didn't touch the first floor." Dorothy adjusted a thermostat on the wall, and Annie heard the sound of a furnace firing below. "Upstairs is offices. Down here we meet in the original rooms. Group therapy."

"A drug treatment program is a nice way to honor Samantha's legacy."

"Her legacy?" Dorothy's expression was bemused. "That's one way to put it." She headed down the hallway towards what looked like a kitchen, and Annie followed.

"The mural outside. Did Samantha paint it?"

"No." Her answer was terse. "That would be Logan. You know who he is I assume?" She looked back over her shoulder. Annie nodded and then followed her through to the large, sunny kitchen. It was far warmer, probably because it faced south.

Dorothy took off her coat and hung it on a hook by the back door. Annie could see her breath in the air, despite the warm sunshine, and opted to keep hers on.

"Help yourself." Dorothy pointed to a large, old-school

commercial coffee brewer sitting on a countertop. If Dorothy thought the behemoth would phase her, she was dead wrong. The church had a brewer exactly like this one, and it had taken a few tries to get the knack of it, but she was an expert now. As she set it up, she thought through what she wanted to ask while she still had the time. Clearly she was going to have to be careful since Dorothy wasn't exactly chatty.

"Did you know Samantha while she was alive?"

Dorothy was bent over, lighting an old range. Annie heard the gentle whoosh of the flame before the woman set a large kettle on the burner. "Knew her, yes. Knew the whole crew. This used to be a neighborhood before the junkies moved in. Steeple Street turned into Needle Street. It's all changed. Nobody knows nothing and no one." She opened the fridge and took out a large container of orange juice and set it down. "Alex hasn't told you much, has he?"

Annie shook her head. "He keeps himself apart. There are only a few people in town he even speaks to."

Dorothy's face grew soft. "He didn't use to be that way. This was a good place to grow up. When they were young, this whole neighborhood was teeming with kids. You'd know where they all were by which house had the bikes parked in front of it. We all treated each other's children as if they were our own. It was safe, then. Not that it was perfect. Most of us worked long hours or two jobs, but when we weren't home, we made sure somebody else was who'd keep the kids in line." Dorothy looked the right age to be the mother of a son Alex's age. Annie was tempted to ask if she had kids and if they'd known Alex, but she didn't want to stop the woman mid-flow.

"We looked out for our neighbors. I know that's not the fashion now. This really was a family kind of place once." She turned to the fridge again and began unloading fruit.

"Alex and Samantha grew up together?"

"And her brother, Eric. They were all friends. There was a pack of them all about the same age. Graduated at the same time. Some stayed, some went off to college or the Army."

"Did they come back?"

"Alex did. Eric joined the army. Heard he'd decided to make a career of it, so no one expected to see much of him again. Their parents didn't stay either. They gave Sam the house and moved south."

"This house? Was it the house she grew up in?"

Dorothy nodded. "Alex's family is two streets over. Parents still there. His brothers aren't too far either, Portland I think." She went back to prepping the breakfast items, gesturing at Annie to help her carry them out of the kitchen. As she talked she led Annie to one of the front rooms. It was set up with rows of chairs and a small table off to the side. It was there they placed the juice, bagels, and fruit. "Alex was a pistol back then. His older brothers were football players, so he had to play basketball. They were troublemakers, so he was an A-plus student, and an Eagle Scout. Classic middle kid had to stand out."

"And he and Eric were friends?"

"Oh yes. The two were tight even when Alex and Sam started dating. You'd think that would bring tension, but it seemed the most natural thing to the three of them."

Annie snapped her fingers in the air. The pieces were falling into place. "She was his girlfriend."

"Yup. Dated right up to graduation, and then something went wrong. Probably the usual–didn't want to be tied down when they went to college. Didn't see much of them after that. Sam came back thinking she could save the world one homeless teen at a time and started this shelter. She talked me into working with her." Dorothy chuckled. "She could talk the hind-leg off a dog. I think I said yes just to shut her up."

"Alex became a cop. He was a bit full of himself, to be honest. Sam was all about the kids." She paused. "Until Logan anyway."

Dorothy headed back to the kitchen and Annie followed. Remembering the coffee, she grabbed the two thermoses waiting to be filled and checked to see if it was done. After filling both she followed her back out to the room and set them down next to the stack of cups and packets of sugar.

"Well, looks like we're all set." Dorothy was giving her the push.

"Can I ask a couple more questions?"

The woman looked up at the clock over the fireplace at the far end of the room. "Five minutes."

"Okay, I know the bare details. I know Logan and Samantha had some kind of relationship, but that night he tried to hurt her?"

Dorothy set her hands on her hips. "Logan was one seriously messed-up human. Sam should've shown him the door day one. He was an artist, supposed to be doing art therapy, but really, he was an addict constantly on the cycle from clean and sober to all messed up. On top of that, he was dealing. What a winner." Her lips twisted in a scornful smile. "Sam had been working overtime to get him clean. Loved him well, but not wisely, you get me?"

Annie nodded.

"Eric kept in touch with his sister. He figured out Logan was more trouble than Sam was willing to admit, but what could he do half a world away? So, he called Alex. Told him to have a chat with Sam. Set her straight. Alex came to the program, in uniform, and read Sam the riot act. Logan saw him leaving. He asks around and figures out that Alex is her ex. He thinks not only is she cheating, but with a cop. He comes back here and tears into her for it. Neighbors called the cops. Logan hears the sirens coming for him, and he pulls a gun out, says he's protecting himself." She crossed her arms and leaned a hip against the table. "Alex and his partner respond to the call. Now it's July, so every window in the place is open. Logan shouts that he's got a gun. Instead of waiting for back up, Alex decides he's gonna play the hero. The man climbed the fire escape." She jerked her head to the side of the building. "Spots Logan through the window and shoots him. He drops dead."

"That's terrible, but if he had a gun—"

"Turns out it wasn't real. It was a starter pistol he kept to scare anyone who messed with him. Had the fool been sober he would have realized the cops wouldn't know the difference."

"Sam must have been upset."

"Upset? She lost her ever-lovin' mind. Cops hauled her to the station, grilled her for hours like any of this was her fault." Dorothy's lips pressed together, and she shook her head. "Girl gets back here, sees the blood on the floor, and jumps out the front window."

Annie closed her eyes trying not to imagine that fall.

"That night ended four lives. Logan and Sam are buried and gone, but Alex and Eric became the walking dead. All the blame shifted to Alex. He acted too fast, he shouldn't have talked to Sam on duty, to begin with, he should have spotted it was a starter pistol, he should have waited for back up... And then Eric comes home to bury his sister, and the two of them go at it on the front lawn of the funeral home." She stood up and checked the clock. "The Moretti brothers had to pull him off. He told Alex he was dead to him, laid it all at his feet, the whole thing. It was ugly. People turned on that boy." She looked down at Annie. "Your Alex, I mean. Samantha was loved, you understand."

Annie nodded, her heart breaking for them all. What a waste of life. The front door opened and a young man slipped in. He gave Dorothy a chin lift and headed to a folded chair. Dorothy motioned for Annie to follow her into the hallway. "You got your answers, now you do something for me." She spoke quietly, urgency in her tone. "Tell Alex no one here blames him anymore. People got angry at him because of their own grief, because that's just how humans are. He should come home, to see his folks if nothing else."

"Okay, Dorothy. I will as soon as I see him." At the door, Annie stopped and turned around. "Thank you. I appreciate you taking the time."

"You saved me about fifteen minutes of set up so, we're even." Dorothy opened the door.

"Goodbye then." Annie slipped out into the cold. She was half-way down the steps when Dorothy called after her.

"Hey, something else. Nobody knows what became of Eric. I heard he might have been discharged. He never comes around this place."

"Okay." Annie wasn't sure why she was sharing that.

"But I've got this feeling he's here again. Maine, I mean." Her expression was dour, and she seemed to be fighting saying anything more. "Someone broke in a few weeks ago but didn't take anything of value, just some letters and stuff from her old office."

"If he were to see Alex again, how would he react?"

"I don't know. But it wouldn't be good." With that, she shut the door. Annie walked back to her car, pausing again to look at the mural. She wondered what inside of Logan had soured so much that he could produce such beauty, but still be so cruel. As she was heading out of the alley and onto the sidewalk to get to her car, she spotted a white pickup truck with tinted windows slow down and pass her at a crawl. Telling herself it was nothing, she picked up her pace all the same. A trickle of premonition ran through her, reminding her of the witch from Macbeth 'by the pricking of my thumbs, something wicked this way comes.' Her thumbs were fine, it was the hair on the back of her neck that was giving her trouble.

Something was not right here. Dorothy seemed to feel it as well. Annie knew better than to believe that a house that saw sorrow and death could be cursed by it, but it felt like it all the same. Samantha's death seemed to mark her former home the way it had Alex. This place needed the grace of God to descend and clear it out. So did he.

CHAPTER TWENTY-ONE

ALEX IGNORED HIS FROZEN FEET WHILE he wrote up the guy trying to discreetly ice fish the lake. The man had rigged up a contraption off the dock thinking he was hiding what he was up to. Not so much. By the time Alex got to him, there had been calls from three residents asking for the wardens to check out the guy 'creeping' around the dock. His excuse had been pretty entertaining too, something about needing the fish for his wife to make up for lousy Christmas presents.

"You're a hard man, Moretti." The fisherman, a Mr. Libby from Sweet River, was giving him the stink eye from the tailgate of his truck, his gear in the bed. The gear he'd packed up, griping the whole time. Alex could read most of these guys now, so he didn't get tense like he might have when he'd first started. Then, every time some fisherman or hunter grumbled under his breath and threw his stuff around, Alex had reflexively adjusted his stance and readied for a fight. Now he knew that most weren't looking to take it there. They wanted to voice their opposition to whatever law they decided was oppressive.

It was a rare occasion that these guys were ignorant of the law they were breaking. Among the men of rural Maine, there was a stubborn belief that all of the wild belonged to whoever had the guts to stake their claim to it. They liked to ignore that the public land belonged to everyone, and that the private land belonged to someone in particular. On some calls, Alex would take the time to explain why the regulation was in place, but mostly he gave them space to grumble, keeping his ears and eyes sharp for when the usual complaining turned ugly. Today he wasn't in the mood to deal with any of it.

"A bit of friendly advice, Mr. Libby? Penobscot County has

like fifty lakes and ponds, and they've been making ice since Christmas. Take the drive next time." He handed him the ticket. "Oh, and you might want to buy your wife a gift instead. Chocolates? Maybe a book?"

"She don't need candy, and she's got the library for books." He slid off the tailgate and stuffed the ticket in his pocket.

"Take her to dinner then."

Libby's expression grew unhappier, and he stomped to the door of his truck, yanking it open. "Thanks for nothing, *Warden Moretti*." He spat the words then slammed the door shut. He'd made the name sound like a curse.

Alex walked back to his truck trying not to chuckle. Grown men acting like preschoolers was not usually this funny. Considering his life of late consisted of dark mornings with coffee he made himself, patrols in the cold, and dinners at home with a bored and lonely Shep, he could use a laugh. He started his truck and blasted the heat. Libby drove off, peeling out and disappearing in a cloud of exhaust. Instead of tearing off after him and writing him another ticket, Alex laughed. It was the first time in a while he'd found anything funny, but something about the sight of Libby's truck puffing down the road was hilarious. He felt a buzz in his pocket and pulled out his phone.

"Moretti."

"Alex, it's Pete. I'm at the Moose having lunch. Heard you were nearby. Come keep an old man company."

"Sure. Be there in ten." Alex drove out to the main road and wondered if this was going to be lunch or an interrogation. It had only been a week since Elaine had posted his picture in *The Lowdown* with a caption designed to let everyone know that he was alone again, but he was sure Pete had heard. People talked. In the winter the talk might move slower, but it would still move. Ever since that first picture had appeared in *The Lowdown*, he and Annie had been a regular item. Alex knew they had gone into this break thinking it wouldn't be a permanent change, but already he was beginning to lose hope. He'd twice started something with her and ended it. This time it *was* for her own good, but she probably didn't feel that way. He wondered if she felt as torn up inside as he did, as if they'd been sewn together and he'd ripped them apart. All his edges were jagged.

Pulling into the parking lot, he headed inside the bar, spotting Pete at a table near the back. It didn't take a genius to deduce that this was going to be an interrogation after all. Pete usually sat at the bar. Hard to give Alex a piece of his mind there. No, he'd picked the furthermost table, which meant there might even be shouting. It was the price Alex was prepared to pay. The only thing he'd rather do less than disappoint Pete was hurt Annie. This was just how it had to be.

"Cold out there?" Pete gave him a smile as he pulled out a chair and sat down.

"A bit."

"Who was the Einstein out on the lake thinking nobody would see him fishing?"

Alex's head jerked back. "Do you have a scanner in your car?"

Pete's lips moved in a sheepish grin. "Don't tell Lauren, but yes I do."

"You're supposed to be retired."

"I get bored." He shrugged. "Besides, it keeps me young."

Alex shook his head. "When I retire I'm going to build a house on the quietest beach I can find, and I'm staying put."

"A beach?"

"Yes. I don't care if it's warm year-round. I like the peace of it."

"Huh." Pete narrowed his eyes. "That's not what I would have expected."

"I'm full of surprises." Alex picked up the plastic menu on

the table and looked it over. "I've never ordered anything but their burgers. What's good?"

Pete pulled his menu out of his fingers. "They've got chili today. I took the liberty of ordering some for you. The cornbread isn't bad either. Not like mama made, mind you. It's the northern sort, a bit sweet."

"I grew up with the Jiffy stuff, so no worries."

"Didn't your mother make you empanadas or something exotic?"

Alex shook his head. His mom found ways to ensure her boys knew their roots, mostly through making sure they knew their aunts, uncles, and cousins, but she cooked to please their father. The way her face lit up when he complimented her cooking, how often she sang or hummed while she worked, Alex could tell it was an act of love for her, not a chore. "She cooks what my dad likes."

"Right, that makes sense. Women do that, sacrifice for their men. My Lauren certainly does. She was a city girl. She hates driving, but she lives in the back of nowhere with me because she knows I like it. That's love for you."

"Wait, I thought she came up here to visit her daughter and met you in the process. Didn't she really move up here to be with Katherine after she and Mac took in those kids?"

"Boy, are you attempting to downplay my wife's sacrifice?"

"What? No—"

Pete chuckled. "I may have been laying it on a bit thick. Yes, she moved up for Katie, but I like to think she stays for me. However, it's not the point I was setting you up for." The waitress arrived at their table with Alex's chili. Pete let him get a few spoonfuls in before he picked up where he left off. "I wondered if you'd had the chance to talk with Dan."

Alex shook his head. It was too weird. How was he supposed to approach the pastor when he'd been to church a handful of times? 'Hey, I'm that messed up guy you met at the New Year's Eve party that Pete warned you about. Can we talk?' Awkward to say the least.

"I thought as much. Couldn't help but notice that you're not seeing Annie anymore."

"No. And before you get on me about that, how can I?" He sat back in his chair. "I've got some guy sending me threats, threatening her. I'm on edge all the time. I went to her place and found out she's been keeping a spare key in an obvious fake rock. Easy pickings. And I yelled at her, Pete. I was so mad she'd left that key where anybody could get it that I couldn't see straight. I made her cry." His gut twisted remembering how she sobbed. "I'm...toxic right now. I poison everything. The best thing I can do for her is to stay away until this all resolves. Somehow." It didn't seem any more likely than it had the day he arrived. His life was still a mess.

"What is it you need, Alex?"

"To fix what I broke. Only I can't do it. I can't make things right. Sam is...Sam is dead. Nothing fixes that."

"You still blame yourself for that?"

"Her brother does. The neighborhood does. And yeah, I still blame me for that, because it was my fault."

"Your fault that she killed herself?"

"Not just that. All of it. Do you know why I broke it off with her when we graduated? It wasn't because it was bad. We were good together, but I wanted to go to college a free man, no limits. I threw her away for nothing. Emptiness. Years of it, knowing it was wrong and doing it all the same." He shook his head. "When I moved home, I wanted to make it up to her, to find a way to be friends, but she froze me out. Said she wanted nothing to do with me. We lived in the same city, knew the same people, but didn't exchange so much as a word until Eric called me and asked me to talk to her about Logan." Alex shut his eyes, blocking out the patient look on Pete's face. He didn't deserve it. Everything he did that day sprung from his ego, not his heart and for sure, not his head. "I went there in uniform as a power play. So she'd know who she was dealing with, so she couldn't slam the door in my face. It was arrogant and stupid. In the end, she's dead because I wasn't thinking about her feelings or her safety. I only thought about me."

They sat in silence for a time while Alex's thoughts went on the trip down memory lane he hated. He relived the moment at Samantha's wake when Eric rushed him in anger, shouting hate, fists flying. Alex wished his brothers hadn't been there, that he'd let Eric beat him to a pulp in front of the whole town. Maybe then he'd have paid enough to find a way to be forgiven. "That's why I'm up here. It's the only way someone like me earns redemption."

"Earns? Nobody earns redemption. We're saved by grace."

"But I have a debt, and I need to pay it."

"That's some mixed-up theology."

"I believe—"

"All the wrong stuff." Pete interrupted. "Maybe you should talk to Mac. He knows a thing or two about redemption."

"That's your solution to everything. Talking." Alex's frustration had him stabbing a finger into the table with each word. "It doesn't change a single cold, hard fact of this whole, stupid mess."

"No," Pete raised his voice. "It doesn't. It changes you!" He let out a heavy sigh and sat back. "I really am getting too old for this."

Alex almost smiled at that. "Listen, Pete—"

"Don't." Pete cut him off and leaned forward again, folding his hands on the table between them as if he wanted to lock them down. "If there is one lesson I learned the hard way, it was that sharing what is weighing you down reduces the burden. Instead of walking around with all that pain and angst like a pile of lead in your gut, you can talk to someone about it, share what you're going through, and maybe even get some advice. No, it won't change that you killed a man."

Alex flinched. It was hard to hear that out loud, and Pete had said it cold, as if it was one detail among many, no big deal. For Alex, pulling the trigger had been the end of the world as he knew it. The man he'd been died with Logan and Sam. He walked away, but part of his soul was still there.

Pete wasn't done. He kept talking in that same, matter-of-fact way. "And it won't change that a girl you once cared for killed herself. And it for sure won't change that a man you once thought of as your friend, wants you to suffer for it." He sat back and leveled a sharp look at Alex. "It won't change that you've hurt someone you might just be in love with." He swept his hand through the air. "None of that changes. But talking about what happened changes how you *feel* about all of that."

"That's a pretty tall order, Pete." Alex took his spoon and dug through his chili, his appetite long gone.

"Not for God."

Alex sighed. "I'm not talking to God, though, am I? You said to talk to Mac and Dan."

"Who are God's instruments on this planet?" Pete's tone betrayed his impatience. "People aren't always what they seem to be. You aren't the only guy with baggage." Pete sat forward, his eyes darting over Alex's face. He knit his fingers together on the table. His lips were pressed flat as if he couldn't decide if he should speak. "It's not my story to tell, but this much I will say. Mac's first wife died with a needle in her arm."

Alex felt the air rush out of him as he lurched back in his seat. Pete didn't react. It was like he hadn't dropped a bomb in the middle of their conversation.

"Seriously?"

"When he was a detective in New York. That's the reason he's here. Like you, he came looking for peace."

"I had no idea."

"He met Katie when she came up here looking for peace of her own. She never planned to stay, but she fell in love both with Mac and the town. They had a rocky road, but it led to a beautiful place."

Alex thought it pretty unlikely that he and Annie had the same trajectory. They weren't walking the same road at all. He felt a buzz in his pocket and pulled out his phone. "Speak of the devil." He shot a look at Pete before answering, "Hey, Mac."

"Hi. Can you swing by the house today? I've got something you need to see." Mac's voice sounded a bit strained. Alex's stomach twisted knowing there was only one thing Mac would call him over to view. It might finally be a lead on the man ruining his life.

"Sure. I'm at the Moose with Pete, but I can be there soon."

"Great. Bring Pete with you if you want. See you shortly."

The call disconnected, and Alex stowed his phone. "You up for a visit to Mac's? He says he has something for us to see."

"Gotcha." Pete caught the waitress' eye and mouthed the word 'check'. A few minutes later they were driving out to Mac's house, Pete leading since Alex hadn't ever been. It was close to where Pete lived. There was an upscale rental cabin on the side of the road and right past it the long drive to a log home built into the side of the mountain. In the distance Alex could see an old barn that looked like it had been renovated recently and a paddock. He parked his truck next to Pete's SUV and headed up to the front entry. Mac's place was huge, but it looked like it belonged there. Some big places looked ridiculous because they were basically suburban houses rendered in 'log' style. Mac's house was different. It had a low profile as if it grew out of the ground. He'd left a bunch of mature pine around it and his outbuildings appeared original to the property. Alex couldn't help but be impressed. Mac might not be a local product, but he'd managed to naturalize like a weed.

Pete knocked on the door, and they waited while chaos, the kid sort, sounded inside. The door swung open and Mac appeared with one small girl clutching his leg and a small boy on his shoulder.

"Hey, c'mon in." He said it like he wasn't being used for a jungle gym. Mac was tall and broad, but not bulky. His black hair was peppered with gray, but he still appeared to be in the prime of life. Good thing since the kids were giving him a workout. Mac grabbed the little boy on his shoulder, tickled him until he was gasping and plopped him into a chair. "Okay, buddy, I need to talk to my friends, so you need to be good." He lifted his head and called, "Olivia?"

While they waited for her to appear Alex took a look around the space. It was a living room, dining room, kitchen all combined together--classy, but very Maine-looking. The timbers of the house had been left natural, and the stuff on the walls and the furniture was what you'd find in a lodge. A nice one, but definitely a lodge. Across the room there was a short staircase that led to a sunken family room with a big leather couch and TV. It looked like a hallway ran off from that to what Alex assumed were bedrooms. Olivia emerged from there, tucking her hair behind her ear and ducking her head when she spotted Alex.

"Hey, honey, can you watch the little ones for me?" Mac gently dislodged the girl wrapped around his leg.

She clung to his arm like a barnacle. "I want to stay with Dad." Mac's face changed, softening in a way Alex had never seen. The guy was usually pretty stoic, but not now. He leaned down and kissed the top of her head. "Be good for your sister. No giving her trouble. I'll be back out in a bit."

Olivia picked her giggling little brother out of the chair and held her hand out for her sister. She darted a glance at Mac, almost like a look of approval, before smiling down at her sister. "C'mon guys. Let's go play." In the end she got them down the hall without much trouble.

"She's good with them." Alex noted more to have something to say than anything else.

Mac watched his children go. "In the group home she assumed a lot of responsibility. It's both a good and bad thing. Hard to give up authority and control once you've had it." Like most of what Mac had to say to him, it felt like those words weren't about Olivia alone. Alex had a lot of ground to make up if Mac was ever going to think he was worth a thing.

Mac motioned for Alex and Pete to follow him down a short hallway beside the kitchen to a home office. The space did not match the man. It had floor to ceiling shelves of stacked fabric, craft stuff, and what Alex could only guess were things for the girls since most of it sparkled. Mac caught him giving it the side-eye and laughed. "This is Katherine's office."

"Okay, that makes a bit more sense. Not that there's anything wrong with a guy being into sewing, but that would be a surprise coming from you."

"I consider myself well-rounded, but my sewing skills begin and end with basic repairs."

"You beat me then."

"Every bachelor should know how to sew his own buttons on, kid. You should get on it." Mac gestured to two hard-backed chairs on one side of the room. He sat down at the fancy-looking desk and pulled a laptop to the edge, tilting it so they could all see. Lifting the cover, he booted it up and opened a window. He popped up a picture, and Alex scooted his chair closer to see it. Pete did the same. It took a minute, but he recognized a string of cabins and in front of it, a man. He had a full beard and was wearing a military-style jacket, jeans, and boots. He had a knit hat pulled low on his forehead, but Alex knew those eyes, the set of those shoulders.

"That's Eric." He reached out and used the laptop mouse to enlarge the photo. How much time had passed since he last saw his friend? Not enough to account for his haggard expression. He'd aged ten years in the space of two. "He looks rough."

"I didn't approach him."

"I know that place." Alex pointed at the screen. "That's a campground outside Nahmakanta."

Mac nodded. "I found out he was stateside, honorable discharge. The only address for him was a post office box in Lewiston. After interviewing a few Army buddies of his, I got the impression he had come north and that he was camping. Got a hit or two that led me to Baxter. There are places where he can pay with cash, stay off the grid, but I got a few leads to the right spot."

"He was never the outdoors type." Alex shook his head. "I barely recognize him."

"I talked to his parents. They're still in Florida and haven't heard from him in months. Talked to former friends, same thing. He's gone dark on almost everyone. If he has a cell, it's a burner. No Internet presence I could find. No vehicle either, which is odd. Makes me wonder how he's getting around."

"So, we have our guy."

Mac tilted his head to the side but seemed to agree. "Probably using library computers to keep tabs on you. I'm guessing he has a friend carting him around or he's hitching. Next step is to make this official and bring him in." Mac sat back, the laptop screen going dark before switching to a screen saver. Alex didn't really want to make this official. He'd rather approach Eric directly and get it all out. What Eric probably wanted was some kind of closure that involved Alex losing a few teeth. Alex was more than ready to take a punch to ease his pain.

Mac seemed to be following his train of thought. "I can see you don't like the idea of having your old friend brought in for questioning, but don't forget, it isn't just you he's targeting."

"He wouldn't hurt Annie, I'm sure of it. He's not that guy. I'm the one he's angry with." But there was a nagging doubt in his gut. He didn't know Eric anymore, as Mac had already pointed out. Then again, he wasn't with Annie right now either, although Eric might not know that. "I broke it off with her last week."

Mac's face bore its usual expression, so it was hard to tell what he thought. "Yeah, heard that. I suppose you think she's safer now?"

Alex didn't know why, but he felt like he had to explain. "I meant it as a precaution, but the longer we're apart I can't help but feel it's for the best. Why ruin her life with my baggage?"

"Everybody's got baggage." Pete pointed out the obvious.

"Maybe so, but mine is armed."

CHAPTER TWENTY-TWO

"WE'RE WHAT?" ANNIE SQUINTED UP AT Erin and Claire. They'd stormed into the bakery at closing and demanded that she come upstairs to their business for a craft night. Half of Sweet River was apparently coming. Annie was not in the mood. The sharp pain of loss was fading to a dull, persistent ache that made her feel tired and irritable. It definitely did not make her want to be around other people, 'testing' crafts of all things. "I'm more confused now than when you started explaining. How is that possible?"

"We're testing out different ideas for wedding favors." Claire folded her arms. "Blame Erin's stepmom, Linda. She's been pushing the bridesmaids to pick one. We've narrowed it down to a dozen different ideas and everyone is going to put a few together and then vote. Katherine and I are the only actual bridesmaids, but all the other local ladies invited to the wedding were invited to this as well."

Erin raised her hand. "Since I know the pain of pouring Jordan almonds into three hundred tiny net bags and cinching them closed with ribbons, I wholeheartedly endorse this plan. Wedding favors can be labor-intensive. This sounds daffy, but it's actually a good idea."

"But your wedding is more than two months away."

"Yes, so we're just in time." Claire clapped her hands together.

Erin turned to Claire and narrowed her eyes. "Now you sound like Linda. If it were up to her, we'd have already had a rehearsal. She needs to chill. I'm hoping putting favors together will do the trick."

"Well, it's natural she'd be excited about your wedding."

Claire waved a hand airily.

"Excited...not sure that's the emotion she's feeling." Erin bugged her eyes at Annie. "Anticipation and anxiety are more like it. You'll see for yourself. C'mon up when you're done."

"Okay." Annie hoped no one was expecting her to be cheerful, happy Annie since that girl hadn't appeared in the two weeks since Alex had put them on 'pause.' She missed him, missed having someone to literally and figuratively lean on. She could count on Claire and Erin, but it wasn't the same.

She finished locking up and climbed the stairs to the second-story where the door stood open to Artsy Crafts. They had two long tables set up with heaps of supplies and women lining the benches on either side. The room was bright and loud. Another table had been set up with refreshments, mainly cookies of all sorts and sparkling-water drinks.

"Here, there's a space by me."

Annie spotted Olivia sitting at the short end of one of the tables, waving and patting the seat next to her. Annie headed there, dumping her things on a chair against the wall. "So you get to join in the fun too?" She asked Olivia when she sat down.

"I got dragged here." She sighed, and Annie wondered if that's what she'd sounded like to Claire and Erin, a recalcitrant teenager. "Still, it shouldn't be too lame. Erin and Claire are hilarious when they teach together."

Katherine took the other seat next to Olivia, and the girl shrunk away from her like she was a stranger. Annie saw the look of hurt register on Katherine's face and then fade. Annie wondered how many times the woman had suffered the same treatment. Annie had to work hard to ignore the urge to give the girl a pinch for it.

Olivia's lips were pressed into a thin line. She crossed her arms and looked away. Annie prayed for the right words to reach her. What she had done, was doing, was cruel and they both knew it, but how to get her to empathize with Katherine? How to get her to see past her own hurting heart to what she was inflicting on someone else? No one could say Olivia didn't have a reason for her actions, but it didn't make them right.

"Well, I'm excited about this." Annie smiled brightly at Katherine. "I've never been a bridesmaid, so this is all new to me. Are we wrapping up candies or bubbles or something?"

"Oh no," Katherine shook her head. "Erin has simple tastes, but her stepmother does not. That, and she's southern, and she's running this wedding, so you know what that means."

Annie waited for someone to tell her.

"They're all going to be 'extra'!" Olivia added jazz hands to her statement.

"Extra what?" Annie tipped her head to the side.

"Actually, that's the perfect word, Olivia," Katherine interjected. "It means needlessly complicated or detailed to be unique and admired." For a moment, Olivia looked impressed with her explanation.

"Ah. I love new colloquialisms." Annie nodded sagely. "I'll add that to my lexicon."

"Okay, whatever." Olivia's cheeks were pink.

Annie looked down the table at the piles of soil, tiny plants, glass jars, pots, sand, ribbons, labels, and had no idea what they were going to do with any of it. "What are we making?"

Claire breezed past the table. "Mini terrariums and succulent planters. Lucky you."

Annie stared back at her. "As a wedding favor?"

"Eco-friendly," Claire replied before moving on to the next table.

"I've got the directions, no worries." Katherine passed her a sheet of paper, and they got to work. In the end, they had made terrariums out of small glass jars that she still wasn't so sure about and planted tiny succulent gardens in clay pots with the names of the bride and groom and the wedding date. It was cute, but for any guest traveling from out of state, it was hardly practical. Annie looked around at the other tables and saw fancy, single-serve hot chocolate containers, local honey samplers, tiny hand-made boxes of curated mints, and several things involving mason jars all in progress. They were definitely extra.

While they worked, Katherine kept darting quick looks her way, and she sensed the woman had something on her mind. She caught one of those looks and waited for her to address whatever it was.

"I saw *The Lowdown*," Katherine said quietly. "I'm sorry." Olivia looked at Annie and her foster-mother but didn't say anything.

"It's for the best." That's the rote answer Annie had come up with. She liked Katherine, but they weren't close enough for her to get into all that happened. This wasn't the place either. But Katherine didn't leave it there.

"The other day I thought I'd have to break up a fight between them." She looked up at Annie. "Mac and your Alex."

Annie sat back in surprise. "Alex and Mac?"

"I know. Weird, right? Mac wouldn't explain. Said it wasn't his information to share." She pursed her lips. "He's an iron fortress when he wants to be. When I saw that you two had called it quits, I wondered if that was related. Mac has strong feelings of what's appropriate and not, when a man is dating a woman. He wouldn't be shy about sharing it."

"He's old-fashioned?" Annie didn't find that hard to believe. He seemed a by-the-book sort of man, not unlike Alex.

"To say the least. He insisted that all our dates be in public places. Wouldn't so much as step a foot inside my cabin until we were engaged. I didn't spend any time in his house until we were married."

"It's Mac's house? Not yours?" Olivia had been listening.

Not only that, she looked like she cared about what she was hearing.

Katherine nodded. "Other than the piano, my sewing stuff, and a few throw pillows, the house and everything in it was his when we married."

"You didn't have any furniture? Didn't you have your own house?"

Katherine's lips curved upwards, as if she was pleased Olivia was still talking to her. "I worked a lot, so I was on the road most of the time. I had a beach house I used to rent out, and that was sort of my home base. I was rarely there, though. The furniture there was for my renters. I pretty much lived out of a suitcase."

"You traveled?"

"All the time. I spent more of my nights in hotels than I did in a house for, gosh..." She raised her eyes in thought... "about a decade."

"Did you have a boyfriend then?"

"No, not then. I was single until I met Mac."

"You were alone for ten years?" Olivia's mouth dropped open.

"Yup." Katherine grimaced. "I was married to my job back then."

"Why?" Olivia's eyes narrowed.

Katherine put down the little plant she'd been adding to her pot and brushed her hands off. Annie knew the story she was likely to share and wondered how Katherine would tell it so that a fourteen-year-old could understand.

Katherine turned in her seat so that she was facing Olivia. "I was engaged once before when I was still very young. That relationship ended in a bad way. It was hard to trust anyone after that, so I preferred to be alone. I had Grammy of course, and my sisters, and my best friend Heather, but otherwise I was alone. In some ways, it was by choice, but I'd also made it hard for people to get close to me. I was still pretty hurt, and I needed to protect myself."

"What did he do? Your fiancé?" Olivia leaned closer to Katherine. "Did he do something bad to you?"

Katherine flicked a look at Annie, but not being able to offer any advice in this she kept her expression carefully neutral. If Katherine wanted to be honest with her daughter, that had to be a decision she made.

Katherine pressed her lips together and then sighed. "We were in a car accident. I was injured, badly, and I lost the baby daughter I was pregnant with."

Olivia sucked in a breath of air and lurched backward. The other end of the table chatted on, oblivious to the sudden silence. A kind of tension grew between Katherine and Olivia. Annie could feel things said and unsaid hanging between them.

Olivia was the first to break it. "That's why you have a scar on your face." She said it quietly, a statement, not a question as if she was putting things together.

"Yes, honey."

The girl's forehead wrinkled. "You were only engaged, not married, but you were pregnant?"

"I am not now, nor have I ever been perfect." Katherine had a lop-sided grin on her face, but it faded quickly. "I believed he loved me and always would. I thought he would protect me, and we'd share our lives together. Turns out I was wrong."

"I'm sorry." Olivia shook her head. "I cannot wrap my brain around you"—she threw out her hand in Katherine's direction—"doing something wrong."

"That could be because you don't know me. You've got an idea in your head of who I am, and any new fact you find has to fit with the ones you've made up yourself. I'm not perfect, and I never was. What I am is redeemed. I hope I've also gained some wisdom along the way. Coming here to Sweet River, meeting Mac, adopting you kids, this is how my life started over."

"You could have had babies with Mac."

"No, I couldn't." Her voice was quiet. "I can't have children, Olivia. The accident did too much damage." Katherine's tone was gentle, but Olivia's mouth dropped open all the same. She looked away for a minute and then back at her foster-mom.

"That's a bummer for you. I'm sorry. I get that's why you wanted to adopt us. I mean it all makes sense now. But I still wish my parents were alive."

"I wish they were too, Olivia. You can't possibly think that Mac and I are glad you lost your mom and dad so that we could replace them. That's awful, and it's definitely not true. I assumed we would put our parenting energy into teaching and coaching. He's the one who first felt the pull to adopt. After a time I could feel it too, and we started looking. God brought you to us."

"I can't thank Him for that." Olivia pushed up out of her seat. "I need some air. Is it okay if I go out into the hall, *Mrs. MacAlister*?" She said the name pointedly like she was intentionally pushing Katherine away, rejecting all she'd said, demanding to return the distance between them. Katherine nodded, her lips pressed tight together, and Olivia fled the room.

Annie had about enough. "I'll be right back." She stood up and followed Olivia out. Once she was on the staircase, she leaned over the banister and saw Olivia leave the building. She followed and found her outside, leaning against the rear wall of the bakery. It was cold, no more than thirty degrees. Annie rubbed her arms as she approached the girl. She knew she should take a breath and calm down before she spoke, but the blood was pounding through her veins, and the words tumbled out. "Your pain"—she began when Olivia looked up at her in surprise—"however sharp and difficult, does not give you permission to inflict it on anyone else."

At first, Olivia seemed taken aback, but then she looked down at her shoes, her hands balling into fists. When she spoke, her voice was full of self-pity. "You don't understand. No one understands."

Anger rushed through Annie. "It's no excuse for how you've treated her. I think you know that. Your heart is telling you that. It's probably why you're miserable. It's probably why you had to run out of the room rather than deal with those feelings."

"What?" Olivia's head jerked up.

"It's guilt, that sick feeling in your stomach, and it's there because of the way you have treated her. Deep inside you know it's wrong. Your conscience is trying to tell you that you need to forgive her for existing, for trying to be a mother to you."

Olivia shook her head. "All I feel is angry, all the time. In there"—she pointed to the door of the building—"I felt sorry for her, and I don't know what to do with that, but it doesn't change anything. My mom and dad are dead. And now I can't even remember them right! Every day it gets harder to remember what my mom looked like, what her voice sounded like. The pictures don't help. I can't feel her anymore; I only feel the empty place she used to be. When I look at Katherine, it just reminds me my mom is dead." She took in a breath. "I can't be what she wants. I can't call her mom. My mom is getting erased every day. The littles don't even talk about her anymore. They're calling Mac 'dad' and the twins…" She sobbed out a cry, but only once. Her fists clenched tight as if she was in a physical fight with her tears. "I will not call her mom. I had a mom. She's dead."

"Then find another word. You're a lover of words, Olivia." Annie wanted to reach out and hold the girl, but somehow she knew that was the wrong thing. "Find the right one. You can't hang on to the past at the cost of your future. No matter what you do, the memories will fade." Annie had a sudden spark of an idea. "You can write them down."

Oliva looked dubious. "Like a diary or something?"

"Not anything twee."

Oliva narrowed her eyes.

"Sorry, that's a British colloquialism. It means…" She tried to think of the American word for it. "Cheesy or overly cute. The real memories you have. The things you want to remember. Put them in a blank book, and you could add pictures or things like ticket stubs. I've got a whole book with pictures of my aunt, ticket stubs from the shows we went to together, even little notes she left me. It helped. Time will march forward whether you want it to or not. I think you'd be happier if you let it do the work of binding you to your new family."

"That sounds so wrong." She shook her head. "I shouldn't have a new family."

"Better that than nothing." The words seemed to burn their way out of her chest. "Better that you have a mother who loved you and a new one trying to do the same than to never have had either." Judging by the look on Olivia's face, Annie's tone was as heated as she was. "I would rather have had a mom that loved me, even if I only got her for twelve years, than never to have had her at all."

Olivia lurched back into the wall. Annie knew what she'd said had been shocking, but it was true. To be loved by her mother was something that had been in Annie's every wish said on a star, tossed with every coin into a fountain, and breathed out with every puff on birthday candles as a child. It was the wish that had never come true.

"If nothing else, give her the gift of friendship. There is a special kind of blessing in the friendship of women. If you can't let her be your mom, let her be that."

"A friend?" Olivia squinted down at her. Despite being more than a decade younger, she had at least an inch on Annie.

"Yes. Start there. If it never grows into anything else, at least you have that."

"I can do friend." Olivia stepped closer, and Annie took the chance that she was amenable to it and hugged her. Olivia lifted her arms and returned the embrace Annie held her for a moment and then pulled away.

"I am so sorry for all you've lost, sweet girl. I spoke out because I don't want you to miss out on all you're being offered."

Olivia closed her eyes and nodded, her long lashes dark against her cheeks. There was a trace of wetness there as if the tears had leaked a little past her iron hold on them. "Can we go back in? I'm freezing." She rubbed her arms, and Annie laughed.

"It was your brilliant idea to come outside." She winked at Olivia. "Let's go up."

The craft supplies had been put away, the winning favor chosen, a hand-made seed packet stamped with 'let love grow,' along with the names and wedding date. The only problem left was choosing what kind of seeds. With only about half the ladies remaining, there were two camps, choose seeds for meaning, and choose seeds for growing. Linda, Erin's step-mother was the leader of the seeds for growth camp. She interrupted Elaine's rather long-winded recitation of the appropriate marriage flowers with her southern drawl.

"Bless your heart, who is going to grow a crape myrtle? Nobody, that's who. I don't care if they are the symbol of marriage. We need something folks will put in the ground, not end up in the junk drawer of their kitchen island. I do not want my baby girl's wedding remembrance stuffed in with the spare batteries, pens, and bread bag ties. Now violas, people can spread them everywhere, and you said they meant love, right?"

Elaine opened her mouth to argue, but Claire got there first. "Violas, they're violets, right? Well, that's pretty. And May would be a decent time to plant them. How about we put it to a vote. All in favor of violas?"

Annie didn't care, but it looked like Elaine was about to be on her own, so she left her hand down in a sign of solidarity.

"That's," Claire squinted around the room. "Six to two. Violas win." There was a light scattering of applause, more, Annie suspected, to celebrate the end of wedding favor testing than the violas.

"If you end up needing help to put them together before the wedding, please think of me." Annie offered to Erin. "I'd be happy to help."

"Well, aren't you sweet." Linda said before Erin could answer. "I noticed you have impeccable penmanship. Probably because you're English."

"She's an American, Linda," Erin explained.

"With that accent?" Linda looked Annie over. "Hmm... With that hair and those eyes, you look like Elizabeth Taylor. Did anyone ever tell you that? She was English."

Erin shook her head, her long hair falling over her shoulder. "No, she was an American too. You're thinking of that movie she was in."

"Nonsense. I know my movie stars." Linda reached out and smoothed Erin's hair back over her shoulder, a touch that struck Annie as uniquely motherly.

"Actually, you both are right." Annie smiled. "Her parents were American, but she was born in London and lived there as a child. I believe she had dual citizenship."

"Do you?" Linda seemed impressed by the idea.

"Yes, my father is British, but I was born in New York, so I'm a British citizen by descent. I only moved to England when I was school-aged. I sort of did the reverse of Ms. Taylor."

"Well, you're both lovely either way, although I hope you will not have her problem with husbands. My goodness, one is enough to deal with. Can't help it if they go and die on you, but divorcing one after another thinking you're bound to get a better one next time?" Linda huffed out a laugh. "I don't think so. There are two kinds of men. The ones that love God, and the ones that don't. You need to pick one that loves God so you can be sure he's going to love you." She pointed a long finger at Annie.

"That's some Bible wisdom for you there." Claire piped up, sliding her coat on.

"Speaking of no-good husbands, how's yours?" Linda asked Claire. Erin rolled her eyes at this and Linda swatted her arm. "Stop that. Ladies do not roll their eyes." She turned back to Claire. "I heard you were having trouble with him."

"Not really." She lifted a shoulder in a half-hearted shrug. "He's around a lot more than he used to be and doing more than he did when we were still married, to be honest. I'm hoping this means he's taking his responsibilities as a father seriously, but some of what he's doing makes no sense."

"Like what?"

"He comes early to get the boys for hockey, and if it has snowed, he shovels my car out." Her eyebrows bunched up as she spoke. "He never did that before. And he brought me a bottle of the hand lotion I like. It's not sold anywhere near here; you have to go to the mall for it. The boys said he spotted it when they were down there at the video game store, and he made them wait while he picked it up."

Linda narrowed her eyes. "What's he buttering you up for?"

"That's the question of the day." Claire picked up her purse. "I have no idea. He'd better not be thinking about moving, that's for sure." She got out her keys. "I will fight him tooth and nail if he thinks he's going to move out of state and take my boys. He can forget that."

"Ask him." Annie blurted. She strongly suspected Paul wasn't buttering her up for anything, but it had to be Claire that found that out. "Ask him what he's up to. I bet he'll tell you."

Claire shook her head. "Men don't work that way." She had a rueful smile on her lips. "Goodnight ladies." With a wave over her shoulder she left.

Annie felt a touch on her elbow and turned around. Elaine motioned with her head to the other side of the room and began to walk away. Annie followed wondering if the woman was going to advocate for crape myrtle again. "What's up?" She asked when Elaine stopped and faced her.

"Tomorrow, could you come to school before the first bell?" Elaine kept her voice low. "I'm having a problem with *The Lowdown,* and I need your help."

"Okay, I'm pretty decent at WordPress, but I'm not a blog expert."

"It's not that." She shook her head. "But I'd rather go over it with you if that's okay."

"Of course." Annie spotted the look of sheer relief on the woman's face and wondered what it was she needed Annie to sort out for her.

"I'll see you tomorrow then." Elaine gathered her coat and purse, and Annie followed suit. From across the room, she could see Katherine and Olivia gathering their things as if ready to leave. Olivia was actually making eye contact with her for once, speaking directly to her. Annie saw Katherine's hesitation and then a smile on her face. Even from that distance, she could tell it was real. She wondered what Olivia had said, but hoped she'd found a name for her new mother after all.

CHAPTER TWENTY-THREE

ANNIE ARRIVED AT THE SCHOOL A half hour before the morning bell. She went straight to the administration office where Elaine would be waiting. She found her behind the reception desk, working on something at the computer there.

"Hey, good morning." She greeted Annie, her voice falsely bright.

"Good morning." Annie pulled off her coat and laid it over a chair in the waiting area. Elaine held up the flip-up section of the counter and Annie passed through. "Is this what you needed help with?" She gestured at the computer screen. On it was the *Sweet River Lowdown's* home page.

"Not quite. Listen, I thought about it last night, and I'm not sure I'm doing the right thing here, but I feel you have a right to know what's going on. I trust Alex, I do, but..." She looked back at the screen, clicked the mouse and brought up a pending comments page. Annie squinted at the screen and spotted her own name a half dozen times.

"What is this?"

"I showed this to Alex last week. It's an anonymous poster. I've never approved the comments because they sounded like threats. I told Alex, and he asked me to screenshot and send them to him when they come in. He says they aren't really threats, but this last one really gave me a turn."

Annie moved closer to the screen and read aloud. "So you scraped her off, Alex? I guess you treat all women like garbage, disposable. Because that's what you do, isn't it? Something's not working for you, you get rid of it? Poor little Annie. She seemed sweet." Goosebumps crept over her skin, and she tried to shake off the feeling. She didn't like this man thinking of her at all, much less thinking she was little and sweet.

"See, that's pretty creepy." Elaine clicked through to a post. "It was on this." The page had a picture of Alex all by himself, in uniform, standing by his truck. "I posted this when Alex asked." She turned her face to Annie. "Why did he ask me to do that?"

"He has someone sending him letters. He was worried about me and wanted them to know we weren't together. The person seems to read the blog. Did he turn this over to the police?"

"Isn't he the police? I mean, might as well be, right?"

"Yes. He doesn't talk to me about these things so I can't know. Not for sure."

"Did I do right in showing you this?"

"You absolutely did." Annie wondered if she could send a message to Alex's stalker. Maybe if he knew that Alex was suffering over Sam's death, he would go away. "Have you ever responded to this poster?"

"No, Alex told me not to."

"Good. I don't think you should. Do commenters have to leave their email address, create an account, anything like that?"

"No. Alex told me I should fix that, but I have to wait for my nephew to help me. Right now all they have to do is to hit a captcha button to prove they're not a bot."

"So no email address to trace or to reply to." The threads of an idea began to knit together in Annie's head. "Would you reply if I gave you a specific message for him?"

"I'm not sure that's a good idea."

"Can you approve this comment so I can reply?"

"Do you think that would be okay?"

"I do. And I'll tell Alex I asked you to do it."

"Okay." She navigated back to the comment and approved it. "I hope you know what you're doing."

"Me too."

Sitting in front of her computer at her desk in the library, Annie pulled up *The Lowdown*. There was the post with Alex's picture and under it the caption *Warden Alex Moretti, single again.* Followed by a short paragraph stating that Alex was spotted out at Maria's and the Smooth Moose on his own during prime dating hours, so everyone should know what that meant. Annie didn't like to admit it, even to herself, but it hurt a little to think the entire town assumed she'd been dumped. "Shake it off." She said aloud into the silence of the room.

Below she found the comment now approved. It was the only one. Apparently, no one needed to comment on their relationship. Annie chose to see this as a good thing. Now that she was about to do it, she had no idea what to say. She wanted the man to understand that Alex was genuinely sorry, even suffering over Samantha's death. He didn't need some anonymous stalker making things worse. It was time to let it all go.

Alex Moretti is not the man you think he is. I should know, this is Annie. You need to make peace with the past. Forgiveness is the only thing that is going to heal that tear in your soul. Hating Alex is keeping your pain alive. It's time to let it go and move on.'

That seemed right. Forgiveness was the only way to heal. Even if the other person didn't ask for it or deserve it. Annie let these thoughts bump around in her head until the bell rang. She got together the materials she was using to teach the third-graders how to start a research project, and she waited for their teacher to guide them down. The noise and action of the first period carried over into the three other classes she taught that day. The kids were restless and ready for a break. They'd have to wait another few weeks though. SRCA didn't take a break in February like the public schools. They had a long weekend on President's day and then a week at Easter, whenever it landed. This year it would be the last week in March.

By the end of the day, Annie felt like she was ready for a break too. It had been a tiring day, both mentally and emotionally. The kids had been a challenge, but that was nothing new. She liked to teach, but it wasn't her primary gift. Annie had nothing but respect for the men and women who managed to do it full time. The emotional drain had come from checking the comments page about eighteen times. No reply had been posted. Before leaving she'd checked with Elaine, and she confirmed that nothing had appeared.

Although she'd rather go upstairs and take a hot shower when she arrived at her building, she checked in at the bakery. The special that day was mooncakes to celebrate the Lunar New Year. She'd avoided any St. Valentine's Day cookies or cakes since she wasn't a fan of the holiday to begin with. The shop was still decked out in reds, but her lanterns strung at the windows and over the counter were far more cheerful than hearts. They were light and warmth. Her heart was sad and tired. When she walked in, Olivia was at the register ringing up a customer's purchase. She gave the girl a smile while hanging up her purse. When the man stepped away, Annie joined her behind the counter.

"How's business?"

"Excellent." Olivia seemed quite chipper. "I have the inventory done already. Claire helped me."

Annie's brows lifted. "Really, wow. That's a huge help. Thanks. Is Claire out back?"

"Yup. She's prepping for tomorrow. Is it okay if I'm running the front?"

"Yeah, I can see you have the hang of things." Annie knew

it wasn't really her business, but she couldn't help wonder if Olivia's chipper mood had to do with improved relations between her and Katherine. She decided one little question wouldn't hurt. "So…Is someone coming to pick you up tonight?"

Olivia shot her a knowing look. "Yes, *Kate* is picking me up at five thirty."

Annie couldn't help but grin. "You did find a name."

"That's what Mac calls her, and no one else but he does. Her mom and Pete call her Katie, you, Erin and Claire all call her Katherine, so I thought I'd pick something different."

"I'm delighted." Annie patted her on the shoulder. "You're a woman of good sense, Olivia Davis."

"Thank you, Annie."

A blast of cold air rushed into the store and Annie looked up expecting a customer, but it was Alex. Her chest contracted like a baby elephant stood on it, and she watched in fascination as he stalked up to the counter, his face like a storm cloud. She had no time to process her feelings as he gave Olivia a lift of his chin which made her blush, and then he took hold of Annie's arm.

"Hey." She protested as he marched her into the back, past a startled Claire, and out the side door. It exited into the first-floor hallway. He slammed the door behind him and then let her go.

Standing in front of her with his hand on his hips, he seemed to be gathering his calm before he spoke. He took in a breath and in a low, measured voice asked, "What did you think you were doing?"

It was stupid, but she was so glad to see him, to have him near, that she didn't really care that he was angry. She knew a lecture was about to come, but compared to not having him at all, that was okay with her. The smile on her face probably didn't help matters. "I was helping you."

He closed his eyes and rubbed a hand over his forehead. "First I get a call from Mac saying Dorothy Beauchamp called him to let him know 'people' were asking questions only to find out it was you." He threw his hand out in her direction. "Then I get an alert that the blog I've been watching for any posts threatening you has a comment *from you* on it." His jaw was clenched. "What are you doing? I'm trying to keep you safe from this guy, and you're engaging with him? He knows where you live." Alex wasn't shouting, but it was close.

"And I know what happened on Steeple Street." She straightened her spine. "I know that you're not to blame for Samantha's death, and that this guy needs to know that too. You are innocent of Logan's blood, and you're innocent of Sam's. And what I learned from Dorothy Beauchamp is that you're forgiven. She said to tell you that. No one blames you for what happened. You did what you had to do, Alex."

He turned and walked a few steps away, shaking his head. She watched his shoulders rise and fall before he returned to stand in front of her. "You don't know anything. I forced that confrontation, Annie. Don't paint me the hero. For pity's sake, not you." His voice was gruff. "I can't take that from you."

"What are you talking about? The man had a gun."

"It was a starter pistol."

"You didn't know that!"

"If I'd let her talk—"

"Alex, you can't possibly know that." She pleaded with him.

"Yes, I can. Sam was trying to back me down, to back him down. I didn't give her the time. If I had slowed down. If I had waited for backup, I could have prevented all this."

"Alex—"

"No." He waved her words away. "This is my fault. I am taking responsibility for what I did. This is where I make it right."

She realized this was where his theology was failing him. This was the sticking point that everything else hinged on. He needed to understand that grace was given, not earned. "You can't. That's the whole thing. You can't fix it."

He jerked back. "Yes, I can. I'm going to find Eric."

Her mouth dropped open. "So you can let him kill you?"

"No. Eric needs to confront me. He needs to see me take a hit, something like that. I don't know what he'll need, but I have to let him have a chance."

Annie shook her head in disbelief. Eric would work out his feelings on Alex with his fists, and that would somehow make it all okay? Alex would take the pain, the injury, and by some strange, cosmic math he and Eric would be even? Would Eric stop when Alex was bleeding, or would he need to keep going until he was dead? "Do you think you owe your life for what happened?"

Alex pushed his shoulders back, his muscles tight. "I took two lives, Annie."

How could he think that? "No, Sam's responsible for her own actions. You didn't push her out the window, Alex."

He winced, and she wondered if she'd been too blunt. She didn't understand his thought process. As much and as often as they'd talked about faith, Alex had seemed to have a solid understanding of the gospel, of God, but this wasn't right or good. This guilt was poisoning him, and he was counting it virtue.

"Annie, I...your faith in me is something I never asked for, but I treasure it. In this though, it's misplaced. This is a hopeless cause. There's only one way to put things right."

"You are not a hopeless cause. Do you think God's grace is so shallow that it can't cover you?"

"What?"

"Do you think that God is so small, so inadequate, that He can't forgive you? Do you think you're so important, so significant, that His forgiveness can't extend to you? That you have to find a way to earn it for yourself?"

"It doesn't work that way, honey."

"Yes, it does." She balled her fists, her nails biting into her palms. "Your theology is weak. God is not."

"Some things can't be forgiven." He looked down at her with pity as if she was the deluded one.

"You really do think a lot of yourself, don't you?"

"What?" He blinked. "No, you're not understanding. I'm—"

"Beyond redemption? Is that what you really think? That what you did was so evil that you can never be redeemed? Wrong!" She pointed a finger at him. "No one is beyond God's love. Don't you know that verse in Romans? Neither death nor life, neither angels nor demons, neither the present nor the future, nor any powers, neither height nor depth, nor anything else in all creation, will be able to separate us from the love of God." She stood back a bit. "They are my favorite verses. 8:38-39. A way to remember that even when I'm alone, I'm not out of God's reach. I used to read that verse when I felt that there was no one on my side, no one who loved me unconditionally. But you, you need to hear it so you can know that no one is beyond redemption. Ask, and forgiveness is yours."

Alex's eyes grew bright. "I want to believe you, but I have begged for forgiveness." He looked away and then back to her. "So many times. And I don't feel forgiven." He leaned close. "I feel cursed."

She reached up and took his face in her hands. "God loves you, Alex. You are not cursed. But there is nothing you can do to atone for what happened. To feel forgiven you need to accept that it's by His Grace alone, not because of something you did or will do. There's no way to pay for what you did. You could pay with your life, and it wouldn't matter. What matters is that you've repented, that you place your faith in Jesus, and that you put your feet on the path and walk it. And Alex?" She stared up into his eyes. "I believe you're there. You're right there, but you can't raise your hand and take the grace offered, because you think you have to do something to deserve it. The secret is, you don't deserve it. None of us do. The redemption road is for sinners. Christ died because we don't deserve God's grace. The atonement was His."

He closed his eyes. "Why can't I accept that?"

"Because you still think you have to earn it. You can't."

He raised his hands and squeezed hers gently before pulling them away from his face. He blew out a long breath, and she was struck by the signs of exhaustion she hadn't spotted in him until now. There were dark circles under his eyes and a scruff on his chin, unusual for him. He reached out and stroked her cheek before letting his hand fall to his side. "I'm strung out, Annie. I feel like I've got nothing left. I'm listening, I promise I am, but I'm not sure how much I can take in. I feel like this is all I can do. I have to find Eric or let him find me, and it's got to be done. I'm tired of running, of hiding. I'm done being the rabbit." His head tilted to the side as he looked down at her. The silence stretched between them before he spoke, his voice broken. "I didn't want any of this to touch you."

"What are we to each other, Alex? What are we going to be to each other?" She hoped all she felt for him showed on her face. "You said what hurts me hurts you. Did you mean it? Did putting us on pause stop you from feeling?"

"No, of course, it didn't." He looked down at his hands.

"Well, it didn't for me either. I..." She wanted to say love, but it was too soon. Her own heart wasn't ready to hear that out loud, and she doubted his was either. "What happens to you matters to me. If you hurt, I hurt."

His eyes shot to hers. "I don't want to hurt you. I wanted to keep you safe. Don't you get that?"

"What is the point of 'safe' if it keeps us apart?"

"Annie—"

She'd had about enough of the safety lecture. Instead of listening to whatever he had to say next, she put her arms around him. "It doesn't matter. I won't leave you even if you leave me."

He held her, and they stood inside each other's embrace for long enough for her arms to ache. His body shook, and she held him tighter. "You're killing me." His words sounded choked out.

"Don't be silly." She fought off the tears clogging her throat. "I'm rescuing you."

He dropped his head to her shoulder, his face in her hair. "You can't rescue me."

"Maybe not, but I can try." She slowly let go of him but held his hands in hers. "I'm not going to give up on you, Alex Moretti. Not for anything. I'm going to be right here, doing my best to help you, whether you want me to or not. What else can I do? You're in my heart."

He closed his eyes and shook his head. "That's my fault."

"No, it isn't. It was my choice." She let go of his hands, hers going to her hips. "I could have let you sit at your table in the corner by yourself and never said a word."

"But I—"

"It doesn't matter anyway. We're together now, even if we are on 'pause.'" She mimed air quotes. "Hearts don't have pause buttons. Now, would you like to come in for a mooncake?"

He smirked at her change of subject. "Will Claire hit me with something if I do?"

"I can't make any promises there, since she isn't particularly happy with you."

"I'm not happy with myself, so there's that." He shrugged.

"Are you ever?" Annie asked it in jest, but the look on Alex's face answered for him. She reached out and grabbed his arm, tugging him toward the door. "Come on, I'll feed you, and then you'll feel better."

They walked past Claire who glared at them with narrowed eyes, and Annie picked up two mooncakes. She towed Alex to his usual table and sat him down, returning a minute later with coffee for him and tea for her. "Did he ever reply? On the blog comment?"

Alex shook his head. "Elaine gave me her admin login. I set an alert so that I'm emailed if any new comment appears, approved or not. I've got nothing."

"Maybe he hasn't seen it yet."

"I hope he doesn't." He gave her a stern look. "You know that wasn't smart. I don't want him seeing you as a target."

"Do you know who he is?"

"I think it's Eric, her brother."

A jolt of fear hit her chest, and she rubbed at it. "Dorothy told me to warn you that she thinks he's here, in Maine. I meant to tell you the minute I got back." She bit her lip.

Alex shook his head. "Doesn't matter. It's a warning I don't need since he is. He was spotted at a campground less than an hour from here."

Annie gasped.

"Oh, it gets worse. He nailed the last letter to my door, and I'm pretty sure he was leaving as I arrived to find it."

"I didn't know." Annie covered her mouth with her hand. The situation seemed much more severe all of a sudden.

"No, and that's my fault. I didn't want you to worry, didn't want you to have to deal with any of it, so I kept things from you. Turns out that was a mistake. I'm sorry."

"Well, the same goes for me. I should have come right to you after talking with Dorothy, but I lost my nerve. I'm sorry I'm only telling you this now. But, from now on, if it involves me or not, I want to know what's going on."

"I'll do my best, but Annie, I really don't want you involved in this. No more visits to the old neighborhood, no digging around like Nancy Drew, and no commenting on that blog." He pointed a finger at her.

"Okay. Fine." She sipped her tea. "But don't hate on Nancy Drew. Those books are the best." She looked over at her shelves. "I'm sure I have one you could borrow."

He carefully folded his hands on the table in front of him. A sign, she'd learned, of his effort to be patient with her. "I'm serious, Annie."

"So am I. Nancy Drew is the best."

He laid his forehead on his hands. "An-n-ie."

"Sorry. I'll stop teasing you. I wanted to break the mood. I promise I'm not going to play Nancy Drew anymore."

His head lifted. "I'm trying to believe you." His eyes scanned her face, spending more time on her lips than anywhere else. "I miss you."

"I miss you too."

"It's going to be over soon. We think we know where Eric has been staying. Just have to catch him there."

"We?"

"Mac has been helping me with this. The department too."

"Good." A wave of relief swept through her. "I was hoping you weren't John Wayne-ing it."

"Not that dumb." His lips tipped up. "Now do you see you don't have to get involved?"

Annie didn't see that at all, but she did feel better knowing that Alex wasn't on his own. "Still, I'm glad I wrote that comment. It was what he needed to hear. If that's Eric, he has to know that he needs to forgive you if he wants to move on with this life. He can't keep carrying that hate around. If he showed up here, I'd tell him the same thing."

He reached out and took her hand. "What am I going to do with you?"

Love me. The words popped into her mind, but there was no way she'd say that out loud. Instead, she shrugged. "You don't need to do anything. I've got your back." She smiled, but he didn't look pleased. He looked heavenward as if praying for patience. She wanted to say something comforting, but nothing was coming to her mind. She looked up too and saw the string of red lanterns there, cheerfully twinkling against the dark glass. "Do you like my lanterns?"

He looked back at her as if she had three heads and they were all revolving. It made her laugh out loud.

CHAPTER TWENTY-FOUR

IT WAS ANOTHER LONG DAY WITH students in desperate need of a day off. Luckily, they'd have one tomorrow. It was the Friday before the holiday and a professional day. The kids would be home, and Annie would have hours in the library with no one to interrupt her work. Sheer bliss after a day like today. She had picked up her mail after leaving school and was trying to juggle both that and her book bag to get her keys in the lock at the back door of her building.

"Annie Caldwell?"

She spun around and saw a man standing a few yards away from her. No one came to the back alley other than the business owners and staff. She didn't recognize this man. He had grubby jeans on and work boots, but his jacket said military. A knit cap was shoved down over his hair, and a full beard hid his face. A jolt of fear hit her. Her skin began to prickle. Beyond him, at the mouth of the alley, a white pickup truck idled. Annie wasn't sure, but she thought she saw someone sitting in the cab.

"So, you're Annie." The man was smiling at her, but there was nothing good or right in that grin. It was sarcastic. "I'm not surprised. You're his type, all curves and sweetness." His eyes ran over her from her boots to her hair, but it didn't feel predatory. More like an inventory. He was sizing her up. "So, Annie." He walked towards her but stopped when she took a step back. He stuffed his hands in his pockets. "I got your message."

"You did." She realized that this was Eric. It had to be. The blood began to pound in her veins as adrenaline rushed through her.

"Yeah, you think Alex is sorry. But I'm not sure I agree." He was soft-spoken, even if his words scared her, his tone didn't, almost like he was making an effort not to be frightening.

"Alex is truly remorseful for what happened." Her heart was beating so hard, she could barely speak. "I don't know how I can convince you of that, but it's true."

"He feels bad. That's nice. My sister is still dead, and it's his fault. He needs to pay."

"With his life?" Her words came out in a rush.

"I'm not going to kill him." Eric leaned in slightly, not enough to spook her, but enough that she could feel the intensity of the anger he was holding in check. "I want his life to be over, but I want him to still be breathing. I want him to walk through the next fifty years–whatever he has left–a ghost. He took her life, he pays with his. No career, no pretty, rich girlfriend." His eyes scanned her face again. "No happy ending."

"What if I decide I'm not going to let that happen?"

She saw a flicker of doubt in his eyes and somehow she knew that he couldn't be the kind of man to hurt an innocent person. This man was not a danger to her. He was more of a danger to himself. That didn't stop her from shaking. She tried to calm her racing heart with a slow, even breath, but her lungs weren't cooperating.

His gaze on her was assessing. "Thing is, Annie. Alex is eventually going to leave you behind. So go ahead, try to save him. He's not about to let you." His lips curved up into a slow, sneering grin. "I know my old friend very well. He used to think he was God's gift, the big man in control of his own destiny. I ended that." His voice dripped with satisfaction. "I made him leave the job he worked so hard for, the job that let him walk all over anyone he wanted to. I separated him from the family that thought he could do no wrong. He left them behind. It's not a stretch to make him leave you too." Eric turned away. "Be sure to tell him I said hi." He spat the words over his shoulder.

"I'm not going to let him leave." Annie surprised herself with those words.

Eric spun back around. The smile on his face was gone, replaced by a kind of bleak resignation. "Then I'll ruin you too."

She shook her head in disbelief.

"Don't doubt it, Annie." He warned, and she watched as he walked away. With her heart still pounding, she fumbled in her pocket and pulled out her cell. At the mouth of the alley, Eric got in the truck. It was gone so fast she didn't have the chance to get a plate. She held the phone to her ear, waiting for Alex to answer. When he didn't, she let herself into her building with shaking fingers and ran up the steps to her apartment. Once inside she locked the door and threw the deadbolt. She got out her phone and tried Alex again. Still no answer so she called Pete instead. He'd know how to get a hold of Alex and Mac. They needed to know that Eric was in town. When Pete answered, it took her a second to get the words out.

"What's goin' on, sweetheart? I can't understand you."

"He was here. At my building, downstairs. Eric. The guy that's been threatening Alex. I tried to call him, and I can't get a hold of him. Pete, you need to get to Alex. He needs to know this man is here, in town."

"Take a breath, Annie." Pete's voice was stern. "Sit down. Is your door locked?"

"Yes, knob and deadbolt, but he walked away. I'm pretty sure he's gone."

"Stay there. Keep your phone where you can reach it. I'll call you as soon as I can." The call disconnected. Annie took off her coat and put away her bag, all with her phone in her hand. Her heart was still racing, and she sat on the couch trying to calm it. Hobbes waddled over to her and hopped up on her lap, meowing in her face.

"Give me a second, boy, and I will feed you." She scratched

under his chin and then pulled his soft, little body into her chest, cuddling him. He didn't love it, but he didn't claw her either. "Thank you for tolerating my hug." She kissed the top of his head and then let him go. The buzzer sounded at her door. She hopped up and went to the video screen she'd had installed by her front door. Relief coursed through her veins when she saw it was Alex. She held down the button to let him in and waited until she heard his feet on her steps. She opened the door the second he knocked. "Alex—" She was interrupted by a hard, warm body knocking into her knees. "Shep!" She reached down and rubbed his ears while he wiggled and tried to kiss every inch of her face.

Alex barked a command at him, and he sat on his haunches, still wiggling. His one floppy ear vibrated with his happy shivers. Alex locked her door behind them. She was worried he was about to shout, to tell her that he had warned her, told her this would happen, so she braced for the lecture. Instead, he pulled her into his arms, crushing her into his chest. "Annie, are you okay?"

"I'm fine. Better now that you're here." In the distance, she could hear the faint sound of a siren. "I'm so glad you were close by. Did you see him? Was he still down there?"

Alex had no chance to answer. A low, guttural sound came from the direction of the couch, and she turned in time to see Hobbes, his back curved in an arc, his fur on end, launch himself at Shep, claws out. "No, Hobbes!" She reached for him, but Alex was faster, and he swooped the cat up. He held the spitting, clawing ball of fur out at arm's length. Annie ran to the hall closet and opened it. "In here."

Alex gently tossed Hobbes inside, and Annie slammed the door shut. Hobbes could still be heard growling through the door. Annie looked at Shep who was still sitting where Alex had commanded him, but he was looking a bit shell-shocked.

"Poor puppy." She went to him and patted his head. "That was Hobbes, and he's a bit mad. I'm terribly sorry."

"He's going to need to get used to Shep or used to that closet, because the dog stays until Eric is sitting in a cell." Alex's words were clipped, a muscle ticked in his jaw.

"Okay. I'll find a way for them to get along."

Alex seemed surprised she hadn't argued. Then again, he probably didn't know how scared she'd been. It was one thing to bravely post a comment that she thought might get her in trouble, but quite another to have trouble arrive on her doorstep.

The buzzer sounded again, and Alex went to the door, checked the screen, and hit the button. "Deputy MacAlister is coming up. You know him, right?" She nodded. "He has Pete with him."

"Why Pete?"

"He's going to stay with you for a few hours. Until we can be sure Eric isn't hanging around waiting for me to go."

"Oh right, do you think he'd do that?"

"No. I think he wanted to scare you and send me a message."

"He said to say 'hi.'" She crossed her arms over her stomach. "I don't know why he said that. It's weird."

Alex pulled her close again. "Don't say anything else until they're up here. I want you to only have to go through it once. For now." He kissed her forehead and then let her go. She stood back as he opened the door. Pete was first through the door.

He gave her a hug and then held her at arm's length. "You okay?" She nodded. Pete towed her over to the couch and had her sit. Mac stood in front of her. He was in full uniform and had his notebook pulled out. All business. She began to shake. It made no sense since now she was safe, but the tremors kept up.

Alex sat down beside her and put an arm around her shoulders. "Mac, Pete, take a seat, will you?"

Mac pulled a stool over from the kitchen and perched at the edge of it. "Okay. Let's go through what happened, as best you can remember. Go slow and don't leave anything out. You can take as much time as you need."

"Got it." She took a deep breath. "I came home from work, and I had my mail with me, so I was having trouble opening the back door." Step by step she led them through what happened and what Eric had said. When she got to the part where Eric said he'd ruin her too, Alex was holding on to her so hard, his fingers were digging into her shoulder.

"We need to put him in a cell." Alex was almost vibrating with anger. "We pull out the stops, throw everything we can at this. He can't be far. We know he's in a white pickup now, that's something."

Mac narrowed his eyes at Alex but addressed Annie next. "The person in the waiting truck. Male or female?"

"I can't be sure, but they were large. If I'd had to guess, I would say a man."

"Passenger side or driver's?"

She scanned her memory. "Driver's side."

"Okay, that helps. Anything else you can tell us about the truck?"

"It seemed older, not new." She tried to pull up a picture of it in her memory. "Rust, it had rust at the bottom of the door."

"That's helpful. Thank you." Mac closed his notebook and turned to Alex. "Not sure how I feel about you heading out."

"I know what he looks like."

"We've got that picture I got of him. It's enough." He pulled his phone out of his pocket. "Which reminds me." He thumbed over the screen and turned it to Annie. "This him?"

She looked at the picture. It was from a distance and not the best detail, but she had no doubt. "It's him." She felt a frisson of fear skate over her skin and shivered.

Alex rubbed her back. "He's not getting anywhere near you. I promise you that."

She looked up at Mac. "You're going to take care of him, right?" She didn't mean Eric, and he knew it. He stared down at her. She had exchanged a handful of words with Deputy MacAlister over the almost year she'd been in Sweet River. He wasn't the sort of outgoing, friendly man that you might otherwise find yourself chatting with. His expression was stony about seventy percent of the time she interacted with him. She'd seen him be jovial, she'd even seen him smile, but he saved all of that for those close to him. As she looked up at him now, she willed him to understand how much Alex meant to her and that he had to come back to her in one piece. He had to. Mac's expression never changed, but he did nod. She took that as a solemn vow.

"Annie, don't worry. We're going to get this guy, and this will all be over soon." Alex kissed her forehead and got off the couch. "Keep Shep with you. Pete can walk him when he needs it. I'll call when I can."

"Okay." She resisted the urge to grab onto his arm and drag him back down with her. Alex and Mac took their leave, and Pete poked around her kitchen. She was about to ask him what he was doing when she saw him put the kettle on. "How very British of you."

Pete raised an eyebrow at her.

"The cure for any upset. Put the kettle on." She shrugged.

After Pete handed her a mug of tea, she wrapped her cold fingers around it, hoping the warmth would penetrate the cold dread she was feeling. She closed her eyes and prayed that God would watch over Alex and keep him safe.

"You calm?" Mac looked him over as they walked to his cruiser.

"No." Alex might as well be honest. His body was humming with tension like a live wire. He was wound tight, ready to spring.

"Give me a good reason not to leave you at the station when I head out."

"I can't just sit there, Mac. I know my limits. I'd do something stupid." Alex held up his hand. "I promise I will do what you say, but you have to let me work this. I'll lose my mind waiting."

"Great," Mac muttered.

Alex wondered if what he'd said would be enough.

"Get in." Mac got into the car.

Alex got in on the other side, relief flooding through him.

Mac turned to face him. "Don't make me regret this." And he pulled out of the parking lot. They headed to the station, and Alex tried to be patient. He wanted to be out and doing something, not conferring with anyone, not checking in with the chief. Mac must have sensed his mood. He called over the radio. "I need to check to see if a Kevin Pelletier has a white pickup truck registered to him."

Alex waited until Mac was off. "You think Eric is working with him? Like I said before, he's a nasty piece of work from the old neighborhood, but I had no dealings with him. Why would he hook up with Eric?"

"Total wild guess. We gotta start somewhere since you're about to come out of your skin."

"I wish you were wrong, but you're not."

Mac huffed and returned his attention to driving. They were about a minute from the station when he swung his head Alex's direction. "Tell her you're serious."

"What?"

"You clearly love her, she loves you. You don't have to have the ceremony tomorrow or anything, but you need to do right by her, and that means to declare your intentions. The only honorable intention you could have at this point is marriage. Seems pretty clear you haven't mentioned where this thing between you is going. You need to do that."

"Boy, you certainly speak your mind, don't you?" He shook his head.

"Life's short. I lost my first wife because I had my head—" He didn't finish that thought. "Don't be stupid. Love is hard to find. It's pretty clear you love her. Since you've found a woman who would die for you if she had to, then I'd advise making it official."

"Annie would die for me?"

"Easily. Written all over her." Mac barked out a laugh. "For an ex-cop, you aren't too observant."

Alex would have had an answer for that, but they'd pulled up to the station. By the time they were through the doors and at the sergeant's desk, they had the answer. Pelletier did have a white pickup registered to him. What's more, now they had a plate. Mac sent out the BOLO, and Alex felt a kind of calm rush over him. Now he had something to go on. They weren't flying blind anymore.

Hours later, he wasn't feeling calm so much as bored. He and Mac had been over every inch of town, and all the way out to the campground where Eric had been spotted. Nothing. They drove back to the station, and Alex called Annie to check in. When she answered the phone, her voice sounded sleepy. It was a sweet sound.

"Hey. News?"

"No, honey. Same as before." He'd updated her two hours earlier with the same lack of information. "I wanted to talk to you one more time before you went to bed, but it sounds like you're already there."

"No, it's okay. Pete's dozing on the couch, and Shep and I are cuddled up reading a book. He's a total bed hog."

Alex closed his eyes. "Tell me you are not letting that dog sleep on your bed."

"Why not? He's warm." He heard her shifting around, jingling dog tags, and Shep's happy groan. She must be petting him.

"Where does he sleep at your house?"

"On his bed, which is on the floor. You're going to spoil my dog." He forgot where he was when he heard Mac's snickering laugh.

"Whatever. Maybe I'll keep him." She laughed. "Although, the needing to go outside to pee thing is annoying. Cats are far superior in their bathroom habits."

Alex had to laugh. "You're right about that. Listen, go back to bed. It's a bust tonight. I'm going to catch some z's in the back room at the station and set out again tomorrow."

Mac pulled up at the station, and they got out of the car. He let Mac go into the station first and waited outside to finish with Annie.

"So I should tell Pete to go home now?"

"Yes. The Captain agreed to put a deputy outside your building tonight."

"Aw, that makes me feel better."

"I'm glad. Tell the old man he can go home, and you get some sleep."

"I will. Goodnight, Alex."

"Goodnight. Hey, wait!"

"What is it?"

"When this is over, I want to talk about...us. Like where we're going. I know we've danced around that, or well I have, and I know we've had some false starts, and those were on me too. But you need to know where I stand, and I want you to know—" He broke off. "Are you laughing?"

"I can't help it." She snickered into the phone. "If you were here I'd kiss you to get it to stop."

"What?"

"Your run-away mouth. I thought it was only my disease, but I guess it's catching."

"Hilarious."

"Don't be mad. Just imagine that I kissed you, and now you can form a thought again. I really do want to hear what you're thinking."

"Oh, no. Now you have to wait."

"What? That's cruel."

"Okay, I'll give you a hint. Mac told me it's time I declared my intentions."

"Oh?" She sounded a whole lot less certain. "And, what are your intentions?"

"Those you'll have to wait for."

"You mean man."

"Let's wait until we're face to face."

"Okay. That sounds reasonable."

"Goodnight, Annie."

"Goodnight, Alex."

CHAPTER TWENTY-FIVE

ANNIE DROVE TO ALEX'S HOUSE TO let Shep eat and pick up his doggie dishes. Alex had given her a key when they were seeing each other almost nightly and hadn't asked for it back. He'd probably forgotten all about it. Annie figured she could grab the things Shep needed and set him up near the kitty counter in her kitchen. Maybe if Hobbes could smell Shep's food and see he was set up to stay, he'd calm down.

Shep rode shotgun. Other than occasionally giving her a sloppy doggy kiss, he'd been a perfect passenger. "Here we are." She parked at the end of his driveway and hopped out. Shep was dancing on his seat. She let him out, and he raced up the porch steps, snuffling the whole way. "Smell some squirrels, buddy?" He was snorting at the door as she opened it. "Go find your dish." She put her bag down and closed the door. Shep ran around the living room sniffing at things. "Weirdo."

She went into the kitchen, found his dog food and scooped some into his dish. "Breakfast!" He popped his head in and then circled around the house again. Then she heard a yelp, a bang, and Shep barking. She ran out into the hallway.

A man stood between her and the front entry, his hand pressed against the door to the basement. A slow, lecherous smile snaked across his face. He had long, dirty-blond hair that was tied back in a ponytail. Shorter pieces of his lank hair hung loose. He was dressed all in black and had several large, thick rings on his fingers. "Well, look what we have here. The Mrs."

Her heart stopped.

Eric came into view behind him. They must have been hiding in the basement. He shook his head. "Annie. I told you to steer clear of this."

She tried to take a breath, but her chest felt tight, and her skin tingled. Fainting felt like a real possibility. All her focus switched to remaining upright. Blacking out would be a disaster in this situation.

"This is the rich girlfriend, right?" The blond man scanned her, but he wasn't taking an inventory, he was leering.

Her lip curled. "Get out."

"We were waiting here to put the hurt on him, but now we have you." The man stood away from the door as Shep scratched and dug at it. "Don't worry, that will hold him." He said over his shoulder. "Now, what are we going to do with you?" He walked towards her, and she backed away. "Where you headed, honey?"

Annie turned around and bolted for the back door. The man caught her, pulling her toward him. "Oh, no, you're not leaving." He grabbed a fist-full of her hair. The sharp pain hit her, and she cried out. He pressed her face-first against the wall. "Eric, take a look in her purse and get out her cell and her wallet."

"No."

The man let go of her, and she slumped against the wall. He shoved a hand in her back, pinning her there. "What do you mean no?"

"She's not in this, Kevin. I'm not about to hurt a woman. Call Alex here, fine. But we don't hurt her." He pointed at Annie.

"I'm not going hurt her." Kevin laughed. "We're going to take her money." He pointed at her purse. "Get out her wallet. She's probably got cards in there, but we want"—he turned to Annie—"bank account info."

"She's not in this," Eric repeated.

"Uh, she's here, so she is."

"No."

"Hey man, we gotta be fluid in our thinking. This girl landing in our laps is a bonus. She's rich, right? We get her to give us the money for the boat, and we skate. No need to mess with Moretti.

No need for the law."

"I'm not stealing her money. What Alex has, he owes me. That's different."

"You are delusional. We've got all we need right here. Give me her purse."

"I'm not doing this. We let her stay, fine. She sits someplace while we get Alex here and follow the plan."

"Plan has changed."

"Kevin..."

In a flash, Kevin struck out, his fist connecting with Eric's temple in a sickening thud. Eric dropped to the floor, senseless. Annie tried to run, but it was too late. Kevin's hand and his rings connected with her cheek. She staggered as a blinding pain tore through her face.

"I knew this kid wouldn't have the stomach." He kicked Eric's still form in the side. "It takes some grit to get it done." He raised his boot and kicked the man's head. Annie, hands covering her face, melted against the wall, her knees about to give out. The man pointed at her. "Don't even think about moving from that spot." Grabbing Eric's ankles, he towed him out the door.

Annie stood up, and her head swam. She needed to move fast if she had any hope of escape. The door banged open again, and Kevin stood in the frame.

"Good to see you cooperating. Now let's get your wallet and get this over with."

Alex walked into the station feeling the last eighteen hours in his bones. He never wanted to see the inside of a police cruiser again. Mac was a machine. They'd checked out every lead, every sighting, and come up empty-handed. All he wanted to do now was go home, have a long, hot shower and sleep for a decade. He headed for the lockers where he'd left his keys, intent on going home at least for a few hours.

"Hey, Moretti!"

He turned around. The desk sergeant was waving him over.

"Some guy has been looking for you. Called about eight times. Edward Caldwell?" He handed Alex a stack of messages.

"What?" Alex snatched the messages out of his hands. "No." He muttered as he read Annie's father's increasingly anxious calls. He pulled out his cell and dialed the number. Edward picked up immediately.

"Is this Alex?"

"Yes, sir. I got your messages. How long ago did you get the call that her account was emptied?"

"An hour ago. I've called her possibly twenty times since. She does not answer. Her phone immediately goes to voicemail. It's not possible. She has never failed to answer a call from me. I've tried her business. They insist she has not been in today. I tried the school, and they say this is a half-day for them and that she never arrived. This is impossible, Alex. Please tell me my daughter is okay."

"She will be. I promise. I'm going to find her, and I'll call you the second I have her with me. I promise." He repeated it. He could hear Edward's ragged breath. "Do you know where the money went?"

"No. The account was emptied into an online exchange. Bitcoin. It could have gone anywhere." He paused. "Alex, my daughter is...my life." His voice broke, and Alex wished with all his heart that Annie was hearing this instead of him.

"She's mine too. I swear to you I will find her."

"Then go." The call disconnected. Alex shoved his phone into his pocket and bolted for the door.

Alex slowly approached his house through the woods. He'd spotted Annie's car but no other vehicles. If they'd arrived on foot, they could have come from any angle. There was no point in looking since he'd already caught movement at one of the windows. He knew he was dealing with one and possibly two suspects and one hostage, Annie. He hadn't called for backup. It might be the biggest mistake he'd ever made, but he had a feeling this was going to go sideways if any uniforms arrived. He hadn't called Mac or Pete either. On instinct alone, he'd gone to the house believing that the only way out was to offer himself up. Get them to release her and then fight his way out—at least, he hoped that was the way it would go.

He crept up beside her car. The back door to the house was not a great approach. The front was the only way to go. He could hear a muffled bark. Shep was alive and probably in the closet if these guys had half a brain. If Eric was in there, they definitely did. Eric had never been stupid when they were young. He was the cautious one. He was the thoughtful one. When they were growing up, it was Eric's words of caution that had kept them out of trouble. How could it have come to this? As he moved, he spotted a body prone in his driveway. He looked closer. It was Eric. Darting out, he grabbed hold and pulled him behind the SUV.

Checking for a pulse, he found one. It was strong and steady. He rolled him over, spotting the nasty cut to his head. Kevin must have pistol-whipped him or worse and thrown him out into the snow. Had he stood up for Annie? Alex slapped Eric's cheek to see if he could get him to come round. The man opened his eyes, blinking rapidly. Alex prayed and waited for him to wake up. This situation was dire. He needed God to guide him. God needed to be the one calling the shots. "Hey." He whispered and slapped Eric on the cheek again. Eric took a deep breath and opened his eyes, focusing on Alex.

"Alex..." his voice was weak, but he was breathing okay and speaking, two very good signs.

"Can you tell me what happened in there?" He jerked his head at the house.

It took a while, but Eric looked around, and Alex could tell he was getting his bearings. "Kevin's got your girl. He's trying to take her money."

"He already emptied her accounts."

Eric tried to sit up but fell back and put his hand to his head, blinking rapidly. "I'm sorry. I tried to stop him."

"It's just Kevin in there?"

Eric nodded. "This is my fault. He said we could live like kings in Florida on your severance package from the cops. Said you'd walked away with a pile. I didn't want you dead, Alex. I wanted you alive to suffer. I'm so sorry, I didn't mean for any of this to happen."

"Annie's inside?"

"I tried to stop him, and he clocked me." Eric sat up, his back against the tire of the car. "Kevin's all about the cash. If your girl gave the money to him, he'll be thinking about getting out. I don't think he'd actually hurt her."

"Kevin Pelletier? You know he ran drugs? He was Logan's supplier. He beat a dealer so bad he ended up in the hospital. How did you end up with Kevin?"

"I messed up." Eric's face crumbled. "I couldn't see straight after Sam died. Kevin met me at Flanagan's after the funeral, and what he said made sense. I fell for it. I'm sorry Alex, it all got away from me. I didn't want to hurt her."

It all got away from him. How familiar was that? "I know. I know." He held Eric up by his shoulders. "

Eric held his head up. "I'm okay." A trickle of blood ran from his nose. Alex let him go.

"Annie doesn't deserve whatever's about to happen if we don't get in that house."

"He's carrying." Eric nodded to his right. "Right hip. If he's got her money already, he'll probably take her car and run. He'll get another ride quick enough. This guy has a network you wouldn't believe."

"And you trusted him?" Alex looked at his old friend. Eric might have been through the wringer, but he was the same man. Grief had touched him, but it hadn't changed him so far as he'd be willing to take a life. He was still in there, somewhere.

"I hope you never have a reason to be angry enough to be as blind as I've been." Eric brushed the blood off his forehead.

Alex pulled a napkin out of his pocket and shoved it into Eric's hand. "You understand what happened that night now, don't you?" Alex locked eyes with his friend. "It's one mistake. One bad decision is all it takes and then the rest falls like dominoes. I never meant to hurt Sam. I wanted to keep her safe. That night it was like everything moved too fast, and it flew right out of my hands and went so wrong…" Alex couldn't go on. He didn't have the words. The silence stretched between them for a matter of seconds, but it felt like an hour.

Eric's eyes slowly closed. "Too much blood."

Alex started fishing through his pockets for another napkin, but Eric reached out and grabbed his hand. "That's not what I mean. I think it's mostly stopped." He touched his forehead. "I mean, her blood. I wanted yours to pay for hers, but now it's your Annie who's doing the bleeding." Each word was a punch to Alex's gut. "We stop it here." Eric reached out and grabbed onto Alex's jacket and pulled himself up. He tipped his head back to look over the bed of the truck at the house and then turned to Alex. "He locked the dog up in the stairs to the basement, and the thing is making a ton of noise. That ought to give us some cover. I spotted him by that picture window in front, so I bet they're in the living room now. I say we go right through the window. You got a couple of big rocks right here. We smash the window in and jump through. He'll be distracted and might not have time to get to his weapon. If he does, he can't get both of us."

For some reason, Alex found himself smiling. "Guess I'm glad I've got a soldier on my side."

"I'm on her side."

Alex winced, but he knew he should be glad to hear that since Annie was going to need them both. It still hurt to know Eric hadn't, or maybe couldn't, forgive him.

Eric lifted his chin. "You ready?"

Everything hurt. Her face most of all. Kevin's rings were not ornamentation. Apparently, he'd worn them for maximum damage since he'd used them with maximum effect on her face. It had only taken one punch before she'd made the call he'd asked for and transferred the remainder of her entire trust fund, all fifty thousand dollars, to him. He'd been very disappointed that it wasn't larger. So disappointed that he'd kicked her in the ribs enough that she was sure at least two were fractured, if not broken. She was praying he was finally done. "You have the money. It's all I have. I promise you that."

"You look like money. You got rich parents?"

"My mother is a socialite with no control of her own accounts. My father owns an arbitration firm. They have diplomatic clients. He has policies in place that prevent ransom demands. You'll get nothing for me. Call him, and you'll see."

He looked down at her. "Maybe." He seemed to be making

calculations as his eyes scanned her face. She was sitting on the couch, a trickle of blood flowing down her cheek from a cut, courtesy of one of his rings. She probably looked as bedraggled as she felt. At least, she hoped that she did. The way he was looking at her, this situation could go wrong in a whole different way.

"Fifty thousand." His head tipped to the side, his eyes fixed on her face. "That's not a lot for my trouble."

"How much did you expect to get out of Alex?"

"Nothing." He smirked. "Eric needed a reason to take things to the next level, so I sold him a line about Alex getting a settlement." He shrugged his shoulders. "I just wanted to kill the guy. He cost me a lot of money when he shot Logan. Having Eric around to take the blame was handy." He moved closer to her, his face an inch from hers. "I don't forgive, and I for sure do not forget. Moretti thinks I'm a joke. Now he knows different." He reached out and grabbed a fist-full of her hair. Her eyes watered as a sharp pain spread across the back of her head. His eyes were searching her face again. "I need to send a message--meth, heroine, coke, whatever it is, you deal it, you work with me. Get in my way, you die. Killing Moretti is going to do that nicely. Question is, what do I do with you?"

Annie was already scared, so his drug lord posturing barely registered. What did was that she was probably going to die, and this man was likely to make it hurt. As soon as that thought settled, it was swamped by her fear for how Alex would react if he found her broken body on his living room floor. It would break him. That wasn't her ego talking, it was a deep conviction that he simply wouldn't survive the guilt of another death.

Annie had been praying nearly non-stop while in the presence of this horrible man, and she knew that the moment her eyes closed on this earth they would open in heaven. Here would be pain, but it would end. Alex though… Her heart ached enough that she didn't really feel the fear anymore. She looked up at Kevin and saw him for what he was, a childish, selfish man utterly devoid of empathy, bent on pleasing himself, deeply insecure and in need of salvation.

"I don't think your quarrel is really with Alex. You know that this life is not all we have. There is a God in heaven who cares what you do, cares for your soul—"

"Really?" He threw his head back and laughed. "Are you seriously going to preach to me?" He sighed. "This is hilarious. Who do you think you are?" He jerked the fist wrapped in her hair so hard she couldn't hold back a cry of pain. In the distance she could hear Shep's paws pounding on the door to the basement. "I'm the only god in the room, baby girl." He let go of her hair and stepped back.

Annie knew what was probably coming next. "I'm rather keen on getting whatever it is you're going to do over with."

"Smart mouth." He grabbed her chin, and she braced. The hit, when it came, wasn't worse than the others, but stars still danced in front of her eyes. He pulled her upright and drew his arm back. A moment later the world exploded, and all around her she heard the sound of splintering wood, rushing paws, breaking glass, and bodies hitting the floor. When she opened her eyes, she saw Kevin on the floor in a pool of blood, Shep standing over him. The edges of her vision grew dim, and blackness descended.

"Edward?"

"Alex." The word seemed to rush out of the man like air from a balloon. "Please tell me this is good news."

"I have her. She's okay."

"Thank God." Annie's father's voice broke.

"She's gonna need to go to the hospital—"

"What? You said she was okay?" Edward's tone changed, his voice even, but angry.

"She's hurt, but not bad. I'll take care of her, I promise."

"What hospital." The words were clipped. In the background of the call, Alex could hear him moving. There were sounds of a drawer opening and shutting.

"Not sure yet. The ambulance is on its way." Alex was sitting on his front steps, Annie in his arms, a blanket wrapped around her. She had regained consciousness, but she wasn't quite with it yet. He'd gotten her out of the mess in his living room and into the fresh air to see if that helped. She was awake, her head on his shoulder, but not speaking. It was probably shock, so he kept her close and warm, hoping that would do until the EMTs arrived. In the distance he could hear sirens approaching. Behind him Eric was slumped with his back against the house, Shep by his side, leaning into him. Apparently, Shep was not a dog to hold a grudge. After a few careful overtures he'd forgiven Eric and let him pet his ears.

"I'm leaving for the airport now. Call me when she's admitted and give me the hospital's information. I also want to know the name of the attending physician."

"Um. Sure." Alex watched a police cruiser speed down his driveway and come to a halt behind his truck. Mac knifed out of the driver's side and started towards Alex. "I gotta go, Edward. I will call you soon."

"I'll likely be in transit. Leave a message." And he disconnected the call.

Mac stopped a few feet from the porch, planted his feet, and folded his arms over his chest. "Details, Moretti. And this better be good."

CHAPTER TWENTY-SIX

ALEX SAT ON A PLASTIC CHAIR in the exam room while a doctor stitched a three-inch gash in Eric's forehead closed. Eric was wincing, his fingers digging into his thighs. The pain was probably excruciating. He'd refused the numbing shot saying he didn't want a needle so close to his eye. Alex doubted that was true. More likely, he wanted to suffer because he felt the burden to atone. They'd both seen Annie loaded into the ambulance crying and confused. They knew that Kevin had worked her over. Alex had been wild with rage--Eric had been silent with guilt. Either way, they were both told to get in the second ambulance. Well…Alex was more pulled away than told. Mac was a whole lot stronger than he looked.

A strange kind of calm had descended on Alex since they'd reached the hospital. Thoughts were skating around in his head. They sounded a lot like the things Annie had been telling him. In trying to atone for Samantha's death, he'd led Eric into a situation where he'd risked Annie's life, and now he was saddled with that same guilt. It was a horrible cycle. Like Eric said, the bleeding had to stop. Getting revenge hadn't helped Eric, and Alex's quest for some kind of atonement hadn't helped either.

Redemption was what they needed. There was only one way to get it—repentance. Alex finally understood. He couldn't just repent for that night. He had to repent for the arrogance that led up to it. He had to repent for the lukewarm faith that let him be in charge and left God as an afterthought. He needed to repent for thinking of himself first, others second, and God a distant third. What had started as an idea on the ride in the ambulance was now a fire burning through his veins. He couldn't sit still with it undone.

"I'll be right back." He slipped out of the room and shut the door. Walking a few paces away he leaned against the wall, covering his face with his hands. He'd been upside down in his thinking for years, hurting the people around him while feeling sorry for himself. His entire focus had been inward. He had made laws for himself, held himself accountable while ignoring the actual sin in his life. That was done. Right there he opened his heart. He prayed for forgiveness, emptying his soul, calling up every act, every dark thought, and laying it all out in the light. He repented of all of it.

The calm that had come earlier returned, twice as strong—and this time peace came with it. Peace filled his chest while a deep kind of resolve flooded his heart. He wanted to fix his eyes on Jesus and not on himself. Never again. He felt the weight of all he'd done, all the bitterness, all the hate and anger, how wrong it all was. And then it lifted. It was like he'd been emptied out. He slid down the wall, sitting on his heels.

Annie blinked. The world was very bright, too bright. It was probably a good idea to keep her eyes closed. There was sound aplenty. Someone was quietly crying as if their heart was breaking. What a terrible sound. She opened her eyes again, and it was still bright, but not as bad. Shapes formed and then edges and lines until finally, she could see straight. She was in a hospital room, lying in a bed. Considering the pain she had almost everywhere, that made sense. She turned toward the noise, and her jaw dropped open. Sitting beside her was her father. He had his face in his hands, his shoulders heaving.

Snippets of memory returned. She'd come-to back at the

house, in Alex's arms. She remembered the look on his face and shuddered. Eric was there too, bloodied, but alive. The ambulance and police had come so quickly. But, she might have passed out again at some point. Her memory was fuzzy. She definitely recalled how Alex had lost it, when they'd shoved him back out of the ambulance when he'd tried to come with her. Mac had arrived, and they'd shouted at each other. Then Mac literally picked him up in some kind of football maneuver and pinned him to the ground.

Alex was going to need someone to talk to. She used the remote control on her hospital bed to raise the back. Her father looked up, his eyes red and puffy. The suit he was wearing was rumpled as if he'd slept in it. She'd never seen him so disheveled.

He immediately stood. "Are you well?"

"I am in a hospital bed, and there are a number of things that hurt, but yes, I think I'm well." She wanted to smile, but her face hurt too much. "You're here."

"Of course. My only daughter was kidnapped, robbed, and beaten. Where else would I be?" He bit his lip.

"I don't know." She laid her head back on her pillow. She'd never seen her father emotional. It was almost too much. "I'm glad to see you."

He sighed. "I'm glad to see you breathing and talking." His lips moved in what probably would have been a smile, but he seemed to lose the will to do it about halfway through. "You have been through a terrible ordeal. I would be angry with your young man for putting you in danger if he hadn't also rescued you from it."

"You talked to Alex?"

"Yes, he had quite a lot to say." He squeezed her hand. "I am so very sorry, Anne. For many reasons." He paused, and she realized that Alex might not have limited his comments to the present situation. Knowing Alex, he'd probably read him the riot act. "Your mother is not here." It was as if he'd heard her thoughts. "She should be…she could be." He looked away. "I flew in from Geneva, and yet it seems the flight from New York is simply too much. I honestly have no answer for her this time."

"Daddy, you don't need to provide an answer for her." She reached out and took his hand. "I know her limits. I used to resent her for them, but I realized that the best thing I can do is forgive her so that I can have peace. I should have done that ages ago. I forgive her." Annie said it, understanding that she meant it. She could feel it now. It was like a burden lifted. "If one day she wants a relationship, I'm right here, but I'm not going to regret what I don't have from her." All her counsel to Alex had managed to sink into her own thoughts. Her mother would probably never ask for her forgiveness, but it didn't matter. Annie was done holding onto the bitterness.

"You always were the best of us." Her father's voice was quiet. "I hope that you can forgive me as well. I have not been what I should have been to you." He took a breath and straightened his shoulders. "I would like to visit more often, to communicate more regularly."

"I'd love that."

"Truly?"

A rather painful smile broke out on her face. "Yes, Daddy. I love you, always have. And if you need to hear it out loud, you're forgiven."

Her father hung his head for a moment. "I did need that. Thank you. I hope you know that I have always loved you. As poor of a job as I've done showing it, you have been the greatest joy of my life. I think I've been afraid to say too much for fear that you'd see the gap between my expression and your mother's. She never planned on children. It was a hard transition for her. In her way, I believe she loves you."

"Love assumes the best. That's Bible wisdom for you." She chuckled and then closed her eyes against the pain. "Oh, my face hurts when I do that."

"I'll call the nurse. Sit tight." He got up and headed for the door. "She should be right outside. I insisted you be in a private room near the nurse's station."

Annie almost laughed again. Of course, her father had bullied them into giving her the best accommodations. She wondered what day it was. Had she been sedated and lost a few? She also wondered where Alex was. Shortly, her father returned with a nurse who examined her and asked her all sorts of questions. She was given a painkiller for her face, which, she was pleased to hear, did not suffer any broken bones. Her ribs were bruised, not fractured, so, all in all, she'd be in pain for a bit, but not for long.

"Where's Alex?" She asked her father when the nurse had finished.

"He'll be here soon enough. You're supposed to be resting."

"I've rested enough. There was something he was going to talk to me about before this happened, and I would like him to tell me now."

"I'll retrieve him." Her father got up and headed out of the room again. It took a few minutes, but Alex appeared in the doorway alone. He stopped there, his jaw hard, his eyes narrowed as if in pain.

Annie raised a hand to her face where the worst of the damage was. "I suppose I look horrible."

"A bit." The smile on his face was wonky. He walked the rest of the way into the room, perching on the edge of her bed. "It's good to see you awake although it hurts to look at you." He winced. "How's the pain?"

"Not that bad. I can't smile or laugh so don't be amusing."

"Yeah, that's not going to be a problem." He fidgeted with

the edge of her blanket. "None of this is funny."

"Hmm… Seeing Mac tackle you to the ground was good for a giggle." She found herself smiling. "Ouch."

Alex shook his head. "Cut that out."

She looked to the window where it seemed to be early morning. That reminded her of the question she'd planned to ask. "How long have I been asleep?"

"Eight hours. They said you'd be under a while. When you first got here, you were belligerent. They said you were still in fight or flight mode, so they had to sedate you. Can't do a cat scan on a patient that takes a swing at the doctor."

"Seriously? That doesn't sound like me."

"They said it's because of the trauma."

She closed her eyes and let her head rest on the pillow behind her. "I don't want to think about trauma. Can you tell me everything?"

"You sure you're ready?"

"I am." She reached out her hand and he took it.

Alex gave her the play by play of how her father knew she was in trouble, how Alex had found Eric and then come after her by throwing a rock through his window and jumping through it. Shep had dug into the door frame around the knob with his front toenails and bitten it with his teeth until it was damaged enough that it flew open. He'd taken hold of Kevin's arm as Alex and Eric were coming through the window. Shep hadn't killed Kevin. Flying glass had severed his artery. His blood wouldn't be on Alex's hands. That was good.

"Did your dad tell you about the money?"

Annie shook her head slowly. She hadn't thought about it since Kevin had emptied her account.

"They got a forensic accountant on it. No guarantees, but they think they can get it back." Alex took her hand in his and gave it a squeeze.

"That's a relief. Not that it matters in the greater scheme of things. Eric never wanted my money. That's why Kevin attacked him."

"Yeah, he said as much. It might influence the district attorney's decision." Alex looked down at her hand in his. "Eric was booked, but the only thing they really have on him is breaking and entering, since the letters aren't something they can act on because I never pursued a restraining order. I'm going to talk to the DA because I don't think he should be charged at all, but it's up to the prosecutor. I told him that Kevin was manipulating Eric, feeding him all kinds of garbage, using him. There's this in-patient counseling program for Vets that the chief suggested. Eric seemed interested. If we can get the okay from the DA's office, he'll go there."

"I'm glad." Annie liked the idea that Eric would get counseling instead of jail time. Healing is what he needed. Maybe with help, he would find a way to forgive Alex, and the cycle of violence could finally end.

Annie got a close look at Alex. He had a fat lip, a rip in his jacket, and a small cut on his hand. "You don't look great either. What happened to you?"

"Oh, right." He rubbed his chin. "Mac has a hard-right hook."

"But are you and Mac okay with each other now? You're not in some blood feud are you?"

Alex grinned. "No, we're good. He was right. The EMTs did not need me in their way. I was a mess."

Annie's stomach tightened. It was what she had been afraid of, but he seemed okay now. Thinking of the blood and glass all over his living room, the state he must have found her in, it was understandable. "It was justified, Alex."

He raised an eyebrow. "Really? I took a swing at Mac."

"You were overwrought."

Alex narrowed his eyes at her. "Anyway, I talked to him a bit ago. He understood and forgave me. He did bust my chops for what felt like an hour, but it was good. He helped me get some stuff straight in my head."

That reminded her. There was something she wanted to hear from him. "Last night, or whenever it was that we last talked, you said there was something we should discuss. I believe it was your intentions."

"Ah, those." He traced the elastic bandage covering the IV in the back of her hand that he still held, his brows drawn together.

She squeezed her fingers together, and his eyes darted up to hers. "Yes, those."

"Well, Ms. Anne Elizabeth Caldwell. I formally state that my intentions are to court you for an acceptable period of time and then to marry you if you are amenable. And then I intend to ensure your happiness for the rest of your life. How does that sound?"

She felt a whoosh in her stomach, and her heart raced. "That sounds grand."

CHAPTER TWENTY-SEVEN

ALEX STOOD AT THE PERIPHERY AND watched the chaos unfold. The shop was filled with Annie's friends and their kids. It seemed the entire town had shown to celebrate the fact that she was alive. He'd given thanks often enough, it was a wonder God hadn't told him to shut up by now. Edward, Annie's father, had flown out that morning to a crisis with one of his clients in London. Annie acted like this was normal, and Alex guessed that to her, it was. But she was still so stunned he had flown in for her that she kept bringing it up. Alex had to reassure her every time. "Yeah, he was freaked when he thought you were in trouble. He crossed an ocean and three time zones to get to you." She seemed to need to hear it again and again. He didn't mind giving her that.

He'd found that there was a lot he didn't mind where Annie was concerned. His heart was about as full as one could get. He was looking forward to introducing her to his family. That was going to take some prep, since she was a little on the shy side, and his mother was likely to lapse into Portuguese and then hug the stuffing out of her when they met. Then she'd have to face the gauntlet that was the aunts, uncles, and cousins. Hopefully, his brothers would be cool. He knew his dad would be. Anthony Moretti was the personification of cool unless he was yelling at one of his sons.

At the front of the shop, there was a sudden commotion. The crowd shifted, and a tall man with a Red Sox cap entered the room. He was hesitant in a way that shouted, 'doesn't belong here,' and Alex's muscles grew tense. He heard Annie softly gasp beside him, and he stepped out between her and the guy. He felt her tug on his arm and turned.

"It's okay, it's Claire's ex."

"He's her ex? He's not here for trouble, is he?

Annie shook her head. "I think we're finally going to get somewhere. Don't intervene."

He stepped back and took her hand in his. "I'm happy to let someone else's drama play out."

Claire rushed up to her ex. "Why are you here?" She seemed to be pleading with him, taking his hand and trying to pull him away from the crowd. The guy wasn't having it. He stood right in the middle, his voice clear and loud.

"There are things I need to say." He was looking down at Claire with an expression Alex was pretty sure he'd seen before. Maybe in the mirror a time or two.

"There are better times for saying them." Claire hissed at him.

He straightened his shoulders like he was about to square off with somebody. "This is my public confession. I've tried to do this for months in small and quiet ways, and it's not working. So I need to do this big and loud."

"Oh, Paul, nobody wants to hear this." Claire tugged on him. "Really.

"The way I left you…" He closed his eyes like the memory pained him. "I need to publicly apologize. I want the entire town to know that I was wrong. Not you." He shook his head. "You were doing your best to make it work, and I ruined everything."

"I'll testify to that, now let's go—"

"Claire, it's more than that. You know it is. I cheated on you."

Claire flinched.

"My infidelity was not because of you or anything you did. I felt pressured, like you had all these expectations I couldn't meet, unreasonable ones. You didn't. It was me. At work I met someone, and she didn't ask anything of me. She thought I walked on water. I wanted to be somebody's hero; I wanted to be somebody's star. You knew the real me, and I didn't want to be him."

"Paul. *Seriously*. This is not the place."

"I created an illusion and then chose it over my family." There was a catch in his voice and a pang of sympathy ran through Alex. Paul got hold of himself and kept talking. "I was running from my responsibilities. I was weak, acting like a spoiled kid, pretending that you were the needy one. I lost myself in her flattery. I lost myself in the escape. I convinced myself that I was the one who was being wronged. And then I destroyed everything I ever wanted or needed. I blew up our lives because I didn't want to be an adult. I wanted to indulge my feelings without consequences. I was running away. My counselor calls it avoidance."

"You have a counselor?"

"Oh yeah." Paul laughed. "I started going when they found that mass in my lung and then went through all the tests. The oncology guy's a Christian and referred me to a counselor who has helped me get my head right."

Claire lifted her hand to her forehead. "What are you talking about?" She sounded alarmed, then again, the stuff the guy said was alarming.

"I was coughing a lot."

"I remember. I told you to get that checked out."

"Well, I did. Had a bunch of tests and they found a mass in my left lung. They sent me to an oncologist after that."

"What?" Claire stumbled back, but Paul caught her by her elbow and held her up. Alex couldn't help but notice he didn't let her go, either.

"It was pretty grim there for a while. I was scared out of my mind. But you know what?"

Claire shook her head. Her mouth was slightly open, and

her eyes were wide. Around the room most everyone was fixed on Paul, waiting to hear whatever shocking thing he had to say next.

"It was the best thing that ever happened to me. I was laying there." He mimed a bed with his hand. "Prepped for surgery, and I was thinking, Claire would find a way to make this funny." He smiled down at her. "She'd have known how to take the sting out. She's the one who believed in me for better or worse. She..." His voice broke.

Claire's eyes grew misty. Annie squeezed Alex's hand. He looked down at her face and saw her eyes get misty too.

"Knowing that it might be the end and that I had done the one thing to put you beyond my reach forever, I realized I messed up. At that moment, I knew that it was all on me. There was no way I could blame you anymore. All that pressure." He laughed. "You know where that went when I was facing death? Gone. 'Cause it never mattered, not for a second." His eyes ran over her face. Claire's expression was impossible to decipher. It looked like she was struggling to take it all in.

"I know it's too late. But I want to at least be friends. I want to hang out with you and the boys. If we can't be a real family again, can we at least build something new? I want Christmases and Easters, and Thanksgivings, but I want them with all of you. If you can't give me that, I'll take what you do give me. I'll take anything at this point. You were my *everything*, and I treated you like trash because I only loved myself. I'm sorry it took me so long to figure it out."

"And are you okay now?" She lowered her voice. "I mean, has the cancer spread?"

"No. It wasn't cancer. The doctor thinks it was a nail I swallowed as a kid. It had been traveling my body all along, then ended up in my lung and a mass formed. Totally benign. Crazy huh?"

"A nail. Paul Murphy. Only you..." Claire dropped her face in her hands and burst into tears.

Paul brought her close to him. He pulled her hands away from her face. "I'm sorry. I didn't mean to upset you. I didn't think you'd care, considering what a fool I've been."

"I want so bad to believe you. I want to have this perfect, happy ending, but you lied, you cheated. You broke my heart." Her voice was watery, but there was no mistaking her anguish.

"I'm not worth believing, but God is, and I promise you, Claire, I promise you, I'm not the man I was. I'm His. Not like before when I said all the right words, but I didn't believe a thing."

Alex could relate to that. He'd been saying the right words by rote for years, never letting his faith get any deeper than a puddle.

"Push came to shove, and my faith was about as sturdy as a wet paper bag. I had to start all over again. I've given Him my life, and where He says go, I go. I want to come home to you and the boys."

"What about that woman?"

"She's long gone. I broke it off with her the second I clued in to what I had done. I haven't seen her since December, before Christmas."

Claire seemed shocked by this, but she regained her composure quickly. "My apartment is small, and I'm not moving. The boys are finally settled in." She argued.

"It would be a palace to me because it feels like home." He pulled her a little closer. "And it has you."

"Annie wants me to be her business manager." Alex looked down at Annie in surprise, and she shrugged. She'd said she was going to make changes, so she was working less. He liked the idea of the shop taking less of her time. More for him. He found himself smiling at that.

Claire fixed Paul with a hard stare. "I intend to take the job. I won't be home every night to cook your dinner or pick up after you. I will not have the time."

"I've been thinking about going part-time at the firm anyway. I can take care of whatever the boys need and give you time to focus on your work."

Then Claire brought out the big weapons. "I don't trust you, Paul. I want to, everything you're saying is so nice, but you've lied to me too many times."

"Trust God. That's all I ask. When I've earned it again, maybe you can trust me. Will you give it a shot? Take a chance with me?"

Claire looked up at her former husband and nodded once. "You get one shot, Paul Murphy, four weeks to see if you can stick with the new you, and then maybe we can talk about a future together. I'm not making any promises. You need to prove you mean what you say."

"I'll give it everything I have. You matter more to me than my next breath, and I plan to prove it to you."

Claire put her arms around his neck, and he wrapped his around her waist. The crowd broke out into applause mixed with "Aw…"

Annie planted her face in Alex's shoulder and sniffled. Alex wrapped his arm around her and held her close. For what it was worth, he believed the guy. He'd heard all kinds of lies from all sorts of liars. Paul seemed to be on the level. It was a sweet way to end the night, watching a couple ripped apart by infidelity come back together. The road to redemption wasn't an easy one, as he well knew, but it was worth it. He leaned down and kissed the top of Annie's head. Yes, it was worth it.

EPILOGUE

Annie clapped along with the rest of the guests as the pastor introduced Dr. and Mrs. Daniel Connors. May in Maine wasn't reliably warm, but as if nature wanted to give the couple a gift, it was seventy degrees and sunny as Erin and Dan walked back up the aisle under the enormous green arbors that had been erected in the garden for the wedding in the hope of good weather.

"Jesus, thank you."

Annie smiled as Linda's voice carried over to where she was sitting with Alex.

"Bill, did you see our pretty girl's smile? Praise Jesus." Beside her Erin's father sat smiling gently, watching the happy couple head to the reception. On his other side, Erin's mother and her husband sat. Annie still found it amazing that all of Erin's folks got along. It was a boon that they did since Dan was very much alone in the world. He seemed happy to have two sets of in-laws. "C'mon, ya'll." Linda waved at the rest of them. "Let's get this show on the road."

An usher escorted Linda down the aisle and then Erin's mom. The reception would probably be like the wedding, elegant, yet homey. Annie was looking forward to the dancing. Alex was not the dancing sort, but Annie was, and she'd secured a promise from him that he'd dance at least two slow songs with her.

She and Alex filed out of their row when prompted. She had to be careful not to catch a heel on the runner. Against her better judgment and with Claire's advice, she'd worn silver high-heeled sandals. They did look awfully nice with her lavender, knee-length dress and its chiffon skirt, but they pinched something fierce. Claire had said beauty equals pain, but Annie ignored it. She probably should have paid attention since her toes were definitely hurting. Walking into the reception hall, she looked around and found their table. Alex headed for the bar where Mac and Pete were chatting as though this was a Sunday dinner at the MacAlisters' and not a wedding.

After dinner, the band started up. They played several swinging numbers that Annie listened to from the sidelines waiting for a slow song. When another fast song started up, Alex took her hand, but he didn't lead her to the dancefloor. He led her out the side door to the formal garden. Boxwood hedges, cement benches, and large ornamental trees gave off the impression of a 19th-century terrace in the English countryside. Alex stopped beside a large rose arbor with tiny, twinkling lights cleverly hidden in its boughs. It reminded her of the night he'd kissed her for the first time, only this was a whole lot warmer.

In the twilight, she could see that the roses were pink, her favorite. From the old-rose scent wrapping around them, they had to be heirlooms. She couldn't resist holding a bloom in her hand and taking a sniff. She revised the list she'd been keeping in her head of the must-haves for the roof garden she planned to have one day. It would definitely need roses. They weren't easy to grow this far north, but the scent alone was worth the effort, never mind their beauty. Alex's hand wrapped around hers and pulled her away to stand in front of him.

"They're beautiful, aren't they? Pink is my favorite color of rose. I think there's a line in *Anne of Green Gables* about pink being the best color for roses. I'll have to look that—"

Alex interrupted her with a kiss. It was just a brush of his lips over hers, but an efficient way to change the subject. He was smiling down at her like he thought she was barmy, but in a way he liked. He laid his hand gently against her cheek, and she watched in fascination as his expression changed from humor to something she couldn't quite put her finger on, but it set off a whooshing feeling in her stomach. She was on that roller-coaster again.

"Annie, I hope you know what you mean to me." He stroked her cheek with his thumb.

"I think I do."

"I'm not great at the romance stuff."

Was he crazy? "Not from where I'm standing."

"I'm not all that attentive."

"I don't need a lot of attention. Claire says I'm low-maintenance." And it was all too true. Her favorite 'date-night' was sitting on the couch with Alex, reading together.

He chuckled. "I want to believe that I'm enough. That you aren't getting shorted by settling for me."

"Okay, now I know you're crazy."

"No, seriously, Annie. I want to be the man you need."

"You are." She wondered what was bringing this on, why the doubts? Things had been rolling along nicely. In fact, they'd been having conversations about the future which made her nervous and yet not, all at the same time. Maybe it was the wedding. Some men got nervous around them as if matrimony was catching. She'd been very careful not to make Alex feel pressured or think she was hinting at a ring of her own. Granted, she'd love nothing more than to spend the rest of her life with him, but he had to want that too. There was no point in rushing things. She turned away from him and cupped a rose in her palm. "If this is all too much...I mean if you think we're going too fast and—"

"Annie."

She turned back to see Alex down on one knee. The breath left her lungs in a whoosh. He fished in his pocket and then held up a ring. It was as if her feet were stuck to the ground and her tongue to the roof of her mouth. He'd taken her completely by surprise. The ring was art-deco with a small diamond. It appeared to be an antique, and she wondered how he'd pegged her style while never once asking a thing about it.

"I was tempted to do this that night in the hospital, but I knew it was too soon. I kept waiting for the right moment because I wanted this to be perfect. Tonight I realized I don't want to wait another second. I know this is stealing some of Erin and Dan's thunder, so it's okay if you want to—"

"Yes!" She flung her arms around him, toppling them both to the ground. Luckily the grass under the arbor was pretty soft. Alex sat up, laughing, and pulled her into his lap. He gave her the ring, and she slid it on her finger, amazed it fit. Usually the older the ring, the smaller it was, and her fingers were not long and slim, quite the reverse.

"It was my Nona's. She and my grandfather emigrated from Italy right before World War II broke out. You remind me of her. She was sweetness and light until you crossed her, then you were in for it."

"Seriously?"

"She was strong and soft all at once. She'd give you a cookie, but she'd beat you with a big, wooden spoon if you made a mess in her house."

"I promise not to beat you with a spoon, or with anything actually. I'm not one for physical violence."

"No, but you can cut a man off at the knees with a look. Trust me."

"When did I do that?"

"When we were apart. You were killing me. I went out of my way to see you, but not let you see me. It was torture. Then, when you did see me, the way you looked at me... I felt gutted."

"I didn't mean to do that."

"No, that's what made it worse. You'd try to be nice even though I'd been cruel to you. All I wanted was to confess everything and beg you to forgive me. I'm pretty sure our kids are going to feel the same. Just shoot them that look."

"You want kids?" Annie's insides, already squishy, turned to mush at the thought of babies.

"Yes. As many as you want."

"Four? Maybe more?"

"I like the sound of that." He dropped a kiss on her forehead, and she slid her arms around his neck, her face tipped up to give his lips a better target.

Alex sat in front of the screen trying not to be nervous. Annie was beside him, his mother and father on the other side. His brother Marc had rigged up Annie's laptop to the big screen TV in the living room and mounted a web cam on top of that. They were in his parent's living room waiting for Annie's father to connect. Before asking her to marry him he'd called Edward, and they'd had a good talk until it turned to his finances. Edward was not impressed with his lack of investment. Alex had then sat through a lecture on how to invest no matter what the salary. He had dutifully filled out the paperwork for the 401k plan the next day.

For all his stuffiness, Edward was a good man. Alex wanted this meeting to go well for Annie's sake. He'd already prepped his parents, asking his mom to stick to English and his dad not to talk sports. He also warned them not to ask about Annie's mom or question why she wasn't there. When his mom had raised her eyebrows at that, he'd had to explain the situation as cautiously as he could. His mom was not above confronting people who were doing wrong even if they weren't related to her. He didn't want to betray Annie's trust. He wasn't sure how comfortable she was with sharing that situation.

A picture popped up on the screen in front of them. Edward sat at a large desk, but he wasn't alone. A woman was sitting next to him. Beside him Alex felt Annie stiffen. She grabbed his hand and held tight.

"Hello, darling." The woman said, presumably to Annie.

"Mother. It's good to see you." Annie's voice was strange. Alex glanced over and saw his mom take Annie's other hand in hers.

Annie's mother was beautiful. She looked like she was mid-thirties, though she had to be at least in her forties. With long, light brown hair, baby-blue eyes, and a thin frame, she looked nothing like her daughter. Nothing but her lips. She had full lips in a perfect Cupid's bow, exactly like Annie.

"It's good to see you too." The woman's eyes seemed to slide his way. "And your fiancé as well. I was so pleased to hear the news." She turned to Edward and then back to face them. "I'm pleased to meet you all."

"Oh." Alex realized in the shock of seeing both her parents he'd neglected to introduce his. "Edward and… Uh—"

"Margot." Annie's mom touched her chest and smiled.

"Margot." He gestured to his mom and dad. "This is my mom Julia, and my dad Anthony." Their parents exchanged greetings and an awkward silence fell over them.

"Well, I for one am so excited to know a wedding is coming. Do you two have a date picked out?" Margot waited while Alex and Annie stared at each other. Annie recovered first.

"Well, yes. We were thinking of December, the week between Christmas and New Year's. I'll be off of work and Alex can get the time off without any trouble."

Margot smiled. "A Christmas wedding sounds nice." Her smile was less certain when she asked, "If you'd like to have it here in New York, I know of a number of event locations that could do that theme justice."

New York? Was she kidding?

"We've decided to have it at the church in Sweet River. We're hoping you and Daddy can fly in for it. There's a resort here, and they have luxury rentals on the lake. It would be beautiful in winter."

"Oh." Margot's face fell.

"We'll be there." Edward turned to face his wife. "We wouldn't miss it." He faced the camera again. "Annie, don't you think you could use your mother's help in preparations? This really is her area after all."

"Sure. Of course." Annie squeezed Alex's hand tighter.

"I'd love that." Margot said it so quietly, Alex almost missed it.

"Yes, I think we could arrange a visit, couldn't we?" Edward asked his wife. "Annie's school is on summer holidays. We can fly out and spend some time at that resort she mentioned."

"You'd come too?" Margot seemed surprised at his suggestion.

Edward's face softened. "I think the firm can spare me, and I'm overdue for a real holiday." Edward's eyes moved to Annie. "And what better place than with our daughter."

Margot nodded, an uncertain look on her face. "Yes. I was thinking of ways to help with the wedding. I…I can do all the research for you and find the best places. And your dress! I can help you with that too. I'll send you some magazines. I know all the best designers and even with your time frame, I am sure we can get something done. Oh, and you could wear my mother's pearls. I know she'd want you to have them. With your coloring they will look divine. In fact, we have a vintage lace veil from your great-grandmother. It would have to be restored, but it is so your style. And are you going to grow your hair longer? You really should. It would be stunning. You have the most incredible hair. I remember those pictures from your high school graduation. It was perfect."

"Margot, my love." Edward got his wife's attention and gave her a wink.

"I was rambling." She blushed.

"I don't mind. I do it all the time." Annie wore a cautious smile. "I guess it's genetic. And I would love to look at magazines with you, and I think wearing grandmother's pearls and great-grandmother's veil sounds perfect."

"I'll bring them."

"Good."

Alex's dad cleared his throat. "With that settled, we'll be sure to set aside time while you're here. We can get to the important topics. Now, I know you folks are from New York, but we're a Red Sox family and any grandchildren will not be receiving any Yankees gear, now will they?"

"Dad, we talked about this." Alex closed his eyes.

Alex gave Annie a leg up, and she scrambled into the tree fort. He climbed up behind her. Together they stood at the window and looked out over Lewiston. From their relative height they could see over the houses near the big brick buildings along the river's edge. It wasn't the most inspiring sight, but it still felt like home, even after all he'd been through. The air around them developed a warm glow as the sun began to set. The sky turned from blue to orange and pink and finally to purple.

"Have you heard from him?" Annie didn't need to clarify who the 'him' was. It had been months since Eric was sent to the program and no, Alex hadn't heard a thing. He'd sent Eric two letters though. Both were full of hope that Eric could know the kind of peace that Alex had found.

"No. But he's got a few weeks left. Maybe he'll come see me when he's out."

"Do you think he's over it?" Annie shook her head. "I don't mean that like it sounds, like her death is something he could get over. I'm wondering if it's enough in the past that he's capable of forgiving you your part in it."

Alex shook his head. "Forgiveness requires that you let stuff go. I don't think he's ready to do that."

"Have you?" She looked up at him, and he saw that some of her old fears lingered. He wanted to banish them forever.

"Yes. Eric might never forgive me, but God has. What was that quote you read to me the other day? The Popeye one."

She smacked his arm. "That's not Popeye, it's John Newton."

"Whatever, I can't remember it right."

Annie shook her head at him. "I am not what I want to be…but still I am not what I once used to be, and by the grace of God I am what I am." She quoted.

"That's where I'm at."

"That's a good place to be." She wrapped her arms around him. "I'm with you. You know that, don't you? Wherever you go."

"Yes. And you can trust me, Annie. I'm with you too. Wherever you go." He kissed her as the sun set on his hometown.

AUTHOR NOTE

There are big themes and little themes in this book. One of the big themes is that redemption is through God's grace, not our works. When we sin, especially when those sins result in hurting others, we twist ourselves into pretzels trying to find a way to get forgiveness on our own. We'll beat ourselves up trying to find a way to atone. Alex quits his job and heads to the woods telling himself he's leaving town to make it easier on his family, but he's running from God. He believes that he is beyond redemption and lives like a monk because he wants to earn forgiveness. He can't, just like we can't. Forgiveness is given. It can be a gift hard to take because it requires humility.

Romans is one of my favorite books of the Bible, not just because it has my favorite verse(s) 8: 38-39, but because of the simple wisdom it drops in every chapter. I especially love the emphasis in 3:23, "All have sinned and all fall short of the glory of God." We're all sinners, redeemed yes, but still sinners. That pastor up there in the pulpit with the suit is a sinner. The deacons and elders who always seem so wise, so put together, are sinners. The director of Christian Ed who wears fluffy pink twinsets with pearls every Sunday and makes you feel like the swamp creature by comparison? She's a sinner. I'm a sinner. You are a sinner. God loves us all. He's given us all a path to forgiveness in the sacrifice of His son. In Jesus, we all get a Redemption Road. Not everyone takes it. Sadly, some get halfway and never finish. They're stuck in one spot thinking that sitting in a church pew, believing in God, trying to be a good person is all enough. It isn't.

If you've been feeling like there's something missing in your faith, you may be stuck halfway. I was a halfway Christian for a long time. I don't think I reached the end until I was in my mid-twenties. That year I decided that instead of giving up candy or chocolate for Lent that I'd give up not going to church instead. I found a church that felt friendly, and I sat in the pew for that entire season. Easter came, and I was still attending. Pentecost came, and I was still attending. Christmas came, and I was still attending.

I can be difficult to read. Most folks assume that I have it all together and need nothing because I project that. I had a difficult adolescence and developed self-sufficiency as a defense mechanism. Sometimes, it works entirely too well. I didn't know how to ask for what I needed, and no one knew I needed anything. But, sitting in that pew week after week, I opened my eyes, let go of the cynicism of my youth, and listened to what God had been trying to tell me all along. I reached out and God made sure there were people there who responded. I found what I needed. I finally understood what God was offering through the sacrifice of his son, and I took those last few steps.

Mothers, good and bad, are also a theme in this book. Olivia Clark, orphaned when her parents died in a car accident, is fostered by the MacAlisters along with her siblings. Katherine and Mac, who assumed they'd be childless, now have a house full of kids they plan to adopt, and it's all sunshine and rainbows, right? But, of course it's not. Getting adopted is not an instant ticket to happiness. Often kids feel loyal to their first family, or adrift without a connection to their biological parents, despite their new family's deep love and commitment. It's not an easy road for anyone involved, which makes it all the more important that people of good faith continue to take it, to make the choice to foster and adopt.

Children are not the only orphans. Many adults, young and old, have been cut or have cut themselves off from their families. Whether it was from abuse, neglect, or some other barrier, there are free-floating, single adults in your town, in your church right now, deeply longing for connection. Some actively seek it out like Annie. Others are unable to reach out and ask. It's up to us to hold out a hand. This is especially important around the holidays when everyone will be talking of, planning to meet, and going to family. There are temporary orphans too, those living away from their families and unable to travel home.

Some of the best people I've met in my life are the 'church ladies' who make it a point to look out for these folks and ask (sometimes bully) them to dinner. One woman I knew would make it a point to collect the 'orphans' as she put it, around her for every holiday. If you went to dinner at her house you would rub shoulders with all kinds of humans but share that same adrift status. She didn't preach a sermon, but through her hospitality she shared the mooring of God's love.

This series has people cut from that cloth, chiefly Pete. He has a sense for when a person he meets needs shepherding. In that way, he's kind of like the old dog herding the puppies away from danger. Reader, if you gained any wisdom from this particular book, I hope it has been to reach out; in your community, in your church, and at work. It can be a hard job for anyone who's had their hand slapped away before but do it and keep doing it until it's second-nature.

Whether you're in need or in a place to help someone who is, if there is anything that can make a difference in our towns, cities, and country as a whole, if there is anything that can unite us, it will be this. Take care of each other.

Blessings,
Christa

Connect with Christa

Website
christamacdonald.com

Facebook
www.facebook.com/groups/1538432676468229

Bookbub
www.bookbub.com/authors/christa-macdonald

Goodreads
www.goodreads.com/author/show/14189014.Christa_MacDonald

Amazon
www.amazon.com/Christa-MacDonald

DISCUSSION QUESTIONS

How do you think Annie's unorthodox upbringing impacted her as an adult?

For most of the book, Alex doesn't believe he can be forgiven for what he did. Have you felt this or has someone hurt you in a way you can't seem to forgive?

Why do you think it was so hard for Alex to accept the forgiveness God was ready to offer him? Have you struggled with forgiveness and what helped you overcome that struggle?

Olivia's loss has made her bitter and angry. What ways can a loss like that change people and how can you help them heal?

Pete is both Alex's friend and his mentor. Have you had a mentor like that in your life? How did it impact your life or any decisions you needed to make?

What did you think when Claire's husband asked her for forgiveness? Have you ever been confronted with someone asking for forgiveness that you weren't sure you could forgive?

Was there a character you identified with? If so, why?

www.ingramcontent.com/pod-product-compliance
Lightning Source LLC
Chambersburg PA
CBHW071743190726
48292CB00003B/849